THE TROUBLE WITH LOVE

NEW YORK TIMES BESTSELLING AUTHOR

CLAIRE CONTRERAS

CHAPTER ONE

ONE YEAR AGO . . .

Bennett

THERE'S a lot to be said about the way we handle betrayal. Some people lick their wounds and walk away, while others, like myself, lick tequila off some random woman's stomach before downing shots of Patrón.

I shake my head after the fifth shot. I haven't done this since I was in college, which feels like a lifetime ago even though it's only been a few years. One thing I'd definitely never done was go to a bar by myself. There's something freeing about the experience of not having to share women with my friends, of not worrying about babysitting anyone, and the likelihood that I'd get into a fistfight was at a minimum without them around to start one.

The woman on the bar sits up and smiles wide at me. I blink a few times to focus my eyes on her, and when I do, I hold up my hand in a peace sign, and walk away without giving her a second glance. Sliding into a booth, I ask for another drink—

bourbon this time. I put my face in my hands and take a deep breath.

My God. How did I end up here?

The week started out promising, but on Tuesday night things took an ugly turn. Paola was crying when I got home and my initial thought was that she wasn't pregnant—again. We'd been trying for two years now and had remained optimistic for most of that time, but I could tell it had been wearing her down for a while now. I hugged her and pushed her hair away from her wet cheeks, and then she dropped the bomb on me—she'd been seeing someone else for six months. She said it casually, as if married people were allowed to go off and see other people. Then she'd shown me the positive pregnancy test. I demanded proof that it wasn't mine. She demanded a divorce. On Wednesday, she took those words back. I got drunk. On Thursday she started packing up her shit, saying she was moving in with Marcos. I called my lawyer. Got drunk again. And today I am on a similar trajectory.

Movement in my booth makes me lower my hands from my face. I blink a few times as a blur of red slides into the booth across from me. She sets down a pitcher between us, pours two glasses, and slides one over. I take it.

"You got a pitcher of vodka?"

"Um. Sure."

I take a healthy gulp and cough, narrowing my eyes. "This is water."

"Surprised you can even tell what it is, considering the state you're in."

"What state is that?" I frown. "And who the fuck are you to judge me? You don't know my life."

"You're right. I don't know your life." She raises an eyebrow. "Anything you want to talk about?"

"Why would I talk to you?"

She shrugs. "Better than talking to yourself like you've been doing for the last ten minutes."

"So, you decided you should come over here in hopes that I'd spill my guts to you?" I eye her suspiciously. *Is she one of Paola's friends? Is this a setup?* I will my eyes to focus on her. No, I'd remember this woman. She has long, thick, wavy blond hair. The kind of long and thick I'd fist and grip as I fuck those beautiful full lips of hers. Her nose is small and thin and her cheekbones are defined and pink. I can't really tell how old she is with all that makeup.

"How old are you?"

"Twenty-five." She frowns. "Why?"

"You sit here uninvited, bring me water, question me about my life." I take a big gulp of the unwelcome water. The bourbon I ordered is taking too long. "It seems like a childish thing to do."

"Oh." She glances away, sipping on her water as if it's the finest Champagne.

"You don't drink? Is that it? You're one of those?"

Her eyes flash back to mine. "I drink when I want."

"Why aren't you drinking now? You're at this bar, wearing a fuck-me-red dress, with that fuckable pout and those long lashes, sitting across from me drinking fucking water. What's your deal?"

"I'm glad you find me so fuckable," she says, looking right at me, into me even. "I'm meeting someone here and I don't want to be drunk when he gets here, so I decided on water. You looked like you needed company, so I sat here. I can move if my presence is really bothering you that much though." She reaches for the pitcher.

I put my hand over hers, our eyes meet—both startled by my move—and lock. "Stay."

She takes her hand from beneath mine and sits back hesitantly. I drink more water. Get more sober. Watch her closer. She's looking everywhere but at me now.

"You think your date stood you up?"

She shrugs. "Wouldn't be the first time."

"He's a fucking idiot."

Her gaze flies to mine. I can't tell if her eyes are brown or green, but they're fucking gorgeous. She looks innocent. Definitely too innocent for me.

"He is an idiot," she says after a beat. "But he's also busy."

"He shouldn't be too busy for you."

"Yeah, well." She shrugs and licks that perfect pout again. "You're here by yourself?"

"Yep."

"Do you always get this drunk?"

"Again with the judgments."

"Sorry." She bites her bottom lip.

"You have the most incredible fucking lips."

She looks away, but the blush that covers her face is impossible to hide.

"You're really twenty-five?"

"Twenty-three." She licks her lips again. "Today's my birthday."

"Well, shit. Happy birthday, twenty-three." I exhale. I remember my twenty-third. Barely, but I know it was fun. "What's your name?"

Her eyes shift to mine again. "Elizabeth."

"Is that your real name?"

"Middle name."

4

I chuckle. This girl is way too innocent. She can't even lie about using a fake name.

"What's your name?"

"Ben."

She nods, sipping on her water. "You look like a Ben."

The waitress comes over with my drink. Fucking finally. I'm definitely closer to sober than drunk now and suddenly I don't want to get obliterated. I sip this drink slower than I did the last. The waitress addresses Elizabeth across from me.

"You sure you don't want anything harder?"

"Thank you." Elizabeth smiles, shaking her head, her eyes on the waitress as she walks away.

"I can give you something hard right now," I say.

Her eyes widen as she turns to me. "Did you seriously just say that?"

"I did."

"Wow." She shakes her head. Her laughter sounds more like disbelief than amusement as it huffs out of those lips, but her eyes are twinkling. "I've heard some shit, but that right there is classic douchebag."

"Classic douchebag?" I bite back a laugh. "I wasn't aware there were different types of douchebags."

"Oh, there are plenty," she says, "but normally out-of-this-world good-looking guys stick to classic douchebag."

"You think I'm out-of-this-world good-looking?"

"And a douchebag."

"I think I'm okay with that." I sip my bourbon and set it down. "You want some?"

She eyes it like she does, licking her lips as she examines it.

"It's only bourbon. It's not spiked or anything," I say, in hopes to settle her nerves. If anything, it makes her eyes widen as if she hadn't considered that possibility.

"I'm fine." She sits back, shaking her head.

I call the waitress over and order Elizabeth a drink to match mine.

"You didn't have to do that," she says under her breath. "But thank you."

"You're welcome."

Her drink comes at lightning speed. The waitress smiles at her and walks away again.

"You know her?"

"Jana?" She glances at the waitress's retreating back, a smile on her face. "Yeah. She's good people."

"Seems like you're good people." I drink, eyes on her as she sips on her own. "I've been coming here for years and I've never seen anyone get VIP treatment," I say. "And this is coming from a VIP douchebag."

She snorts. "VIP douchebag."

"Happy birthday." I lift my glass and clink it against hers. She blushes like she didn't remember she'd said that.

"Thanks."

"So, birthday girl, what do you want for your birthday?" I ask. "And how long are you going to wait for the non-classic douchebag who stood you up?"

"He's worse than any douchebag." She sighs. "I'm done waiting. And the only thing I really want is a good lay."

My brows shoot up. Little Miss Innocent is straitlaced and straightforward and it's such a fucking turn-on. "That can be arranged."

"You're too drunk to be a good lay."

"I take offense to that. Even in my most drunken state I'd probably be a better lay than half the men you've slept with."

She laughs. "You're so full of yourself."

"I'm not. It's the simple truth."

"Yeah, okay."

I set the bourbon down and slide it away, then reach for hers. She slaps my hand away.

"Don't you fucking dare."

Her outburst makes me laugh. "I've been turned on from the moment you sat across from me, but this is taking it to another level."

"That's interesting." She cocks her head. "Considering you looked like you were either crying or falling asleep when I sat across from you."

"So why sit here?"

"Because I'd rather sit across from a guy who looks like he's on the verge of a breakdown than sit alone anywhere else in this bar and have to deal with lame pickup attempts."

"How are you going to get laid if you don't let people try to come on to you?"

She shrugs again, taking another sip of her bourbon. "And there lies the crux of the story. I want to be wanted, but I don't want to be pursued."

"That's such a woman problem." I shake my head. "Why are women so fucking needy anyway?"

"Women are needy?" Her eyebrows shoot up. "Men are the reason the word *needy* even exists."

"Right." I scoff. "If needy is synonymous to men, how would you describe women?"

"Survivors."

She says it with such sureness, that I almost think she might be right. Then I think about Paola and the situation we're in because of her particular neediness. You'd think I didn't try to fuck the woman nightly. She rejects me more than she accepts, and that's why this is so much more difficult to process. I look at the woman sitting across from me. She probably won't go home with me tonight, with the way she's analyzing the fuck out of me, so I might as well have a normal conversation until I'm sober enough to take her to a diner. I'd kill for chicken and waffles right now.

"Have you ever cheated on a boyfriend?"

Her eyes widen. "No."

"Does it disgust you? The thought of cheating?"

"I mean . . ." She sighs heavily and takes another sip of bourbon. "My parents were cheaters and my ex was a serial cheater, so yeah, it bothers me."

"Which is why you've never cheated on a partner?"

She frowns. "I guess I've never understood the point of cheating. If you don't enjoy the person you're with, you might as well move on and sleep with other people at that point. It's really not that difficult."

I scoff. When she puts it that way, it seriously pisses me off. Fuck it. I bring the bourbon back, and just as I'm lifting it to my mouth, Elizabeth reaches out, her thin fingers tentative on my hand, her big brownish-greenish eyes on mine as she lowers the drink from my lips.

"Hey, Ben."

"Yeah?"

"Let's go have sex."

CHAPTER TWO

Morgan

YOU KNOW that feeling you get in the pit of your stomach when your whole life is about to change? That's exactly how I feel as I approach the building of SEVEN. I've beaten the odds in every other aspect of my life—escaping my shitty life in Vegas, getting into my dream university, putting myself through said university, and landing great internships as well as working with incredible companies. This moment, though? It feels like the biggest moment of my life thus far.

I take a deep breath and let it out, shaking my arms and legs the way boxers do in the ring before a big fight. I got this. I got this. I totally got this. I remind myself that it's not even a legit interview, which honestly scares me a little more than it should. I've never been one to accept a handout, but when my brother spoke to Mr. Cruz about me he'd been so impressed that he offered a job without even meeting me. I'd be an idiot not to take the opportunity. Ever since I was in college, I had my eyes on SEVEN—a tech company that creates everything from websites to apps and also invests in the making of robots and different kinds of technology. As a person who's obsessed with apps, from building them to the way they cater to specific people, this company is my dream. Aside from not wowing Mr. Cruz, the other thing I'm worried about is them giving me a temp job instead of a permanent position, but honestly, right now, I'll take what I can get. I exit the elevator and smile at the receptionist, letting her know I'm here for a meeting with Mr. Cruz.

"Junior or Senior?" she asks.

"Um. Senior?" I frown. "I think. I hope."

I've seen Mr. Cruz Junior only once while Devon roomed with him in college, and it was definitely an experience sixteen-year-old Morgan would truly love to forget. I'd walked in on him and a girl making out—heavily making out. His hand was underneath her shirt and she was grinding against his crotch. I'd been secondhand embarrassed, yet felt like I was burning from the inside. I ended up having to tell Dev I had to go home immediately because I felt like I'd come down with a cold. Needless to say, I never met the guy face-to-face and I'm still mentally preparing myself for the moment it finally happens, mostly because I've thought about the sounds they were making and the passion they'd shared more times than I can count. Reconciling his face to that experience may completely ruin it for me or fuel it further.

"He's ready for you," the receptionist announces. I walk forward and stand by the door to his office. "You can walk right in."

When I do, I'm met by the smell of old books. I inhale and instantly feel a little calmer than I felt five minutes ago. An older man stands behind the desk. He's wearing jeans, a polo shirt, and a huge smile on his face. Definitely not what I was expecting.

"Miss Tucker," he says as he rounds the desk. "I've heard so much about you, I feel like I know you."

I extend my hand and let out a surprised, "Oh," when he doesn't give me a business handshake, like I'm expecting, but rather a hug. He pulls back, the crinkles around his eyes prominent as he smiles.

"I see the resemblance," he says. "Devon has become like a son to Barbara and me. I hope you feel comfortable enough here to come to see us as family as well."

"Thank you so much, Mr. Cruz." I smile. "And thank you so much for this opportunity."

"Charlie," he says, waving a hand as he walks back to his chair behind his desk. "Call me Charlie."

I take a seat across from him and wait for him to address me again.

"So, how do you like it here? You two grew up in Vegas, right? Have you gotten used to this concrete jungle?"

"I love it." I smile. "I went to college here, so I've felt at home here for a while."

"Magna cum laude." He glances at one of the papers in front of him. "From that school, especially, that's quite an achievement."

"Thank you."

"So, what are your goals?"

"My goals?" Goals was not a potential question on the list I'd made myself in preparation for this interview. I go with a short description of what I'm being hired to do. "Um. I'd like to help your clients with their social media presence."

"Right." He sets the papers aside and folds his hands on his desk. "But what are *your* goals? You went to an incredible school, got out of a bad environment, as far as I know and I don't know much." He raises his eyebrows. "So, what is your passion? What are your personal goals? According to Devon, you have a lot of those. That's what I'm interested in. Forget all the BS you're supposed to impress me with and tell me what you see yourself doing in the future."

"Oh." I blink. "I create apps for fun as a side gig. It pays and it also serves as practice. Right now, I have two apps, which run independently and need back matter updates only a few times a week, but my goal is to create a foolproof, successful dating app that stands out from the rest."

"That's impressive. What purpose do your current apps serve?"

"They're primarily friendship apps. One is so people don't have to eat alone. It targets specific high schools. The other is for used books for my university."

"Wow. That's—"

The door opens behind me and Mr. Cruz pauses. He smiles at whomever is walking in. I don't turn around because I want him to know that regardless of how chummy he is with my brother, my focus is on him and this job.

"Morgan," Mr. Cruz says, "this is my son Bennett. Come join us, B."

I stand up and turn around with a smile in place and my hand extended, and when he closes the distance between us I feel as though I may just faint because *no*. There is absolutely no way life can be this cruel.

"I will. I came to meet the elusive—" He frowns. "M-Morgan?"

"Hi. You're . . ." I try to hide my panic, but I'm pretty sure my heart is going to explode out of my chest. "You're Bennett?" The tremor in my voice spreads to my hand, arm, and now most of my body. I lower my hand to try to hide my nerves. *What the fuck? What the fuck? What the fuck?* This is Bennett Cruz? This guy? Of all of the millions of guys in the city it had to be him?

"Oh, you've met," Mr. Cruz says behind me. "I thought you said you hadn't."

"No." Bennett clears his throat. "I mean, we met once in passing but I didn't realize . . ."

"Yeah, that's so crazy. Small world, wow," I add quickly and lamely because what are we supposed to say? We met and fucked once and it was the most magical experience of my life and no man after him has really come close to recreating that with me?

"Sit, sit," Mr. Cruz says. "Morgan was just telling me about her love for dating apps."

"You're on a dating app?" Bennett's question is barely audible. I don't think he's gotten over the shock just yet.

"I build them." I lick my lips, suddenly feeling way shy. "I mean, my dream is to build one that will lead people to true love. A lot of today's apps are very much for instant gratification, and that's cool, but I feel that if we took the pictures off them and keep the anonymity we had once upon a time with AOL and such things, we can get back to a place where people stop sending . . ." I hesitate.

"It's all right, you can say it," Mr. Cruz says with a chuckle. "I think I know where you're going."

"Well, where people stop sending nudes and start having deep conversations," I finish.

"So, your goal is to be Cupid," Bennett says beside me.

I shrug, meeting his eyes for the first time since he arrived. "My goal is to help as many people find meaning in their lives past just a good lay."

"Sometimes a good lay is the only thing people need."

I will myself not to react. I'm good at that, but this is a true test of my poker face abilities.

"Forgive my son, Morgan. He's out of touch with love," Mr. Cruz explains. "A bitter woman and even more bitter divorce will do that to you."

"Oh." I rear back slightly. *He was married? When was he married?* "I'm sorry."

"Yeah. Shit happens." Bennett rubs his forehead as if he wants to be anywhere but here.

"Anyway, Morgan, we are thrilled to have you here at SEVEN and look forward to helping you reach your personal goals as well as seeing growth in this company."

"Thank you so much." I smile wide. "I'm really grateful for the opportunity."

"Patty will show you around the building. Keep your eyes peeled for an email from us about your assignment and where to report to on Monday." Mr. Cruz stands up when I do and comes around for another hug. "And we'd love to have you over for dinner this weekend if you can make it. I know you've been living here a while, but having family far away can get a little lonely. Barbie makes a great sweet potato soufflé and I'll be grilling."

"I would love that. Thank you." I smile again.

Bennett stands up and rebuttons his suit, his amber eyes meeting mine as he extends a hand for me to shake. I take it, my pulse quickening with the contact.

"Look forward to working with you," I say.

"Likewise."

I drop my hand as if I touched hellfire—and in a way I did. I walk out of the room, fighting the sudden urge to scream at the top of my lungs.

CHAPTER THREE

BENNETT

"YOU HAD SEX WITH HER, didn't you?"

My attention snaps to where my father is standing. "What? No."

"Either you already did or you're thinking about it and my advice to you is to kill that thought as quickly as you can. This is Devon's baby sister."

"She's not a baby," I mutter.

She sure as fuck doesn't look like one. She looks like a goddamn wet dream in that sleek black pencil dress and those sneaker wedged shoes. What kind of a woman wears sneakers to an interview? A year ago, she'd said her name was Elizabeth. *Her middle name*, I remind myself. Still. What the fuck?

I walk over to my father's desk and pick up her resume, reading it over quickly.

"She's qualified," he says. "She's overqualified."

"Yeah. I see that." My scowl deepens as I look at the top of the page—Morgan E. Tucker.

Fuck.

If Devon finds out—if he even gets an inkling that I fucked his kid sister—he'll kill me. As a two-hundred-plus-pound wide receiver, it wouldn't even be a hard feat for him. Fuck. Shit. Fuck. If I was home, I would've hit my punching bag already. Twice.

"What department did you assign her to?"

"I haven't yet."

"Hm." I look at her resume. It's pretty impressive. The girl has interned at major companies. It makes me wonder why she used her brother's connections to work for my company instead of taking a job at one of those. "Social media needs help."

"So do you," he says. "You need a new assistant."

"Fuck no." My eyes widen. "She's completely overqualified for that position."

"I agree," he says. "We can have her doing more than one thing. She seems perfectly capable."

"Dad." I stare at him.

"Just a couple of weeks, Bennett, until I figure out what department she's a better fit for. I'm leaning toward development since she's already doing that on the side."

"Conflict of interest. We want to build a dating app, she builds dating apps. That's a recipe for disaster."

"Maybe we can buy one from her."

"She's barely out of college." I shoot him a look. "You think she can make something worth buying?"

"You saw her resume." He raises an eyebrow, challenging. I back down because he's right. "You were in college when you started this company."

"Good point. Do as you wish. Hiring new talent is your job, not mine." I set her resume down with a sigh. "Did you go over the contracts? I'm meeting with Ricky at ten."

"Patty emailed them to you."

"Good. I'll see you later." I turn around and start walking out of the office.

"Ben."

"Yeah?" I turn around to look at him.

"I expect you to be on your best behavior around Morgan Tucker."

"She's too young for me, Pops." I wink at him and walk out, heart pounding. I really do need to get my shit together if I'm going to have to see her every day.

CHAPTER FOUR

MORGAN

"REWIND, please. I'm pretty sure I just heard you say that the best lay of your life is Devon's best friend," my friend Jamie says.

I'm on a three-way phone call with my friends Jamie and Presley, recounting everything that happened this morning. After my interview, Patty showed me around the building and introduced me to some colleagues before sending me home, but I haven't been able to shake my encounter with Bennett.

"Talk about a bad first impression," I mutter as I walk around my apartment.

"Second impression," Presley corrects.

"Pretty sure you made a great first impression," Jamie adds with a laugh.

I shut my eyes but laugh despite myself. "What am I supposed to do?"

"What can you do? Take the job and pretend he's not there," Jamie says. "This is too good of an opportunity for you not to."

"She's right," Presley says. "Just don't succumb to temptation again."

"Funny, coming from you."

"Well, I'm not leading by example," she says. "But seriously, this is a different situation. This job can open up so many doors for you. I have no doubt you'll be creating an amazing concept and actually getting credit for it by the end of the year."

"You're right. I mean, it's not like I'm going to tell Devon or anything." I bite my lip. "Do you think he'll tell him? What if he tells him? My brother will flip out."

"I doubt he's going to tell him."

"It was a one-time thing."

"You're overthinking this. I bet you he's over it already."

"Yeah, I doubt he paid much attention to it," I say. "Apparently, he's divorced, so I doubt I was ever at the forefront of his mind." My phone starts beeping with another call. "I have to go. It's Dev."

"Good luck."

"Love you."

"Love you guys." I switch over. "Hey, Dev."

"Hey," he says, "I was in practice earlier so I couldn't call. How'd it go this morning?"

"It went well. I guess. I mean, I don't know what I'll be doing, but apparently, there are tons of positions I qualify for so they just have to pick one."

"Yeah, Bennett was telling me he's looking for an assistant."

"I can't." I blink. "I mean, that would be . . . I'm pretty sure I qualify for other things."

"You probably do." He sighs. "I miss you, Morgie. When are you coming to visit?"

"Nobody told you to take a job with the enemy," I say.

He chuckles. "Come on. Come to a game. Maybe you'll become a fan. Nora did."

"Nora is a fan of you, not that team. No chance in hell I'll become one. I'll go to a game though." I laugh. "When does the season start?"

"First home game is in two weeks."

"'Kay. I'll be there then."

"Perfect. I'll tell Nora."

"Mr. Cruz invited me to their house this weekend for a barbecue."

"That'll be fun. You should go."

"Can you come too?" I hold my breath because I know it's unlikely. I'm sure he and Nora have plans already.

"Yeah, why not? Nora will be in Florida visiting her parents anyway. Can I crash at your place?"

"Always." I laugh. "Technically it's *your* place, Dev."

My brother bought this apartment with his first NFL check. There have been many checks and many purchases after it, but I know he'll always consider this two-bedroom apartment his first home. I moved in last year when the apartment I'd been renting with a roommate reached the end of its lease, and my brother basically made me move here on the basis that it was empty and he needed someone to look after it anyway.

"It's our place, Morg. I'll see you this weekend."

And with that, we hang up and I feel a helluva lot more comfortable with the idea of going to a barbecue that Bennett will no doubt be attending.

CHAPTER FIVE

"WE'RE GOING OUT."

I GLANCE up from my computer and look at my brother, standing in the doorway of my room. "I'm good."

"No, you're not good. We're going out."

"Um. No, I'm not." I shoot a pointed look at the glass of wine beside me and the computer on my lap. "You go."

He walks into my room and sits on the edge of the bed, his weight sinking half of it. "Nora will kill me if I go out by myself and I want to go out."

I shut my laptop with a sigh. "Why are you so restless? Why can't you just stay in?"

"Because I can't." He shrugs. "I mean, I can, but it's all I do these days, stay in, stay in, stay in."

"Okay." I swing my legs off the bed and stand, stretching. "Where do you wanna go? Presley opened her brewery."

"Nah, we can go there Sunday. Let's go to this new bar they opened up the block."

I frown. "There's no bar up the block."

"Yeah, there is."

"What's it called?"

"It Has No Name."

"The bar has no name?"

"No. It Has No Name is the name. It's an all-black building . . . you've never seen it?"

"Oh." I frown. I have seen it. I walk by it all the time, but it literally has no name. "Okay cool. That's not far. I can do that. Does it have a rooftop?"

"It does, actually. You'll feel right at home."

"Yeah, 'cause there are so many rooftops in Vegas." I roll my eyes.

The mention of Vegas instantly shifts his mood. He stands up and strides out. "Can you be ready in an hour?"

"Yep."

I GREW up holding my brother's hand, and it's exactly how we walk into the bar with no name. There's something comforting about it. A part of me feels like he's ruined me by being such a good male figure in my life. He's not much older than I am, but he's old enough to have that effect on me, especially when our own father was such a deadbeat before he finally walked out of our lives for good. Devon took on the role of father figure pretty quickly, from teaching me to tie my shoes to taking me to buy tampons the first time I got my period. Come to think of it, he took on a full parental role. He seriously deserves all the good things.

As we walk in, people turn their heads, some of them say his name, others look at him, then at me, then back at him. I squeeze his hand tighter. I don't know how Nora puts up with this scrutiny all the time. I can't imagine having to deal with every single woman looking at me like they know they'd be a better fit for my partner.

We're escorted to the second floor, to a secluded section where there are three guys laughing. When they see Dev, they shoot out of their seats. He lets go of my hand to match their overly excited greetings. After a round of hollering and jumping around, he turns to me.

"This is my sister, Morgan."

The three of them take turns giving me hugs, until the third one, Jermaine, gives me a huge bear hug and lifts me up from the floor until I'm laughing. When he sets me down my brother yanks his hand from my waist.

"Little sister," Devon adds with a growl. "All of y'all are bad news, so don't fucking get any ideas."

They all laugh. I roll my eyes but laugh as I take the seat next to my brother on the oversized couch. Devon gets a couple of bottles of Champagne and pours me a glass, and I listen as they talk about football—two of them play with Dev, and one of them, Jermaine, plays for the local team here. They're mid-conversation when Dev suddenly gets up and starts jumping like a kid again.

"I thought you weren't gonna show, motherfucker!"

I look up and watch as Bennett walks over to us with a date in tow. All the guys make a huge fuss about him being there.

"Where's Nora?" he asks as he takes off his jacket before turning to the woman he came with. "This is Stacy."

"Nice to meet you," Dev says. I take a bigger sip of Champagne. "You met my sister, Morgan, right?"

"We met." My smile is flat but polite as I nod, completely avoiding his eyes. I look at his date and smile. "Hi, Stacy."

"Hi." She smiles back. "Kinda glad you're here. I didn't realize I was crashing a guys' night."

I smile while I sip, wondering if Bennett usually sees my brother when he's in town. How have we never run into each other before tonight? Well, except for that one time when . . . I shake off the thought. My stomach is uneasy enough without the added reminder of our night together. If there's any chance I'm going to make it out of here without losing my mind, I need to keep my head down and my thoughts in check. It does nothing to calm my nerves when Bennett decides to fill the empty spot beside mine. Thankfully, we all fall into easy conversation about football coaches and roster changes.

"You should tell your boss to hire my brother," I say, smiling at Jermaine. "That way we can do this all the time."

"Or I can just ask you out and we can do it without him." He winks.

"Hey, I'm not objecting." I laugh.

"I'm objecting," Dev says loudly. "Every man sitting around this table can either keep their hands to themselves or lose a limb."

My gaze instantly finds Bennett's. He's sipping his drink nonchalantly, smiling like the cat that ate the canary. I'm grateful for the dim lights, because I know my face is flaming red right now. I look away.

"Aw, come on, Dev. You gonna tell me someone who looks like she does doesn't date?"

"Maine, I love you like a brother, but don't go there," Dev says, his tone final. "Besides, you couldn't fucking handle her even if you tried."

Jermaine laughs. I sigh, draining the rest of my drink before leaning over to whisper in my brother's ear. "I'm going to go to the bathroom."

"Want me to—"

"I need a break from your overprotectiveness." I shoot him a look.

He chuckles. "You're going downstairs?"

"For a little while, but I do need to use the restroom. I'll be back in a little while." I ruffle his hair and walk toward the stairs.

Downstairs, I feel free. They have a DJ playing music, and a full bar. I walk over to the edge and lean against it, waiting to catch the bartender's attention. When I get it, I order an Old Fashioned.

"Make that two."

My gaze snaps up at the sound of the voice beside me. "What are you doing down here?"

"Getting a drink," he says. "What does it look like I'm doing?"

"Following me."

He chuckles. "You're a little sure of yourself."

"Am I?" I turn to face him fully and this time I force myself to keep my eyes on that intense amber gaze of his. "We have a personal waitress upstairs."

"Yet here we are."

"Look, I get it. This is weird and awkward and you think I'm going to slip up and say something to Devon, but you're wrong. We had a one-night stand. I'm sure you haven't given me a second thought since it happened. I mean, you were married, divorced, you're obviously with someone now, and that's great, I'm glad for you. My point is, you don't have to worry about me saying anything at all." Our drinks come. He pays for both. I cut him a look. "You didn't have to do that."

He shrugs a shoulder. "I wanted to."

"Well, thank you." I take my drink and move away from the bar, closer to the corner. When I look up, I can sort of see the area where we were sitting upstairs. I see the couches, their feet, but not much else. Bennett sidles up beside me. I frown. "Is Stacy in the bathroom or something?"

"No."

"So why are you here?" My eyes widen. "Shouldn't you be upstairs? I already told you I'm not going to mention anything."

"I know." He sips his Old Fashioned. Watches me. Sips again. "I wasn't really worried you would tell him."

"So why are you here?" It's the millionth time I've asked and I'm at the point where I'm exasperating myself, but he's totally killing my vibe and the reason I came downstairs in the first place.

"Why are *you* here?"

I blink. "Because, as you can see, I have a helluva overprotective brother and I'd rather take my chances down here."

"You're trying to see if you meet someone?"

"Yes and no."

"Okay. Now I'm intrigued."

"I like talking to people, especially single people looking for people to make a connection with."

"Playing Cupid." He hides his smile behind his glass as he takes a sip of his drink.

"Not exactly. I mean, I'm not pairing people together at the club, if that's what you're getting at."

He chuckles. "Because that would be ridiculous. People come here to have fun, get drunk, dance, and maybe leave with someone they connect with on an animalistic level. You want to turn that experience into some sappy romance novel."

"First of all, that is not a fair assessment on why people go dancing. Secondly, finding love isn't sappy and neither are the majority of romance novels. You should do your research before you make those kinds of statements."

"Sure. I'll wait for a list of romance novels I should read, or will you lend me your paperbacks so I can see everything you highlighted?"

"I don't remember you being this obnoxious the first time we met."

"But you do remember screaming my name until the crack of dawn." His slow spreading smile is trouble. As a matter of fact, everything about this man says trouble with a capital T. I'd never really understood that statement until this moment.

"You should probably run along. Wouldn't want Jermaine to put the moves on your girl." I lift my Old Fashioned. "Thanks for the drink."

"He can have her." He gets closer still, until our arms are touching and our backs are against the wall underneath the staircase we should both walk up right now. "I get bored easily."

"Is that why you got a divorce?"

"No." He pulls away.

"Hm." I take another sip. "Do you have kids?"

"No."

"Hm." Another sip.

"Do you want kids?"

"Are you asking me if I want to practice making them with you?" He raises an eyebrow.

"Are you asking to get your balls chopped off by your best friend?"

Bennett chuckles, tossing his head back and resting it against the wall behind us. As his laughter fades, he says, "I can't stop thinking about you."

His admission makes my heart skip a beat. I ignore it. On

top of Bennett being my brother's best friend, we're going to be working in the same building, so this feeling bubbling inside me needs to be shaken away as soon as possible.

"You've seen me twice since our one-night stand a year ago." I look at him. "Otherwise, I'm sure you wouldn't be thinking about me at all."

"I'm sorry I left."

"We agreed it was a one-time thing."

"Did you forget about me after that day?" He straightens a bit and takes another sip. His eyes are so close, his mouth is so close, his chest, his arms. I could lie to him but decide not to.

"I think about you all the time actually." I sip my drink, not taking my eyes off his. "I get off to you almost every night. Even named my vibrator Ben."

"Fuck." He bites his full bottom lip and groans as he comes closer still, his breath fanning my face as he closes the distance between us. "I want to kiss you so fucking bad right now."

"But you won't?"

He shakes his head, and our noses kiss for us, Eskimo style. "Dev's my best friend. He wouldn't approve."

"I agree." I lean in closer. His lips are a breath away from mine. My heart is pounding against my chest, against his. "It would be a really bad idea."

"Terrible."

"Once you start work on Monday, this can never happen again," he whispers. "Ever."

"No more sneaking kisses?"

"No more anything."

"Why?"

"Because I promised my father I'd stay away from you."

"Okay."

"Okay."

Our lips touch. His mouth is soft, so soft, the kiss light and warm. When he sneaks his tongue into my mouth, we both groan, a vibration against my chest that rumbles through me until it hits my knees. I bring a hand up and grip his strong biceps, holding my drink with my other. He brings a hand down and grips my waist tightly, to the point of pain. He drags it down and back to my ass, squeezing, pulling me to his body until one of his legs is wedged between mine. The short dress I'm wearing rides up slightly, and suddenly I can feel the friction of his jeans against my panties. He moves with the beat of the music and even if I hadn't already fucked him I would know just by this display how good he'd be in bed. The thought comes with a wave of heat as we continue to kiss. We both come up for air at the same time, my eyes hazy, needy, as I look at him. The look in his matches mine.

"You should go," I say finally, remembering he brought a date here. The thought fills me with horror. Is it a girlfriend? It can't be if he's been here with me most of the time. "Someone is waiting for you upstairs."

"Does that bother you?" he asks. "That I'm here with another woman?"

"No." I scowl. "Is she your girlfriend?"

He shakes his head.

"But you're going home with her." I lick my lips. "She'll be the one screaming your name tonight."

He brings his hand to cup my neck and pulls me in for another kiss—hard, fast, unyielding. "I wish it could be you."

With that, he leaves.

CHAPTER SIX

I SHOULD HAVE NEVER AGREED to come to a barbecue at Bennett's parents' house. Thank God my brother is here. Otherwise, I would have had to come up with an excuse to leave. His parents are lovely and welcoming and make a mean steak, but Bennett's presence is making me edgy. It's the way he looks at me, that hooded amber gaze filled with dirty promises that takes me back to that first night and the other night, when he kissed me underneath a stairwell. My heart pounds a little faster, a little harder, at the thought of his lips on mine, his tongue sliding inside my mouth. I blink away from his lips and smile at his mother as she tells us about the Alaskan cruise she and her husband went on over the summer.

"The ice was all melted," Mr. Cruz says.

"It was definitely not what we were expecting," Ms. Cruz adds. "But it was still a good time."

"You were both drunk the entire time," Bennett says with a laugh. "Every time you called to check in, you were slurring your words."

"The alcohol was good," Mr. Cruz says, shrugging.

"And the ice was melted," Ms. Cruz adds, offering an explanation. "We couldn't even go sledding with the dogs."

"How's your mother doing?" Mr. Cruz asks, looking at Dev.

I feel myself stiffen but manage to keep a smile on my face. I'm not sure how much my brother has told these people about our parents or family life. A big part of me wishes he hadn't told them anything at all. It's embarrassing enough to have lived it, and letting outsiders in feels painful even if they do mean well.

"She's doing great," Dev says, smiling that carefree smile of his.

He looks over at me and we hold that familiar stare, doing that thing that only siblings and best friends can do with their eyes, and I know he hasn't told them much about anything. I relax. Having a drug addict for a mother is hard enough without the outside scrutiny. It's something I don't speak to anyone about, partly because I'm ashamed of it, but also because my friends wouldn't understand. They were born with silver spoons in their mouths and even though they've faced their own hardships, none of them have come in the form of a mother who'd rather shoot up than take her daughter to ballet.

"So," Mr. Cruz says, "Morgan, I hope you don't mind me doing this, but Paul is a good friend of mine and I happened to run into him the other day so I asked him about you. He said you developed the Global Trust website and came up with the concept."

I feel myself blush. "I did."

Devon puts a hand on my knee. "Morgie doesn't like to talk about her hard-earned achievements. She has also revamped a ton of NFL teams' websites."

"That's not on your resume," Bennett says, frowning.

"It was pro-bono work I did last year, to gain experience." I shrug. "I had to make room for other things in my resume."

"She's also working on a ton of great ventures," Dev adds, smiling proudly. "One of these days she's going to come up with a concept that's going to blow our minds."

"What is your goal?" Ms. Cruz asks, walking back over with a case holding a bottle of wine and glasses. She sets it all down and pours some for us.

"I want to change the scope of online dating." I smile at her as she hands me a glass and take a sip. "I feel like there's so much potential there."

"What would you do differently than what's already out there?"

"A few things. For starters, I don't like that we seem to be overlooking the importance of intimacy and obsessing over looks and hooking up." I set my wineglass down and go for my iced tea.

"How would you do it, then?" Devon asks. "No pictures?"

"Well, I mean, I have a few concepts. A few are no pictures in the beginning, so you'd have to communicate with someone for three weeks before you get a picture."

"How can you be sure they're not exchanging pictures on the side?" Bennett asks. The curiosity in his voice makes a little thrill run through me.

"Well, I can't." I shrug. "But I guess if they do, that's their problem. I'm just trying to help them find a more meaningful connection."

"Tell them about the workplace app," Dev says. I shoot him a look, feeling myself flush again. He chuckles. "Morg, this is what they do for a living. They're not going to judge you."

"He's right," Mr. Cruz adds. "Besides, you've been the most

interesting houseguest we've had in over a year." He gives Bennett a meaningful look.

"Okay." I take a deep breath as I gather my thoughts. "Eighty percent of the single people I've interviewed say they haven't found love in person or on a dating app because they have no time, and when they finally make time, the people they match with aren't interested in the same things they are." I pause, making sure I haven't lost any of them. Their interested expressions keep me talking. "So the idea is to create this app where the singles in each company have a chance to get to know each other based on interests, no pictures, no names, no departments. In workplaces that do not have a fraternization policy, obviously."

"So basically what Facebook was for college students before everyone's mom started joining," Bennett says, grinning at his mom's reprimanding frown.

"More or less."

"I like that," Mr. Cruz says, nodding slowly, as if he's giving it some thought. "Have you created this app already?"

"Yeah, I mean, it's not final, but it's in development."

"It's a pretty simple concept," Bennett says, pursing his lips. I try so hard not to stare at them and fail, but staring into his eyes is so much worse, so I end up looking away.

"Why don't you report to Bennett's office first thing tomorrow morning, Morgan?" Mr. Cruz says. "I'll speak to him about a few things once you leave here tonight. I'm sure he would love to hear about more of your concepts."

I nod slowly, in disbelief. People like Bennett and his father have the power to make or break my career. They have the power to turn my abstract concepts into globally established companies.

CHAPTER SEVEN

I REALLY DO plan on reporting to Bennett's office as soon as I can, but first I stop by the break room to brew myself the cup of coffee I couldn't have this morning because I was busy taking my brother to the airport. The door opens as I'm standing by the counter, waiting for it to finish brewing, and a tall guy wearing a Mets baseball cap and plain black T-shirt walks in. He pauses when he sees me.

"You're the new girl."

"That would be me." I let out a laugh as I extend my hand for him to shake. "Morgan."

"Wesley." He nods back toward the door. "I'm in development."

"Oh, nice. I'm . . . actually, I'm not sure where they're putting me. I'm meeting with Bennett this morning about that. It's either social media or marketing though, so I guess we'll be working in close proximity."

"You're entirely overdressed for our department." He eyes me up and down. "Not that you don't look great, but we're more ripped jeans and Converse kind of people."

"And Mets caps." I look at the hat on his head.

"And Mets caps." He smiles.

"Want some coffee?" I pour myself a mug.

"No coffee for me. I'm a tea kinda guy."

"Mets and tea. Got it."

"You're not a Yankees girl, are you? Is that why you're drilling me about my hat?"

I laugh. "No, I grew up in Vegas. No baseball for me."

"Only prostitutes and gambling." His easy laugh makes me laugh.

"You got me completely figured out." I wink.

The door opens and shuts. We both look up to see Bennett walking in. Our eyes lock instantly, and I swear my heart goes into a frenzy. He looks great in jeans and a T-shirt, but Bennett in a sharp blue suit is on another level of hot.

"Wesley," Bennett says as way of greeting, taking his gaze from mine for a second before he looks at me again. "I see you've met Morgan."

"We were just getting to know each other." Wesley meets my eyes. I can't help but smile. He has kind eyes that make me feel comfortable, unlike Bennett's dark, explosive gaze.

"We have a meeting in four minutes, Miss Tucker," Bennett says.

Wesley's eyebrows shoot up at his tone. "Guess I'll see you later? I take my lunch break at twelve-fifteen. I'm going to the bar down the block for a burger, if you want to join me."

"Sure. I'll —"

"Excuse me, please," Bennett cuts in, walking toward me. "Some of us actually need to get work done today."

I move away from the pot and wave at Wesley, laughing at

the way he rolls his eyes behind Bennett's back. When the door closes again, I let out a breath and look at Bennett.

"You're not very nice to your employees."

"They're my employees. I don't have to be nice, I just have to be fair. I'm not here to make friends."

"Hm." I watch as he pours his coffee. "Good to know."

"What's good to know?" His eyes flick to mine.

"That we're not going to be friends." I walk out of the break room, heading to the reception area of Bennett's office. He follows shortly after, walking straight to his door and holding it open for me.

"You coming, Cupid?"

The way he says that makes my entire body burn up, but I ignore it as I walk into his office and take a seat across from the chair he's going to take. I take a sip of my coffee as I watch him take off his jacket and hang it up on the rack behind him. He rolls up his sleeves until most of his golden forearms are exposed and I focus on the way his muscles flex with the movement. I blink rapidly and look away. I can't sit here fantasizing about a guy who's technically my boss. It doesn't matter if we already slept together. He sits down across from me and takes a sip of his coffee, sighing as he sets it down.

"So, my dad wants to give you the opportunity to try that workplace app here." He says it as if it's no big deal at all. It takes me a moment to break free of my shock before forming a reaction, because seriously, *what?*

"What?"

"Devon's been talking about you and your ideas for years, and I guess you won my father over during dinner the other night," he says. "He believes in it."

"You don't." I study his face. God, he's gorgeous, like a beautiful work of art those ancient guys in Rome used to make.

"It's not a secret that I don't believe in love or wasting my time on those kinds of apps."

"I get it. It's not for everyone." I lick my lips. "He really wants me to try out the app here?"

"Guess so." Bennett nods. "Are you on any dating apps?"

"No."

He chuckles. "Seriously?"

"I think the ones out right now are cool and all, but I want to meet someone who likes me for me, not for the shape of my ass."

His lips lift in a slow smirk, but he doesn't say anything. He doesn't have to. My face goes up in flames nonetheless.

"So, there's no fraternization policy here?"

"Nope." His gaze heats on mine.

"Good to know."

"That doesn't change anything between us."

"Who says I'm asking because of you?"

"Good point." His mouth twitches. "I can give you access to the database so you can pick the singles out and ask them if they want to participate."

"Okay." I take a deep breath. "Is that what you want me to work on? Like . . . as my job?"

"No." He lets out a low chuckle. Even that sounds sexy as fuck. Ugh. "You're going to be my assistant for the next few weeks. It'll give you enough time to get your app running so we can gather data and explore the dating app world. Dad's really interested in that and he liked your concept. I don't have an assistant right now, and to be honest, I'm a bit of a control freak when it comes to my things. I won't need much, but I will require a few things like scheduling and meetings because I hate doing that."

"Okay. I've never assisted anyone, so you may have to be a little patient with me."

He waves a hand at my comment as if he won't mind. "You'll have access to my personal and business emails, which you'll respond to on my behalf every morning."

"Sounds simple enough."

He watches me. I watch him, unsure of whether or not I should get up and leave. Finally, after a couple of beats of discomfort, I clear my throat and ask, "Should I leave now?"

"That would be helpful," he says. "I have to get on a call in two minutes. Welcome to SEVEN, Miss Tucker. I look forward to working with you."

With that, he dismisses me.

CHAPTER EIGHT

I'M GOING through the database when Wesley shows up in front of my desk. My gaze flies to the time on my computer. Twelve-ten.

"You're punctual," I say.

"I'm serious about food." He smiles. "You ready?"

The phone on my desk rings. I shoot Wesley an apologetic look as I reach for it. "Bennett Cruz's office."

"I see he got a new flavor of the month," a woman says.

"Excuse me?"

"Did he get bored of his previous assistant or did she get tired of him treating her as if she was second place?" The woman doesn't wait for me to respond before adding, "News-flash, you will always be second place to me, so I suggest you don't try to fill my shoes."

"Who am I speaking to?"

"Mrs. Cruz, and you'll do well to remember that."

"Um . . ."

She ends the call before I can get another word in. I put the receiver back in its cradle and look at Wesley, wide-eyed.

"That was the strangest conversation."

"Tell me about it on our way to lunch." He pats his stomach twice.

"Yeah. Sure." I blink, trying to figure out why she'd call my line to say those things. Bennett is divorced. Why would his ex-wife put his new assistant on notice? I'm bending down to get my purse when Bennett's door opens behind me.

"Going somewhere?"

"Lunch." I straighten, heart pounding. He eyes me like he knows I'm hiding something. I'm not. I'm going to tell him about the call as soon as I get back.

"Hm." He looks between me and Wesley. "Can you grab me a sandwich while you're out?"

"Sure. What kind?" I pull out my phone to take a note.

"I'll text it to you," he says, walking over to me and taking the phone from my hand. He types something in there and fishes his phone out of his pocket. He hands mine back, holding my gaze. "Thank you."

"Of course."

"SO, from what I hear, his ex-wife is crazy," Wesley says as we're wrapping up the foil of the sandwiches we just ate. "She'll keep calling like that. The best thing to do is ignore her."

"I just . . . how did she even know he got a new assistant?"

Wesley shrugs. My phone buzzes for a second time with a text from Bennett and I'm once again regretting having given him my number.

Bennett: Are you on your way back?

Me: Not yet.

Bennett: . . .

Me: You're legally obligated to give me a one-hour lunch break.

I smile when I see the typing bubble appear and disappear, revealing he deleted whatever response he was going to send.

"You ready?" Wesley asks, standing.

"Ready." I pick up the bag containing Bennett's lunch and let him guide me out of the sandwich shop.

On our way back, we talk some more about software development, which is Wesley's first love. He tells me about the video games he's in the middle of building and how SEVEN may buy it from him if they decide it'll be popular in today's market. We talk some more about the software they've purchased in the past and what they've been able to do with them. I'm not entirely convinced I would want to hand over my dating apps to them, but I like knowing my options. Wesley walks me all the way back to my desk, still talking animatedly about his software.

"You have to check it out," he says. "It might help with the back matter of the workplace app thing."

"Maybe. I just worry about being involved in the back matter at all, even though it is all anonymous. I don't want people to think I'm trying to play Cupid." I frown as I say the words, thinking about Bennett.

"I think you should be fine. Someone definitely needs to make sure it's running properly though. Are you going to sign up to make sure it is?"

"I would, but what if I end up getting matched with someone?"

"There are worst things than finding love." Wesley shrugs,

then smiles. "Come on. You can't be the girl trying to make everyone else happy and putting yourself second. You'll end up alone."

I want to tell him that in the end, we all end up alone, but that wouldn't be on brand—it wouldn't match the fun, carefree, obsessed-with-love persona I've worked so hard to create. He departs with a little wave and the promise that we'll do it again tomorrow, and I go to Bennett's door, knocking twice before opening it. He looks up from his desk and signals me over as he talks to someone on the phone. I shut the door quietly behind me and walk around his desk, taking out his food and setting it over the table neatly—sandwich in the middle, chips to the left, water bottle on the right. When I'm done, I walk around the desk again and head back out.

The rest of my day is spent working on the app and website, and I completely forget about the call I received this afternoon.

CHAPTER NINE

"HEY, NORA." I smile at the sound of her voice.

"Morgan, I was going to FaceTime you after my yoga class today," she responds. "How are you? How's the job? Is Bennett being an asshole or is he treating you right?"

"He's fine." I laugh. "He's not an asshole."

"Good. Do you like what you're doing there?"

I spend the next five minutes telling her about the app and how my colleague thinks I should sign up to make sure everything is functioning properly.

"That sounds messy," she says. "Hold on, your brother just walked in. Let me put you on speakerphone."

"Hey, Morgie."

"Hey, Dev. I was just catching Nora up on the app stuff."

"I heard. You're going to sign up for it and let yourself get matched?"

"I mean . . . you know how I feel about that, but I do need to make sure it's running smoothly on all accounts. If this does well, SEVEN may give me a huge opportunity."

"Fuck it. What do you have to lose?"

"What if you meet the love of your life?" Nora adds.

"I don't know . . ."

"She's right, Morg. You may meet a really great guy on there."

"I don't know if great guys exist. Aside from you, of course," I add quickly.

He chuckles. Nora laughs. "Anyway, I wanted to FaceTime you to see your reaction, but being that we're all on the phone right now, I think this is the right time to tell you that . . . "

Nora lifts her hand up, showing me a huge ring on her left hand. "We're getting married!"

"Oh, my God." I squeal. "It's about time!"

Dev laughs. "I thought so too."

"I'm so excited, you guys! Congratulations. Do you know when you're getting married? Big wedding, small? Tell me everything!"

"We're thinking small and intimate," Nora says. "And I want you to be my maid of honor."

"Oh, my God." I feel myself tearing up. "Of course, I will!"

"Don't tell Bennett yet," Dev warns. "I want to call him later today to ask him to be my best man."

"Okay." My stomach does a little flip. "Anyway, I have to let you guys go. I just got to work, but yay! Congratulations! Love you both."

"Talk to you soon."

"Love you!"

I run into Wesley in the lobby and we ride up together, talking about the app the entire way up and as he walks me to my desk.

"So basically, I just need to make it pretty and it's done. I already emailed all the singles on the database and sent them a signup link should they want to join."

"I already joined." He looks me in the eye. "Wouldn't it be cool if you join and we end up getting matched?"

I smile. "It would be interesting. I mean, it would mean we have a lot in common."

"I think we have a chance."

Bennett's door opens. He frowns when he sees me standing there with Wesley. "You're supposed to be in my office, Tucker. What are you gossiping about this early in the morning?"

"I was just telling her that I joined her app. I'm kind of hoping it matches us together." Wesley winks at me as he walks away. I blush and look away, busying myself with taking things out of my purse before putting it away.

"I'll be in your office in ten minutes. I'll get us coffee." I don't bother to look up.

I know he's still standing right there, staring at me, because I feel his eyes on me, but I can't bear to confirm it. What must he be thinking? I just started this job and I'm already flirting with some guy, or he's flirting with me, whatever. It wouldn't be so awkward if we didn't have all this stuff between us. I go to the break room and brew a fresh pot of coffee. The door opens and closes, and I glance up to see Bennett walk in.

"I told you I would get your coffee." I frown.

"I didn't tell you how I like it."

"Oh."

He walks over and stands beside me. It's impossible for me not to smell him, impossible for me not to feel him. He lifts an arm and reaches over me to get two mugs from the top shelf of the cabinet. I stop breathing. He's not touching me. He's not doing anything inappropriate. He's just a man getting mugs of coffee. A good-looking man. A really good-looking man who's got a really nice dick and who knows how to use it. Not that I'm thinking about that or anything. I will my heart to stop pounding. He brings the mugs down and places them on the counter, then clicks the off button of the coffeemaker and taps the hand I'm using to grip the pot.

"I think it's done now," he murmurs, his voice too close to my ear.

I shut my eyes. "Wesley wants me to join the app."

"Yeah?"

"Yeah."

"Are you hoping the app matches you together?"

"Would it bother you if it did?" My eyes snap open. He's standing too close to me. Kissably close, which is a problem.

"No." His gaze flicks from mine to my lips and back up.

"Okay, then."

"I take my coffee black." He pushes away from the counter and walks toward the door.

In his office, I sit across from him with the laptop provided to me. We're going through his business emails first. He reads them from his desk, and tells me quickly what to respond to whom, according to the schedule I made him yesterday. He then goes through his personal email and tells me what to jot down on the schedule according to that.

"I have to go to Vegas for a conference in a couple of weeks. I want you to come."

My gaze flies to him. "To Vegas?"

"Is that a problem?" He tears his eyes from his monitor to look at me.

"No."

"You and Devon really don't like going back there, do you?"

"Not really." I look back at the laptop in front of me.

"But your parents are still there?"

"My mom is."

"What about your dad?"

"I . . . he's not in our lives," I say, finally, and it feels like a weight is lifted off my shoulders.

"Oh. I didn't know that."

He eyes me with intrigue, but lets it go. I don't know what my brother has told him, but based on the way he phrased this question and the way his parents talked the other night, I can only assume it's not much. That is definitely a conversation I'd rather not have.

"Anyway, Wesley is helping me with the coding for the app. It should be up and running in a couple of days," I say. "I already met with your dad about it and showed him how it runs and everything."

"Wesley seems to be very interested in this." His gaze shifts from the computer to me.

"I mean, he's a developer. It's fun."

"A developer who's dying to get in on the action. He's hoping you join the stupid thing as a user and that it pairs you together." His gaze never leaves mine. Mine never leaves his.

"It very well may pair us *if* I joined, which I won't. We have a lot in common." I glare at him, not because of anything other than the fact that he called it stupid.

"Do you ever wonder how much we have in common?"

"No." I glance away. "We're . . . obviously compatible in bed, but that doesn't mean anything."

"Doesn't it?"

"I'm compatible with a lot of people in that way."

His gaze heats. "So your goal is to find love?"

I bite my tongue. That question makes me feel like a phony.

After a few seconds of debating whether or not I should answer, I clear my throat.

"I like the idea of helping other people find love. I'm not really interested in it myself. I mean, I just . . . I've had really bad luck in that department."

"I understand that." He nods. "But don't you want to find your soul mate?"

"Don't we all?" I smile. This is a ridiculous conversation. "For now, I'm perfectly content playing Cupid."

"So you're not getting on the app?"

"Just to make sure it runs well. It's a huge opportunity that you're even letting me test it out on a smaller scale." I don't say everything it could mean if it works and they end up loving it and buying it from me.

"My father's giving you the opportunity," he says. "I'm not against it, but I want to be clear that I'm also not rooting for it. We have enough app ideas to go through on a daily basis. Everyone wants SEVEN to back them."

"With good reason. Anyone who's anyone in the tech world knows SEVEN can make or break you."

"Is that why you chose to come work here instead of where you were interning?" I can tell he's fighting a smile. "I wasn't aware you loved this company so much."

"I think it's incredible what you and your father have accomplished with it. I mean, I don't know of another story like yours. It's not really a surprise that the tabloids are always looking for an interview. You come from a family of immigrants that have achieved the American dream. That's not to be taken lightly."

I'm not one to fangirl, but SEVEN is by far the most impressive and superior tech company out there right now. It's even more incredible that Bennett didn't inherit this. From what I understand, he wasn't rich before this. His parents weren't poor, like Devon and I were growing up, but they didn't have the kind of wealth they're rumored to have now. His dad was an engineer for a big computer company and when Bennett came to him with his vision for the future while he was still in college, playing football with my brother, they launched. I'd never heard of anything like it before. He finished his program at school, graduated at the top of his class, went to graduate school even though he didn't need to because by the end of year one, SEVEN was already worth millions.

"Thanks for that." He smiles, the lines around his eyes crinkling. "It's going to be a little harder for me to voice my next concern, though." He chuckles. "Dating apps is not something I want this company to be known for. Dating apps get messy. We spent an entire year clearing our name after that affair app went wrong with the leaked information and the software malfunction. It's not you I don't believe in, or your concept, it's love in general. It's too messy for business."

I blink. "I guess I see your point. It can be messy. Love can be brutal and leave you aching, but it's also impossible to live without love, to grow without it. Don't you think?"

"If we're talking about a parent's love, yes. A mate?" He shrugs. "I mean, we were made to fuck, obviously, to procreate, but I'm not sure we absolutely need to love one person for the rest of our lives."

I'm still stuck on the "we were made to fuck" part, and because of that, I feel my neck starting to heat up. In an effort to fight it, I lick my lips, pry my gaze from his, and focus on my laptop. I cannot talk about this with Bennett Cruz. He looks at me and I get hot, but innuendos from his lips take me to the point of combustion. I change the subject and give him access to the workplace app and explain to him how the coding is set up, but the way he's looking at me as I speak does nothing to control my rapidly beating heart.

CHAPTER TEN

ONE WEEK LATER . . .

I'VE BEEN STARING at my phone for two minutes, waiting for it to hit nine o'clock. That's when the app will go live and pair the thirty-seven people who signed up. I scroll down to refresh. Thirty-eight people. Interesting. At least it'll be an even number. I was kind of worried about someone being left out. At nine o'clock, my phone buzzes with the message I set up: Welcome to *Meet Me at SEVEN*. It's a silly name, but it was the only thing I could come up with for the company. The message that follows reads: Congratulations! You've been paired!

I scroll past the warnings and general rules that I know by heart until I get to the main chat. When everyone signed up, they were asked ten questions. Depending on how you answered the questions, the app paired you with whom it thinks you're the most compatible. We are all anonymous, save for our screen name, and even that is generic and provided by the app. Mine is a Robin. My pair's is an Owl. That makes me frown. I don't think those birds even go together. I'll have to tweak that once the three weeks are up. In the future, I could also just have people use their first names, or maybe a nickname, or just a name they like. I jot it down, noting it as the first issue to fix.

Owl: Good morning

My stomach flutters because oh, my God, an app I created entirely myself is actually running. That feeling never gets old. Also, the Calibri font I used looks good. Also, holy shit, the stupid thing matched me even though I was on grey and it wasn't supposed to. Another glitch I definitely need to fix, but oh well, now that I'm on here, I decide to roll with it anyway.

Me: Hey

Owl: So, how does one talk about things without actually talking about things?

Me: LOL we can talk about anything. We just can't share pictures and locations and stuff like that.

Owl: Can we talk on the phone?

Me: Seriously? It's day one. No.

Owl: I mean in general

Me: No.

Owl: After three weeks?

Me: If we both agree we're compatible.

Owl: Can we sext?

Me: Reminder: it's day one.

Owl: I'm just trying to figure out what the rules are

Me: There was an entire rule section before you got to this chat

Owl: Skipped it

How the heck did I end up with someone who skips the rule portion of the app? I sigh, tossing my phone on my bed as I stand up and walk over to the kitchen. I have three requirements for today: strong coffee, a hot shower, and a good book. Beyond that, I'm not doing anything at all, except ordering food when I get hungry later.

Owl: I wonder who came up with birds for screen names? Kind of lame.

I glare at the phone screen, resisting the urge to respond with *You're kind of lame!* Seriously, day one and I already feel like the compatibility sequence must have missed a mark somewhere before pairing us together. It doesn't matter. I can't respond anything remotely like that because if I do, he has a higher chance of figuring out who I am and that would defeat the purpose of this entire thing. He doesn't send any more messages the rest of the day, and I don't know what to send him, so I don't either. As much as I like the idea of people finding love with technology, I'm not sure I'm quite open to it, which makes me feel a little bad for the person paired with me.

I'm getting ready for bed when my phone rings and I see Bennett's name on the screen. My heart kicks as I answer it.

"Hey."

"Hey." He clears his throat. "The Vegas conference starts on Wednesday, not Friday like I'd planned. Is that okay?"

"Um. Yeah. I mean, if you need me there, I'll be there."

"Perfect. I hate to ask this of you since it's a weekend, but the flights are selling out quickly . . ."

"You want me to book our trip?"

"Yes."

I pause. "You wouldn't want to do that yourself? I mean, because you know what you like, seats and hotel-wise. Or will you tell me?"

"I can stay on the phone with you while you do it."

My eyes dart around my living room. Obviously, I'm alone, but he hasn't even asked to confirm that. I could easily be out on a date or out with friends or have people over. The thought makes me frown. "How do you know I'm not busy?"

"Are you?"

"No, but how do you know I'm not?"

"I don't know. You answered the phone. If I'm busy, I ignore the call."

"Oh." I blink, pulling my laptop over my lap. "So, coach? First class? How many tickets? When do we return?"

"Let's book Tuesday night to Sunday. Is that doable for you?"

I stare at the screen. That's almost a full week. It's not like I'm taking a week vacation. This is part of my current job, but still, six days in Vegas? The thought makes my skin crawl. I hate Vegas. Hate the smoke, hate the Strip, hate the memories I have there, hate everything I left behind.

"Morgan?"

"Uh, yeah, that's fine. Tuesday to Sunday," I repeat.

"First class. Two tickets," he says. "Two rooms at the Aria. That's where the conference will be held. Might as well stay there."

I nod at my screen as I click away, booking the trip.

"I'm sure you'll have some free time to visit family while we're there," he says. I nod again, this time a little faster, my nerves ticking in my neck.

"Sure."

"If you need to take the day off tomorrow, you can. I know I sprung this on you at the last minute."

I shrug a shoulder. "It's fine."

"Just take the day."

"Okay." He doesn't really have to tell me twice. I just didn't want to take advantage. "I'll email this to you now. See you Tuesday, then."

"See you Tuesday." He hangs up.

I forward him the emails and exhale, lying on the couch. I can do this. I can totally do this.

CHAPTER ELEVEN

I END up coming into the office late on Monday anyway because there are a few things I want to tweak and I can only do it from my computer here. While I'm at my desk, my phone rings. I answer it, not really paying attention to the caller ID. Bennett isn't in today anyway so I'll just take down the message.

"You're still there."

It's the woman again. I frown. "Do you need something?"

"Just wanted to let you know that I have eyes on you. If you sleep with him like his last assistant, your career will be over before it even begins."

"Excuse me, ma'am." I blink at her tone and her words, trying hard not to let them get to me. He slept with his last assistant? Is this something he does on the regular? For some reason, it's not a welcome thought. "I would never sleep with my boss, so I can assure you neither of us has anything to worry about."

"That's what they all say." She scoffs. "Google Amanda Matters. Raquel Velazquez. Fionna Erickson."

"Why would –" I start, but she hangs up the phone before I can even finish my question.

Jesus, she really is crazy. I roll my eyes and ignore the call. Wesley said this was exactly what the last assistant put up with and the woman drove her out of a job, so I'm not going to sweat it. I'm here to work, not play. I'm here to make my dreams come true, not worry about Bennett's dirty laundry. Still, I stand up and walk over to Wesley's desk and recount the conversation. He lets out a low whistle, tossing his Mets cap on his desk, and running a hand through his dirty blond hair.

"That bitch cray."

"My thoughts exactly." I lean against his desk. "I haven't told Bennett about the calls. Should I?"

"Honestly?" Wesley makes a face, shrugging. "If she's really bothering you, tell him. Otherwise, ignore the crazy witch and let it be. She'll get tired of calling and you're being moved to this department soon, so who cares? Let the next girl deal with her."

"You're right." I nod. "Do you think it's true? That he slept with the last girl?"

"I guess there's no telling," he says. "But if I had to bet money on it, I'd say he didn't. I'm sure you've noticed he's not very open to work relationships, despite there being nothing against it in the rule book."

"Yeah. I've definitely noticed." I absentmindedly pick invisible lint from my pants.

"So, you're leaving to Vegas soon."

"I am."

"I like the app, by the way."

"Oh." I smile wide. "You were matched."

"I'm hoping I was matched with a particular person." He winks. "The bird names are a little funny, but whatever."

Oh, my God. We stare at each other for a beat, then two. Curiosity will not get the best of me. It will not. So, on that note, I push off his desk, fluff his hair and walk away.

"See you next week."

"See you." I hear his chair turn as I'm walking away and I know he's looking at me.

The thought makes me smile. Wesley is an entirely different person than Bennett is, but he's just as attractive, in a different way. Bennett is more the jock turned businessman and Wes is the tech dork that didn't lose his surfer edge. He's sexy, and I would definitely not be mad if we did get matched.

CHAPTER TWELVE

OWL: Tell me a secret. Something nobody knows about you

Me: I was engaged once

There's something about anonymity that gives people a sense of bravado. Maybe it's false bravado, something I'll regret once these three weeks are up and this stranger knows me better than I know myself, but in the moment, it feels good. I decided late last night that I would throw caution to the wind and open up the way I hope everyone using my apps does. I figure it's hypocritical to ask them to do this without doing it myself.

Owl: Wow. What happened?

Me: Broke it off, which was good because we would've ended up getting it annulled shortly after our wedding date. Britney style.

Owl: Would it have been a drunken Vegas wedding?— Britney style

Me: Probably. The engagement was lol

I smile. The engagement was very drunken and very stupid and mostly we were a couple of kids who wanted to know what everything felt like. We wanted every experience within our grasp and we took it. We talked about marriage like it was just a thing on our checklists and not something to be taken seriously, and maybe that was the crux of our problems. Maybe we never really took each other seriously enough.

Owl: That you regretted accepting?

Me: I didn't regret it until later on

Owl: Did you give the ring back?

Me: Threw it at his face. The only thing I regret is not eloping. I kind of wanted that experience.

Owl: Even knowing it wouldn't have worked out?

Me: Haven't you done stupid things in your life?

Owl: About a million stupid things. Getting married in Vegas has never crossed my mind though

Me: Maybe you should

Owl: I think I'll leave that off my bucket list

Me: Tell me a secret

Owl: I cheated on an ex of mine

I stare at the phone. That's my number one deal breaker. Like, complete and total deal breaker. *This isn't a for-life kind of thing, Morgan. This is a fun, experimental app. Stop being judgy.* But I can't. I can't not be judgy about this. With a deep breath, I call my best friend, Presley.

"Hey, Little. What's up?"

"Hey. Nothing much. What are you up to? How's the brewery?"

"It's going. Nathaniel's on his way here to check on this Wi-Fi because I've tried everything and it won't connect."

I laugh. "Good thing you have an expert at your disposal."

"Shut up." She laughs. "What's going on? This is the week you leave for Vegas, right?"

"Yeah. Tomorrow, actually."

"Oh, wow. How long will you be there?"

"Tuesday through Sunday."

"Oh. Wow. With Bennett?"

"Yep."

"Hm." She doesn't comment further, but I can hear her thoughts as clear as if she was screaming them at me. "You'll be okay? I mean, obviously you're not sharing a room or anything, but will you be able to handle seeing him every day in a city where no one knows you?"

"I'm not following."

"People tend to get closer when they travel."

"Right. No. Not going to happen. He treats me like a little sister or something."

"Somehow, I doubt that. He kissed you."

"Before I started officially working with him. He's been on his best behavior since."

"Boring," she says. "So what's up with the app? How'd the launch go?"

"It has a few glitches that I've caught, but nothing major. Yet."

"Did it pair you with someone who seems compatible?"

"Not really, but I'm making the best out of it. Or I was, until he told me he cheated on his ex."

"Deal breaker," she says.

"Right? Total deal breaker."

She's quiet for a couple of beats. "Tell him it's a deal breaker. See how he reacts to that."

"Okay. I think I will."

We hang up with the promise to see each other when I come back from my trip and I continue packing. Owl has sent a few messages asking if I've completely disappeared.

Me: Cheating = deal breaker for me
After that, it's radio silence.

CHAPTER THIRTEEN

THE MORNING ARRIVES QUICKLY and soon I find myself sitting in a little cubby in first class beside Bennett, not that we can see each other. That's probably my favorite part about it, if I'm being honest. When we land in Vegas, the first thing I do is switch my phone out of airplane mode and text my brother, Presley, and Jamie, letting them know I landed okay. I put them all in a group text to make it easier, and I know Devon is going to have my head for it, but I don't have time to text message multiple people the same phrase right now. I also check the app and cave into turning on the push notifications for it.

Owl: How's your boss? I know we're not supposed to talk about work, but I have a few bosses, so I figure it's not giving anything away

Me: I have two and they're both nice.

Owl: Nice is better than total assholes

I laugh. *Agreed.*

Bennett looks up from his phone and meets my gaze. "What?"

"I was laughing at something . . . " I shake my head and decide not to finish my sentence. If I tell him I'm on the app, he'll make fun of me the entire trip. "Nothing."

"Did you hear what they said about our bags?" he asks as we step out of the airplane. "My phone is acting like it's still on airplane mode."

"We'll figure it out. We don't have to be anywhere tonight, do we?"

"Nah." He glances at his watch. "We could go to dinner though. Or a show? How many of these shows have you seen?"

"Not many. I didn't really hang out on the Strip aside from the times I was working."

"Where did you work?" He's looking up at the screen listing different baggage claims. I'm looking at him because I try so hard not to when he's paying attention to me that I've resorted to sneaking glances.

"A couple of casinos."

His eyes jump to me. "How old were you?"

"Old enough." I shrug a shoulder. Age doesn't mean much in this city. In certain circles, being young makes you more desirable.

"Did your brother know about these jobs?"

"No." My eyes widen. "And I would appreciate it if we kept it that way."

His eyes assess me momentarily, as if he's sizing me up, or examining how many secrets hide inside of me. It's not something I'm used to or appreciate, so I glance away, looking at the screen above us.

"Carousel three," I announce and walk away.

WE CHECK into the hotel and take the elevator up, walking to our rooms in silence. He's still walking beside me when I reach mine. I turn to look at him and realize our rooms are beside each other.

"Dinner?" he asks.

"Sure."

We walk into our rooms, the doors shutting heavily behind us, and I notice there's an adjoining door that separates us. One that I do not plan to open under any circumstances. I start unpacking. If I don't unpack the minute I get into a hotel room, I feel unsettled the rest of the trip and that is a feeling I can't afford, not now, not with Bennett, and not on this trip. I take out one of my little black dresses and hang it up by the closet, placing a pair of black pumps that Devon and Nora gave me for my birthday last year. I snap a picture and send it to the group chat.

Me: Does this look like a date outfit?

Devon: Who are you going on a date with? Aren't you in Vegas for a work conference?

Me: *eye roll emoji* not going on a date, that's why I'm asking, otherwise I'd just wear it

Jamie: I like it! Could be business chic

Presley: I like it!

Me: Thanks!

The minute I hit send, I get a phone call from my brother.

"Seriously?" I say. "Is this about the date outfit?"

"No." He pauses with a heavy sigh. "Are you going to call Mom?"

"No." I plop down on the floor by my bed. "Do you want me to check on her?"

"I don't know."

"That means you want me to."

"Not true. It means I don't know. I don't know what I would do if I was there."

"You'd probably call, and then she'd call you back every five seconds until you visit her with a wad of cash."

He's quiet. I'm quiet. We both know I'm right.

"I'll let you know if I speak to her," I say after a moment.

"Be careful."

"Always."

I hang up the phone and toss it on the bed. I love my brother and I'm so grateful for everything he did for me growing up, but after he left for college my life was flipped upside down. No amount of advice or phone calls to check up on me could've helped me during that time. It's not his fault. None of what happened was, but it doesn't change the fact that it happened and he doesn't even know the half of it. My phone buzzes. I lift my head and look at it.

Owl: So, cheating on my ex is a total deal breaker for you?

Me: I hate liars, cheaters, etc., so yeah, I guess it is

Owl: Even if I had my reasons?

Me: We tell ourselves anything we have to in order to make our wrongdoings acceptable. It doesn't make our actions any less wrong.

Owl: Ouch

Me: It's the truth

Owl: I understand. Friends?

Me: Sure. Friends :-)

THE EFFORT I put into this outfit, my hair and makeup, are worth it when Bennett's eyes run along my body, taking it all in. I know I shouldn't feel this sensation inside of me, but I can't help it. I can't stop feeling when I'm near him, and that's a lot more than I can say about anyone else I've dated these past few years. He's wearing a checkered blue button-down tucked into dark jeans, dress shoes that match his belt, and a navy suit jacket over it all. He looks like a fucking wet dream, with his dark hair brushed back, that shadow on his golden skin, and those auburn eyes that seemingly glow when he's looking at me. I sigh, shaking my head.

"I know," he says.

"Know what? That you look good?"

"That we shouldn't be thinking what we're thinking about each other."

I lick my lips, looking down at my shoes. "I'm not thinking anything, other than the obvious, you look hot, but you know that."

He steps forward, his dress shoes tapping against the tip of mine. "Doesn't mean I don't like to hear it from a beautiful woman."

I glance up, heart pounding in my ears. "I work for you now."

"Which is why this week is going to be the ultimate test," he says. "Even if I didn't know how good it feels to be inside of you, it would be the ultimate test."

I can't speak. Or think. But somehow, I manage to blink away all of the thoughts running through my head and turn around, toward the elevators, Bennett at my heels. This is definitely going to be the ultimate test.

CHAPTER FOURTEEN

OWL: What's your favorite color?

    Me: Cherry red. You?

    Owl: Black

    Me: LOL

    Owl: Favorite movie?

    Me: Shutter Island. You?

    Owl: Seven

    Me: Guess we are matched up pretty well, huh, new friend?

    Owl: Guess so

    Me: Favorite food

    Owl: Indian. You?

    Me: ME TOO!

    Owl: Biggest regret

    Me: I can't.

    Owl: We'll come back to that one

    Me: Doubt it. I can't say it aloud

    Owl: I'm asking you to type it

Me: It might be worse to type than to say aloud, then I'll have the mistake staring back at me

Owl: It's already staring back at you every single day. Might as well let it out into the universe and forgive yourself for it

Me: Not today

Owl: Fair enough. Mine is the cheating thing

Me: Are you just saying that because you know it's a deal breaker and you want to jump over the friend zone hurdle?

Owl: No. I'm serious.

Owl: But is it working? The jumping out of the friend zone thing?

Me: No. Nice try, though ;-)

"You're smiling again."

Bennett's voice beside me startles me. "Jesus."

"Just Bennett."

I roll my eyes. "Stop sneaking up on me."

"I'm not sneaking up on you at all. I'm getting food." He shoots a pointed look at his plate. We're standing in line at a buffet. "You're holding up the line by staring at your phone with a goofy smile on your face. Did you get yourself a boyfriend?"

"Not exactly."

"Oh, God." He reaches over for the tongs and serves himself salad. "You're not on the app, are you?"

"I have to keep an eye on it." I try to hide it, suddenly embarrassed by the entire thing.

"Yeah, for maintenance. I didn't think you'd actually join for love."

"I didn't join for love." I take the tongs from him and serve my own salad. "I joined for research. I've already found five glitches."

"Hmmm. It's a good thing you're testing it out, then."

"Yeah." I glance away from his hand.

"You're still smiling."

"I'm not allowed to smile?"

"You are." He stares at me, a small smile forming on his lips. It's not a wanting smile or a seductive one, but a soft one that makes the plains on his face look soft instead of intense. It's a smile that makes my heart dip into my stomach and bounce back up. "It's cute."

"My smile?"

"All of it. You say you don't want to find love, but I think it's pretty obvious you do, Cupid."

"Hm." I walk to an empty table. He sits across from me. I glance up and meet his gaze as I'm setting the napkin on my lap. "You know, if I had to call you something, I'd call you Trouble. That's what you are. Trouble with a capital T."

He grins. "Is it the dimples?"

"Yeah."

"The perfect smile? The bulging muscles?" His eyes twinkle with each description of himself. Each accurate description that makes my pulse skip twice. "The natural tan? The six-pack?"

I roll my eyes, laughing. "You're so full of yourself. It's no wonder you and Dev get along so well."

His smile drops at the mention of my brother. He clears his throat and starts cutting into his steak, quiet as we both enjoy our meals. When he looks up, his eyes are different, a little darker, a little secretive. "So, you are dating someone on that app?"

"Not dating. Just talking."

"You think it's Wesley?"

"I think Wesley wishes it were him." I laugh. "I honestly don't know much about him, so it very well could be him." My smile falters when I look up from my plate and see his scowl. "What?"

"Nothing. I just didn't think it would bother me this much."

"Me and Wesley?"

"You and anyone." His gaze locks with mine. "You and anyone that's not me."

"You said . . ."

"I know, and I meant it. I did. It's not a good idea. Fraternization policy or not, it wouldn't be fair for me to go after you being your superior. It definitely wouldn't go over well with your brother. You say I'm trouble with a capital T, but you don't even know the half of it."

He is trouble. I bite my lip. I want to though. I want to know all of it.

CHAPTER FIFTEEN

DAY one of the conference is a success. Bennett and I went to a few panels together and then split the rest of the day, agreeing to catch up tonight over dinner. I'm walking back to the elevators when I spot him smiling at something a woman in front of him is saying. She has a hand on his arm, looking up at him like he's a god, and I'm instantly flooded with hot jealousy. He's a sweet talker, like my brother. He plays mind games. I don't like either one of those things, so why is this particular man getting under my skin? After the whole Justin fiasco, I've gone for straitlaced boys. The ones who don't think to swerve out of their lanes. The ones who don't really question what I'm doing or saying or go against the grain. The wallflowers that don't have women draped all over them all the time. Bennett is not that. He's bold and gorgeous and rich and smart and is definitely not a wallflower. The two walk into the elevator together, the only people in there right now. I fight the urge to run and catch it so they have an audience. Instead, I wait and watch as the numbers tick above the door, stopping on our floor. Ugh.

I catch the next one and keep my head down as I walk, checking my app once more. There's a notification I missed an hour ago.

Owl: Radio silence from you today

Me: Working

No response. Also, no sight of Bennett or the woman he was speaking to downstairs. I walk into my room and pause when I hear voices in the room beside mine. Definitely his. Probably hers. My stomach clenches. I shouldn't want to listen, but I press my ear to the door nonetheless. I can't make out their conversation but I can hear that they're having one. Better that than sex noises, right?

Me: I think I have a crush on my boss

Maybe I shouldn't say that to this stranger. In three weeks, he'll know who I am, and if it's Wesley, whom I like, I'll have no chance with him. But also, I need to say it to someone who's not my friend. I need to say it to another male, one who can't possibly like me yet. It's too soon for that. I toss my phone on the bed and head to the shower. I calculate that I have enough time to shower, lay in bed in my fluffy robe for an hour, and still have time to get ready for dinner, so that's what I set out to do. Better to busy myself and ignore whatever is happening next door. I mean, I have absolutely no reason to be jealous of whatever is happening. Jealousy is an emotion though, and emotions don't really make sense.

I'm lying in bed when my phone vibrates with an alert from the app.

Owl: Sorry. Work was crazy today. So . . . you like your boss?

I close my eyes. Maybe I shouldn't have said anything after all. While the anonymity is freeing, this is the kind of thing that could come back and bite me in the ass.

Me: I said I think

Owl: Maybe you should tell him?

Me: NO! I would never.

Owl: Is it bad that I'm glad you're not going to tell him? Gives me an opportunity to win you over or at least cross the friend zone line

Me: LOL. Anyway. Do you like what you do? At work?

Owl: I do.

Me: Me too

Owl: What's your ultimate goal? Get this on your resume? Move up in the company? Start your own?

Me: I would love to start my own, but that requires money, which I don't have

Owl: I hear you.

My alarm goes off and I shake myself and bolt out of bed. I have a pending dinner work date with Bennett that I am not going to miss. I dress quickly, opting for a more casual look today, in tight jeans, a tight black shirt, and another pair of stilettos. I sweep my hair into a bun and walk out of my room, opening my tiny shoulder bag to make sure I grabbed my room key.

"Whoa."

I look up and startle when I see Bennett standing in front of me. He's wearing a similar outfit to yesterday's—jeans, dress shoes, dress shirt, and blazer.

"Whoa yourself."

He smiles. "You hungry?"

"Always."

"Good." He chuckles as we start to walk toward the elevator. "I'm starving."

"Anything in particular you feel like eating?" I ask as we step in.

He looks at me, his eyes aglow, and I know the answer he could easily give me. It's the one I crave to hear, but don't question because I'm afraid I'll get the answer I want. I'm afraid I'll get one I don't. I change the subject instead.

"I saw you talking to someone."

His brows pull momentarily, before realization settles. "Lana."

"Didn't catch her name." I step out of the elevator. He follows. I glance up as we walk through the noisy casino. "She was in your room earlier."

"Keeping tabs on me, Cupid?"

I roll my eyes, hiding the disappointment, wishing he'd add more to that, give me details even though I know they'd grate at me. Why do I care? WHY DO I CARE? Ugh. He steers me toward the Japanese restaurant and asks for a table for two.

"Away from the noise," he adds.

The hostess smiles and asks us to follow her. We walk to the back of the restaurant, through a door, and are ushered into a dimly lit room with a table for two at the center. On the floor. I look at her. Look at him. Look at the table. Look back at her.

"Um."

"This is perfect. Thank you," Bennett says.

"This is super private and I feel like I'm going to have to give you a hand job in here," I whisper shout when she walks out.

He throws his head back and howls out a laugh. "Seriously?"

"Yes, seriously. Don't tell me that wasn't your first thought."

"It really wasn't, but now that it's in here." He taps his forehead. "It can't be ignored."

"Well, it's not going to happen." I look at the pillows on the floor. "Am I supposed to take off my shoes? I'm kind of afraid my pants will rip. They're really freaking tight and only a little stretchy." I gnaw on my bottom lip. Bennett laughs louder. I shoot him a glare. "It's not funny. I don't know the etiquette here. I've never been to a place like this before."

"Take off your shoes. I'm sure your pants will be fine, but if not, I have a jacket you can use."

With that, I take off my shoes, and walk over to the pillows, getting down on all fours and crawling to the middle of the table.

"You have no idea how sexy that looks," Bennett murmurs.

I glance up, still on all fours, and nearly gasp at the look on his face. I sit down quickly and pick up the menu. I need to control this ridiculous feeling. He takes off his jacket and tosses it over the chair on the other side of the room and meets me on the floor, lifting his own menu.

"You like sake?"

"Never tried it."

"Ever?" He lowers his menu, raising an eyebrow. I shake my head. "We'll have to order some shots, then."

"Okay."

We go over our respective days in panels and what we learned. At one point, I feel like I'm probably talking way too much, but Bennett just sits there with a look of interest, so I keep talking until he frowns.

"You lost me."

"Where?"

"Why are they uploading PDF files into a program and cross-checking them with other PDF files?"

"To find out whether or not the people plagiarized the other titles."

"Who would plagiarize *Wuthering Heights*?"

"Stupid people." I shrug. "I don't know. I just thought it was pretty amazing that she was able to create this program for this specific audience. It's a big audience, too. Publishing houses are already contacting her to cross-check things."

"Impressive." He takes a sip of his beer. "Note to self, don't hire a ghostwriter."

I laugh. "That's what I said."

He smiles, his eyes looking all over my face to the point that I'm forced to look away and pick up my drink.

"You don't like attention, do you?"

"Not really." I'm looking at the beer in my glass as I take small sips.

"You're beautiful," he says, his voice low. "You should be used to attention."

"I hate it." I glance up, meeting his gaze.

"Being told that you're beautiful or the attention being beautiful brings?"

"Both." I swallow. "When I was a teenager, I cut my hair like a pixie in hopes that it would drive guys in the opposite direction."

"Did it work?"

"Yes and no." I take another sip. "They definitely made fun of me, but they didn't stop trying to grab my ass in the hall."

"I would've killed them." His jaw flexes. "Devon should've."

"Devon wasn't there. He was in college, as he should have been."

Besides, that wasn't the worst thing that happened back then, but I don't say that. I can't get into that part of my life with a stranger, and as much as Dev has always said Bennett is his best friend, he hasn't told him about our family issues. Not that I can blame him. I haven't told my best friends about those issues either.

"Did he know?"

"Seriously, Bennett, that was a long time ago." I set my drink down. "Tell me how you started SEVEN."

"Do you want the honest answer or the one I give the media?"

"Honest."

"I kept seeing all of these apps and websites that had so much potential but no real brain power behind any, so I got a group of likeminded guys and started offering our services to them. My dad had already worked at a global tech company for years and managed to end up in a position of power, so I asked him to quit and come on board."

"And he did." I blink. "Just like that?"

"Just like that. He's my dad, after all. Wouldn't your parents do whatever they could to help you out?"

I reach for one of the shot glasses full of sake and take it. I take the next one right after. And the next. Then, I wash it all down with the beer.

"Jesus, Morg. You're not going to be able to wear your heels out of here if you continue at that pace."

"Maybe you should catch up." I shoot a pointed look at the shot glasses in front of him.

"Fuck it, we're in Vegas, after all." He chuckles and copies me. "And you know what they say –"

"I swear to God, if you finish that sentence, I will spill this beer over your pretty little head."

He laughs loudly and thankfully changes the subject.

As it turns out, sake is strong as hell. So strong that even the four rolls of sushi we share aren't enough to stop my head from swaying.

"I think I'm drunk."

He chuckles. "I think I am too. I feel like a lightweight."

"We took like six shots."

"And the beer." He lifts the beer.

"Oh, my God. And the beer."

I look over at him. He looks over at me. My eyes fall to his lips. I think about the last time they were on mine, how good they felt. I've never been entirely comfortable around men, but for some reason Bennett has always made me feel wanton. I wonder if all women feel this way around him.

"Did you sleep with her? The Lana woman you took back up to your room?"

"No." He licks his lips. "Didn't touch her. Didn't kiss her. Didn't do anything with her except talk."

"In your room?"

"In my room." His gaze darkens. "I was too busy thinking about the beautiful woman staying in the room beside mine."

"Liar."

"I am a liar, but I'm not lying."

I swallow. "What was she doing there then?"

"Just talking. I had some papers she wanted to see."

"What happened to email?"

"Nothing that I'm aware of, but they were already printed and in my room, so she followed me up." He searches my eyes. "I swear it was innocent."

"If I kiss you, I'll regret it," I whisper.

"If you kiss me, I won't be able to stand it, so you better not."

"Hm." I close my eyes and lean against the pillow behind me. "I could easily fall asleep here."

"As soon as we get the check, I'll take you up to your

room," he says. My eyes fly open. I turn toward him. He smiles. "So you can go to bed, Cupid. Don't get any funny ideas."

"I wasn't." I close my eyes again, go back to getting comfortable. "Maybe it's for the best that we're just friends. I swore off men anyway."

"When did this happen?"

"At some point last year. Between breaking up with my ex-boyfriend and hooking up with a really hot one-night stand."

"How long were you with him?"

"On and off about three years. More off than on, so I guess less than that." I open my eyes when the waitress approaches with the check. As she clears our plates, Bennett hands her a card. I don't even think to argue. It's a business trip, therefore, a business expense.

"What happened?"

"He cheated with someone I loved."

"Ouch."

"Tell me about it. I have enough daddy issues to sustain me through a lifetime. The last thing I need in my life is a man who doesn't value me."

"Hey, at least you know your worth and what you want." He smiles. "And now you're building apps to help everyone find what they've been searching for as well."

"Those who can't, teach, right?" I reach for my shoes and start to put them on, carefully standing up to make sure I can balance on them.

"You can," he says after a long moment. We start walking out, his hand at the small of my back sending tingles up and down my spine. "You'll find a man who treats you right. And if he doesn't, send him my way and I'll kick his ass."

"Maybe you should hook me up with a good man." I glance

up at him with a smile. "I'll give you a list of qualities I'm looking for."

"Well, consider my curiosity piqued. How soon can you have this list ready?"

"Definitely by –" My phone buzzes in my purse and I stop walking and fish it out. No one calls me at this time. There's an unknown number on the screen though. A local number. My heart dips as I ignore the call. I'll call back when I'm in my room—alone. "Sorry about that."

I keep the phone clutched in my hand as we take the elevator to our floor. We go over tomorrow's schedule and agree to meet for breakfast at eight o'clock before our long day starts again. When we get to my door, I turn around.

"Are you going to tuck me in?"

"You have no idea how tempting that offer is," he says. "So tempting that I'm going to be a good boy and go tuck myself in before I do anything stupid."

I smile. "I didn't take you for a coward, Trouble."

"I didn't take you for a temptress, Cupid." He steps forward and leans toward me slowly. I shut my eyes, part my lips, my heart swooshing in my ears as I feel him draw closer still, his lips brushing against my temple. I gasp quietly, waiting, savoring it, but he pulls back. I open my eyes and meet his. "Good night, Morgan. Get some rest."

CHAPTER SIXTEEN

MY PHONE WON'T QUIT RINGING throughout the night. I tried to ignore it as much as possible, but at one-thirty in the morning I decide enough is enough and answer it.

"What?"

"I heard you were in town."

I shut my eyes. "What do you want?"

"I haven't seen you in over a year and that's your first question?" she asks. "That's no way to treat a mother."

"I have no money for you, if that's what you're getting at."

"Hm." She sniffs. "That's not what I called for. I miss you."

I want to laugh, or argue, but there's a rock in my throat I can't swallow past, let alone speak through, so I'm grateful when she speaks again.

"I can come see you," she offers. "I just got off work at the Waldorf."

"I'm at the Aria." My words fly out of my mouth before I have a chance to fully think them over, to fully protest. "I can meet you in the lobby."

"Bar."

"Okay."

"See you soon, Buttercup."

I hang up the phone and wipe my face. I'll be damned if she sees me crying. I move quickly, deciding to leave my outfit on and trade my stilettos for pink slides. Grabbing my phone on my way out, I check the app.

Me: I want to share a secret

Owl: Share away

Me: I hate my mom

Even as I type it, my eyes fill with tears. It's something that annoys me to no end.

Owl: You're not alone. I think most of the universe has parental issues. Want to talk about it?

Me: Not really. I just needed to say/type that aloud right now. I'm about to meet with her for the first time in over a year.

Owl: Wow. Good luck.

Me: Thanks.

Owl: Report back when you're done. I'm here if you need to vent some more ;-)

Me: Thanks.

The elevator doors open up to the lobby and I head toward the bar. There are many bars here, but I know the one she means. It's the type people go to when they want to be seen— when they want to be looked at and flirted with. My mother is nothing if not flashy. I spot her immediately. She's standing by the bar in a short little black number that shows off a body that would make a twenty-year-old envious. She flips her long blond hair, so much like my own right now, box-blond looks good on our golden skin tone. I wish I could smile at the sight, it should make me feel good that I got these rockin' genes, but nothing helps the dread growing in the pit of my belly. My feet continue to move, at odds with the emotion to flee the scene unscathed, but it's too late for that. I'm not unscathed, nor will I ever be.

She looks up when she senses my approach, then gives me a once-over, making a face. "Why are you wearing flip flops at a bar?"

"Because my room is upstairs and I'm not looking to fuck anyone tonight." I shoot her a pointed look. She smiles. I sigh. "What do you want?"

"I can't want to see my beautiful daughter?"

"No."

"Seriously, Morgan." Her expression falls. "I've tried to call you countless times to apologize. I've asked your brother to speak to you."

"Devon doesn't know the half of what you did to me. If he did, he wouldn't speak to you either."

She waves my words away. "Boys don't understand."

"You would say that." I scoff as the bartender hands her a flute of Champagne. "So, what did you want to see me about? Need me to pay for your fancy drink?"

"No." She blinks, annoyed. She would scowl if it weren't for the Botox that keeps her face wrinkle-free. "I have a boyfriend and he's very rewarding."

"I bet."

"Want a drink?"

"No, thanks."

I don't mention that my head is still swimming in all the sake I had with Bennett. As a matter of fact, I decide I can't mention Bennett at all. I don't know if she's met him or not, but the thought of her even looking at him makes me feel a little sick.

Ugh. What is wrong with me? He's no one of importance to me.

My mom starts walking away from the bar and toward a booth, and I follow, sitting across from her.

"You look well," she comments, her eyes on my face.

I look at her arms, searching. She was marred with scratches the last time I saw her, both from altercations and the needles she injected herself with occasionally.

"I stopped using."

My gaze meets hers. "When?"

"Around the same time you told me to go fuck myself." She smiles. It's sad, thoughtful. "Funny what your own daughter saying those words to you will do."

"Yeah, well, I still mean them." I glance away, back at the bar.

"You're a cold bitch, Morgan Elizabeth."

I purse my lips, fighting a smile. Anyone else says that and it would be offensive. My addict, whore of a mom says it, and it's instant gratification. It's the kind of thing she says to the girls who work for her, the ones who sell their bodies in exchange for monetary value. I never had anything but respect for her and those women. Sure, it's easy to frown upon things like that, but when they're behind closed doors with their powerful clients, they wield their bodies with power, as they should.

"Are you here with someone?"

"I'm here for work." I meet her gaze. "Why? Hoping to fuck another one of my boyfriends?"

She sighs heavily, setting down her glass with a clink. "You never let me explain what happened."

"It doesn't matter what happened, what matters is that it happened—period. Who does that? What kind of mother sleeps with her daughter's boyfriend?"

"I was high."

"All five times?" I laugh. "That's your excuse?"

"I was in bad form."

"And you expect me to believe he took advantage of that? Please, Mom."

"Fine. I can see I'm not going to change your mind about what kind of person I am, but I really am sorry." She glances down at the table. "Dev told me you landed a solid job. Playing with computers, the way you like."

I scoff. *Playing with computers.* "I did."

"Got out of this shithole."

"I would've done that with or without you fucking Justin, if that's what you're getting at."

"That's not what I'm getting at." She sighs again, exasperated. My phone buzzes on my lap. I glance at it.

Owl: I peed my pants at a football game once

I blink at the screen, then smile, shaking my head.

Me: One that you were attending or playing in?

Owl: That is the question, isn't it? ;-)

Me: LOL you're crazy

Owl: I hope you're smiling.

Me: Maybe I am

"When your father left, I didn't know what to do with myself," Mom says. "I was so lost."

"You cheated on him with his brother." I look up, setting my phone aside. "Both of his brothers. How'd you think it was going to end?"

"I don't know." She shrugs. "He cheated on me with his secretary and I stayed."

I roll my eyes. "You seem to have a real issue understanding what commitment means. It's a wonder Devon is in a stable relationship. You and Dad both seriously messed us up in the love department."

"Men are always fine as long as they're getting somethin'."

"You're not wrong."

"I let go of my girls. Passed the baton to Celia and let her take the reins."

"You quit?" My brows raise in surprise.

"I figured it was about time." She licks her lips. "Rodney, my boyfriend, didn't like me being involved in that life."

"So you'll live off him now? You must see that there's a pattern you keep following. You keep putting all your faith in people thinking they're going to be your savior. People are flawed and selfish and when push comes to shove, we all reach for our own life rafts first."

"I guess you're right. I used to have faith in you and then you left me here."

"To go to freaking college, Mom. Jesus Christ." I slap my hand on the table. "What are you going to do next? Blame me for your betrayal?"

"No. I'm not saying this to excuse my behavior with . . . Justin." She clears her throat. "That was a mistake. You left me to go to college. I was alone and lonely and . . . he was there and I was there and . . ." She shakes her head, blinking glassy eyes. "I really am sorry, Morg. It was wrong."

I learned more about life from watching my mother than I did from anything she ever said to me. I learned that you can bargain anything, that nothing is ever final, that when it comes down to it, you'll always pick yourself over someone else. I would love to argue all of it, but thing is, life has taught me that these things are true.

"I'm not ready to forgive you."

She looks struck by this. "I understand."

"I don't think you do, and because I've already agreed to this meeting, I'm going to humor you on Girl Code 101," I say.

"First, you don't ever go after a friend's significant other. This is probably a difficult thing for you to understand considering your line of work and the amount of married men you see, but it's quite simple. Second, if the man pursues you first, you turn him down and immediately tell your friend. Third, if you decide to throw caution to the wind and ignore both of those things, you have to accept that your actions terminated your friendship. In this case, replace 'friend' with 'daughter.' Even if I forgive you someday, you will never be invited into my life. Ever."

"I'm your mother. We're family. We're bound by blood."

"If I could drain myself of your blood, I would." I shrug, sliding out of the booth. "I've done the next best thing though. I've decided to choose my family from now on."

"But –"

"I'm done. I'm glad you're doing well. I'm glad you're clean and no longer using. I'm glad you have a boyfriend and you're happy and well taken care of. Despite everything you did to try to fuck up my life and ruin me, I'm happy for you."

I walk away slowly, with my head held high and my shoulders pushed back. I hold this bravado until I get inside the elevator, and then I start shaking vigorously. When I step out on my floor, I start silently weeping, and by the time I'm in the confines of my room, I start to sob loudly. I manage to shower, wash away as much as I can of the meeting, of the memories— of my fourteen-year-old-self having sex with a stranger because my mother is too fucked up to open the door and I know he'll beat her to pieces if she doesn't give him what he asks for. Of myself alone after dance recitals, guitar lessons, and having to turn down every single friend when they ask to come over to my house. I wash away every broken promise and heartache she's caused, including seducing and having an affair with my boyfriend of two years, a guy I genuinely thought I would marry. I stay in the shower and cry until my eyes are puffy and my fingers have pruned.

When I turn the water off, dry myself, and wrap myself in the too-large plush robe, I feel my shoulders shake with more sobs. At the sound of a knock on my door, I gasp, wiping my tears quickly. The knock gets louder. I make my way over and look through the peephole at Bennett, standing on the other side. He's wearing a gray T-shirt and plaid pajama pants, his hair in disarray, those too-wise amber eyes meeting mine through the peephole. I know without question, that I look like a complete mess. I know, without question, that if I open the door right now, I'm going to let him see me at my most vulnerable.

"Morgan." His voice is firm. "Open the door."

I do, slowly disengaging the locks and pulling the door open. I step back, looking at the floor, at my red toenails, and his clean bare feet.

"I . . ." He starts. "It sounded like you were crying."

"I'm fine."

"If you need something," he says, "If you want to talk –"

"I don't."

He steps forward, blocking the doorway. I let go of the door handle, but otherwise remain unmoved.

"Do you want to be left alone?"

I nod my head, biting my tongue to hold back the tears that don't seem to want to stop forming. I'm always alone. Always alone, but never lonely. It's something I'm okay with; something I take pride in. Instead of leaving, he steps inside, letting the door slam shut behind him and reaches for my left hand, tugging as he steps toward me. He smells of Christmas—pine and cinnamon wrap around me as he brings his other arm around my body, pulling me against his chest, and then the other until I'm fully cocooned inside a shell of muscles. I start to cry again. I leave my arms down at my sides, unable to bring myself to open up completely, despite the notion that my chest is currently split open, purging emotions. His hand moves slowly up and down my back, strong yet comforting. After a while, I stop crying, but I stay with my head resting on his chest because I don't know how to pull away and wipe my tears without him seeing me. It's stupid, really. His shirt is soaked in my tears, yet I can't bring myself to fully admit I let myself do that. I take a deep, shuddering breath and force myself to pull away. He takes his arms away reluctantly, slowly, as if he's afraid I'll tip over without him. The defiance inside pushes me to wipe my tears quickly and turn my chin up. I offer him a sheepish smile.

"Sorry you had to witness me being such a girl."

"Don't do that," he says. "Don't use your femininity as a crutch for your emotions."

"You're right. Women are stronger than that." I nod. "I'm sorry you had to witness me being such a guy."

He smiles. "Want to talk about it?"

"Not really."

"Okay." He stands there, looking at me, waiting. I look down and realize I'm still in a robe.

"I need to change."

"Do you want me to leave?"

"While I change?"

"In general."

"Can you stay a while?"

"As long as you want."

I move and grab my pajamas, taking them to the bathroom and changing quickly. An overview of my appearance in the mirror confirms that I look like a hot mess—crazy hair, puffy eyes, blotchy skin. No wonder he didn't even look at my robe or check me out. Jeez. I brush my hair and dab my face with cold water, hoping it helps. It doesn't. With a shrug, I turn and head back into the room. He's sitting at the edge of the bed, phone in his hand as he types something.

"You're not telling my brother, are you?"

"No." He glances up at me. "I should though. Something is obviously wrong."

"Please don't tell him anything." I walk until I'm standing directly in front of him, my legs between his. It seems to be all he needs to toss his phone aside and look up at me, bringing one of his hands to my waist. I inhale sharply.

"Are you trying to seduce me?"

"Is it working?"

"It doesn't take much." He chuckles lightly, tugging me forward.

"For you to be seduced?"

"By you," he clarifies. "It doesn't take much for me to be seduced by you."

"Good answer." I lean down slightly, closing my eyes as I press my lips against his softly. His grip tightens on my waist as he pulls away from the kiss.

"Morgan." He looks up at me with such longing, I feel like I'm about to burst. "We really shouldn't do this."

"How can you look at me like that and say that?"

"I'm trying to be rational."

"About something completely irrational." I bend a knee, bringing it up between his legs, feeling how hard he is. He groans, shutting his eyes, fingers digging into the flesh of my hip. "You want this."

"You have no idea how much." He opens his eyes again. "But not tonight. We shouldn't. Not after . . . I don't even know what happened or why you were crying . . ."

I sigh, pulling away and crossing my arms.

"Don't do that."

"Don't do what? Be upset that you're not letting this happen?" I glower. "I don't let emotions come between myself and an orgasm."

"Good to know." He raises a brow. "I normally don't either, but you're not just some random woman at a bar anymore and for some absolutely insane reason I want to get to know you."

"Absolutely insane reason? Not because I'm hot and was a good lay the first time around?"

"That's part of it." He stands up, reaching for me. When I don't uncross my arms for him, he just grabs on to my left as he comes closer still. I tilt my head up. He's stupid-tall when I'm barefoot. "Also, because you're smart and funny."

"We can get to know each other tomorrow."

"We will." He puts an arm around me and holds me to his chest, his shirt still wet from before, a reminder that I already sort of let my guard down with him. "Tonight, let's rest, okay? We have a long day ahead of us."

"Okay," I whisper against him.

He leads me to the bed and we lie under the covers, our bodies facing each other as his fingers lightly run over my arm. I'm asleep before I even have a chance to ask him a question, and that's how I end up spending the first full night with Bennett.

CHAPTER SEVENTEEN

WHEN MY ALARM GOES OFF, I groan and reach over to turn it off, but instead, hit a wall of a person and instantly open my eyes, wide awake.

"Turn that shit off," Bennett grumbles.

I smile. Even first thing in the morning the man looks like he can be on the cover of a magazine. It's extremely unfair. A part of me can't believe he stayed the night. I can't believe I let him. Oddly enough, I don't regret it—yet. I push myself up and out of bed, heading toward the bathroom. Taking a look at myself in the mirror, the gravity of last night actually hits me and I find myself wishing Bennett wasn't in my bed right now. He probably thinks I'm crazy. When I emerge from the bathroom, he's sitting up in bed. He glances up from the phone in his hand.

"It's seven o'clock. We don't have to be down there until nine."

"I know." I start looking for the clothes I'm wearing. "I like to start getting ready two hours before."

"Two hours?"

I glance up at him. "Yeah."

"Why?"

"Just something I do." I shrug. "I like to be prepared."

"Such a little perfectionist," he says. "How's your app doing? I keep forgetting to ask."

"Good." I clear my throat, busying myself with the underwear drawer, which was difficult to do, since I only had three clean underwear left and one of them was already in my hand, but what was I supposed to say?

"Just good? Has anyone dropped the app? Or deleted it? Or complained? I haven't seen any data. Have you been reporting to my dad?"

"Everyone is still active. I told your dad I would accumulate the data over the three weeks and then give it all to both of you in one shot." I grab all of my clothes and start walking to the bathroom. I don't want to give him a chance to ask me if I'm on it. It's not that I'm embarrassed. I mean, I developed it, after all, but still. "I'll be ready in an hour. Feel free to lounge here or go back to your room."

OWL: You okay? Never heard back from you

Me: Yes. It was weird, but I got through it. Your joke helped.

Owl: Good. It wasn't a joke though.

Me: LOL Well, either way, it helped. Any more secrets for me today?

Owl: You need more?

Me: I'll tell you one if you tell me one.

Owl: Okay but I get to ask the questions

Me: Okay. Going into a meeting though so I may not respond right away.

I set my phone on silent, put it in my purse and walked out of my room. Bennett is standing in the hallway.

"We should open the doors between our rooms."

I raise an eyebrow. "That sure of yourself?"

"I was before you gave me that answer." He chuckles as we head toward the elevators. When we stop in front of them, he gives me a once-over. "You look beautiful."

"Thanks." I feel myself blush despite the fact that I spent an hour on my makeup, trying to hide the blotches and puffiness that came with last night's grief. That memory comes with a wave of uneasiness. I look up at him. "I'm sorry about last night."

Of course, the elevator opens the exact moment I say this and I find five pairs of eyes looking at me. One of the guy's smirks as if he suspects what I'm apologizing for.

With a light chuckle and a large hand at my lower back, Bennett ushers me to the back of the elevator.

"You don't have to apologize for being human," he says, low and near my ear.

"I pride myself in not having reactions like that to situations."

"I wish you would tell me what happened."

I glance away. Not going there.

He sighs but doesn't comment. When we walk out of the elevator, we step to the side.

"Guess we can grab breakfast here." I eye the tables crowded with pastries and coffee.

Bennett pulls out a paper and unfolds it, brows slightly pulled together as he scans it. "We can do software development

—" He stops talking and glances up at me at the sound of my laughter.

"You own a tech company and you're not using the app for this conference?" I pull out my phone and scroll, feeling his eyes on my screen. He taps my hand, his touch sending a shiver through me.

"You're on the app?"

"Seriously?" I laugh. "Stop looking at my screen."

"Are you?"

"Yup." I click on the conference app quickly.

"Morgan."

"Yes." I meet his questioning gaze. "I have to make sure I can keep an eye on it and fix whatever glitches need to be fixed."

"You seem to be more invested in this than just a developer," he says, his tone grating. I ignore the statement.

"There's a really interesting panel with a robot today." I scan the description of that one and smile when I see it's Presley's boyfriend's company. "I definitely want to go to that one."

"Morgan." He covers my screen with his hand. My eyes snap to his. "Did you join the app? Did it match you with anyone?"

"Yes."

"And?"

"It matched me. End of story."

"You don't want to talk to me about it." His eyes narrow.

"I don't see why it's any of your business."

"You were ..." He lowers his voice, coming closer still, until I'm dwarfed by him. "You were coming on to me last night. I told you I want to get to know you."

"You've said yourself that you don't believe in love. I don't see how this has any bearing on us hooking up. We're here two more days. We can hook up tonight, tomorrow, and be done with this pull by the time we get back to the office on Monday. It's not like I'm sleeping with him."

"So you want to talk to him and just fuck me without letting me get to know you, is that it?" A muscle in his jaw jumps.

"That's not —"

"Bennett! Hey, man. Long time, no see." We're interrupted by an older man who clearly knows Bennett.

I step aside and go over to the table filled with food. Grabbing a plate, I put a few things on it before moving on to the coffee. Every few seconds, I glance up and catch Bennett watching me as the man continues to talk his ear off.

WE END up taking a car because the hotel the lunch meeting is taking place at is not on the strip. I'm relieved because it's the first time I actually get a chance to text my friends back.

Me: Pres, is Nate Dog here this weekend?

Presley: He is! I think he's meeting with your boss, actually.

Me: Ha. Funny story, I think I'm on my way there right now.

Dev: How much are flowers supposed to cost?

Jamie: Like a bouquet?

Presley: Depends where you buy them … duh.

Me: same answer ^

Dev: For the wedding, assholes.

Jamie: WHAT WEDDING?

Presley: YOU AND NORA ARE GETTING MARRIED?

Me: Omg. I thought I told you guys?!

Jamie: NO

Presley: BAD FRIEND

Dev: Ballpark price, Jamie. Isn't that part of your job?

Jamie: It honestly depends, but I'll do your flowers for free! I just want an invite to the wedding ;)

Dev: You got it. I'll tell Nora to call you

Jamie: YAY

Presley: When is the wedding?

Dev: We're thinking winter

Me: OMG! SO SOON!

"What are you all smiley about?" Bennett asks beside me. "Chatting with your suitor?"

I roll my eyes. "Maybe."

"Is it so wrong for me to not want you to be on that app?"

"Yes, actually." I slip my phone into my bag and look at him. "You don't see me questioning what you're doing with your life. As a matter of fact, I've had to deal with your psycho ex-wife telling me all kinds of things about you and I haven't once brought it to your attention."

"What? What are you talking about?"

"Your ex-wife. She's crazy and has been calling the office every single morning around ten-thirty like clockwork to tell me all about your sexcapades and how all the previous girls quit because they couldn't handle you. Or her."

"Why didn't you tell me?"

"What's the point? I'll be out of that desk when we get back."

"Hm." His jaw seems to be working overtime, with the way it keeps twitching. "My father assigned you to another department?"

"Development."

His gaze catches mine. "With Wesley."

"And twenty other people."

"Are you hoping it's him you're chatting with on the app?"

I stare at him for a beat. "How's Stacy, by the way? Are you still dating her?"

"I was never dating her."

"Oh, I'm sorry, fucking her."

"Would it bother you if I was?" He raises an eyebrow. I pull back slightly, realizing that it would bother me. Why though? I try to make sense of it, but he's staring at me, waiting for a response.

"Maybe it would."

He leans a little closer. "Why do you think that is?"

"I don't know," I whisper. He comes closer still. I feel my pulse quicken.

"I like that it bothers you."

"Why?"

"Because it means you care." His lips crash down on mine before I can form a response and suddenly I'm entirely too aware as to why I would care if he was sleeping with someone else. His mouth is familiar, as if it's been on mine an entire lifetime, yet it feels exciting, as if it's my very first kiss all over again. As the kiss deepens, I toss a leg over him, half straddling him in the backseat of the car as I tug his hair. In the back of my mind, I remind myself that there's a driver, but I don't care. Right now, I want this. As his large hands explore my body over my blouse and stretchy pencil skirt, I want nothing more than to rip it all off. The car comes to a stop and the driver clears his throat.

"We're here." I register his door closing as he comes around to open ours, and I pull away and sit back down, fixing my outfit and my hair, running a finger under my lip to make sure I don't look a mess.

Bennett takes a deep breath beside me and looks over,

bringing a hand to my cheek. "I'm not sleeping with anyone, Morgan."

"Good." I smile.

He chuckles, shaking his head as he gets out of the car and helps me out.

CHAPTER EIGHTEEN

"I SHOULD PROBABLY MENTION I know who we're meeting with before we go in there," I say as we walk toward the restaurant.

Bennett looks down at me. "How?"

"A friend."

His brows pull together slightly, but the hostess approaches us before he can ask more questions. Bennett walks behind me as she leads us to the table, pressing his hand slightly on my lower back. I want to shake it away, because the meeting isn't making me nervous, but the way his hand feels certainly is. I spot Nathaniel first, sitting in the center of the table, talking animatedly with his business partner, Ryan. I'm relieved to find that it's just them and one more man I've never met. Nathaniel stops talking and stands up, laughing when he sees me. I walk around the table and laugh when he throws his arms around me, lifting me off the ground in a hug.

"Did Presley send you to spy on me?"

"No." I roll my eyes as he sets me down and turn to say hi to Ryan, in a much more appropriate way. I don't know Ryan the way I know Nate though. "Hey, Ry."

"Morg." He kisses me on both cheeks. "This is Elias."

I turn to the man I'd never seen. "Nice to meet you, Elias."

"Likewise. I've heard a lot about you." When he smiles, his dimples are on display. "All good things. Impressive things."

"Good." I turn to find Bennett saying hello to Nathaniel and Ryan, and turning toward Elias and introducing himself.

He raises an eyebrow at me. "I didn't know you were so popular."

"I'm not."

"We go way back," Ryan says. "College."

"And Nathaniel is engaged to my best friend," I add.

"I don't know how I pulled that off." Nate chuckles. "Luckiest man alive."

"I agree." I smile.

"I do too," Elias adds. "I've only met her a handful of times but I don't know how he managed to score that one."

"Years and years of work." I wink.

"Do you want to get down to business or you want to wait until after we eat?" Nathaniel asks, looking at Bennett.

"I have nothing in my stomach to get rid of if you start throwing numbers my way right now, but I'm good either way," Bennett says. He looks over at me. "You hungry, Morgan?"

"A little." I start scanning the menu in front of me. "But don't let me stop you from starting your meeting."

"Let's eat first and talk after," Ryan says. "I'm starving."

"Morgan, how do you like working at SEVEN? I know you can't say anything bad in front of your boss, so wink your left eye if you hate it," Elias says.

"Oh, my God. I love it." I laugh. "Nothing to hide."

"My father's her boss," Bennett says beside me. "Most days I feel like she's bossing me around."

Nathaniel raises an eyebrow, looking between us. I shoot him a look to stop it, which makes him laugh.

"Bennett is Devon's best friend," I say, staring at Nathaniel with my best stern look, but my words only stoke his curiosity.

"That is definitely interesting," he says.

"I feel like the odd man out. Did all of you attend college together?" Elias asks.

"Not together," I say. "I'm way too young for these geezers."

They all laugh.

"Too old?" Bennett asks beside me.

"You are." I bite my lip to keep from laughing at the expression on his face, even though I know I'm blushing fiercely. "I was Nate's fiancée's little sister in our sorority," I explain.

"Damn. You are young," Elias says, his features pulled into a surprised frown. "I thought I was the young'un here."

"I figured you weren't as old as these guys."

"Nope." His smile widens. "Still under thirty."

"Okay, we get it, we're old, now if you two can limit the flirting about your ages until after we talk shop, that would be awesome," Nate says.

Elias and I share a laugh. Was I flirting? I replay what just happened and think, no, I wasn't. I glance over at Bennett, who doesn't seem the least amused by what's transpiring and rethink my conclusion. Maybe he thinks I was too. Maybe I don't really care.

"Lay it on me," Bennett says, looking at them.

"It's not really a secret that we've recently decided to

expand our investments from just tech to other things: breweries, restaurants, nightclubs, etcetera," Ryan starts. "We're looking for someone to merge the tech portion of the company with and we thought, who better than SEVEN?"

"Where do you come in?" Bennett asks, looking at Elias.

"I have a few things I want developed that I was hoping to sell to these guys, but they decided it may be in my best interest to sit in on this, see how it goes, and potentially sell it to your company instead."

"Interesting." Bennett sits back in his chair, keeping the arm closest to me on the table as he drums his fingers absentmindedly. "When you say you want to merge the tech portion, how much of it are we talking? Do you want me to buy out your client catalog or stay on board for decisions that need to be made?"

"It's our catalog," Nate says. "Essentially, we'd be your client. We want our team focusing on other things and would rather have a company like SEVEN work on development and coming up with new ideas on ways to push what we currently have."

Bennett is quiet for a long moment. I feel like I'm sitting on eggshells, holding my breath. When he speaks, it's to Elias again. "What are you trying to sell?"

"I have an idea for a dating app."

It takes everything in me to restrain my gasp, especially when Bennett looks over at me and I see the amusement lighting up his eyes. He looks at Elias again.

"What makes you think I'd back your idea?" Bennett asks. "I have a million people with ideas for dating apps."

"It's not a dating app as much as it is a friendship app," Elias says. "It involves travel and food. And I'd pay for it to get done. I have ideas and money, but no experience or anyone who can develop them for me."

Bennett nods slowly in understanding, then looks at Nate. "What are you offering?"

Instead of spending the rest of the time eating a healthy lunch, I stuff my face with bread and butter because this meeting has my nerves on edge, as if I'm the owner of SEVEN and not just a lowly employee.

"See, Morgan, if you'd have come and worked for us instead of picking SEVEN, you could've done this and more," Nate says, smiling.

I know he's only half joking. He'd offered me a job and a salary that was more than I'm currently making, but SEVEN has been my dream company for too long to turn the opportunity down.

"She could've stayed working for the company where she interned," Bennett says.

"I would have." Ryan laughs. "I mean, hell, if they want to hire me now I'd sell all my shares to Nate and run over there."

"Shut up," Nate says, laughing.

"It's impressive that so many people want you on their team," Elias says. "Do you have experience with development?"

"Back off, Elias. This one is mine," Bennett says. His tone is neither playful nor harsh, but his words make my heart skip nonetheless. "You may have a chance to work with her though."

"I look forward to that," Elias says, smiling at me. "Have you gotten a chance to develop any apps while you've been there?"

"I'd like to note that I've only been there two weeks," I start. "But yes. Actually, dating apps are kind of my thing, and SEVEN has been graceful enough to let me test out a workplace dating app idea I've been brewing for a while."

"Wow." Elias exchanges an emphatic look with Ryan and Nate.

"Isn't that messy?" Ryan asks.

"That must be the go-to male response." I roll my eyes, not even bothering to hide my annoyance.

Bennett chuckles. "Because it is messy."

"We've already discussed this." I meet his gaze.

His smile drops slowly as he looks at me, his expression going from pointed to something else . . . something that makes me forget how to breathe for a second. For someone who doesn't believe in love in the least, he sure knows how to make a woman believe she has a shot with him. I force myself to look back at the men across from us.

"Anyway, it's going well so far."

"Do tell," Bennett says. "I haven't received feedback or data from this marvelous app. So I'm hearing this for the first time."

"Bennett has his reservations about dating apps," I explain, "which is fair. I get it, but this one is going to show him that real love isn't as hard to find as he may think. I haven't conducted the first interviews yet. The questionnaire goes out on Saturday morning, which will be a week after the app debuted. So far, no one has dropped it or filed a complaint though, and that's good. As far as I know, the users have remained anonymous –"

"Wait, they don't even know the names of the people they're matching with?" Nate asks, frowning.

"They're assigned names. Birds, actually. Canary, Blue Jay, Owl, Cardinal."

"Birds." Bennett shrugs. "I mean, if it works, it works, right?"

"But if you were to expose this app to the real world . . ." Ryan starts.

"They'd pick a nickname that suits them. The birds are just

for our trial in the office. I figured if they were allowed to pick a nickname, there was a higher chance of people piecing two and two together. For all you know, you're matching with the person who works beside you."

The three men across from me blink. And blink. I shoot Elias a look. "Didn't you claim to be into dating apps?"

"As a business. Sure."

My mouth drops. "I will refrain from commenting on that out of respect to the man sitting to my left, but please note that if he wasn't here and I wasn't at risk of getting fired, I would say some really mean things right now."

They all laugh, including Bennett. "Hey, I'm not your boss. My dad is. I can't really fire you."

"How does that work, by the way?" Nate asks. "You started the company and brought him on, but he has a higher position than you?"

"It depends on how you qualify positions. I created the company, but my father was a big boss in the industry for a long time. I'd be an idiot to think I was smarter or more business savvy than he. So, I begged him to come on board, offered him the CEO position, which he tried to decline, but I was just a kid. Smart, sure, but a kid nonetheless. The rest is history." Bennett shrugs a shoulder.

I blink up at him. I wasn't expecting that answer. As a matter of fact, it's a question that's always been on my mind. Every time I read an interview with him or his father, I wonder if that question just doesn't get asked or if they'd rather not answer it publicly. Whatever the case, I didn't think this would be the answer. It's a surprising one. Not many men I've met would be willing to take the backseat to anyone, especially not a father. It seems to me that most men are always in competition or trying to surpass their father somehow. Not Bennett though.

He continues talking to the guys, and I find it harder and harder to concentrate on the words coming out of his mouth. I just keep staring at his full lips and sharp jaw with the five o'clock shadow that makes him look hotter than he did two days ago, if that's even possible.

Thankfully, the food gets here and I stop staring and start eating. We fall into a comfortable conversation about where the companies are going and how tech is an unstoppable phenomenon that just keeps getting bigger.

"You sure you want to give it up?" Bennett asks Nate. "It sure sounds like you don't."

Nate's eyes jump between Bennett and me. "I don't, but I know Presley wants me to be more present in her endeavors and wishes we'd do more business together." He shrugs. "And Ryan is about to have another kid, so I think he'd rather have the money in his pocket and not work as much for it." Nate looks at Ryan with a laugh.

"Damn right. Kids are expensive," Ryan says with a chuckle. Once it dies down, he gets serious again. "We trust your vision, Bennett. We've been watching you for years and have seen what you can do for people. We've gone over every other company from New York to the Silicon Valley and yours is the one we keep coming back to."

"That means a lot," Bennett says. "I trust we can make this work, and that we can get your ideas off the ground for you, Elias."

We all stand up to say our goodbyes. Bennett, Elias, and Ryan keep talking, while Nate and I are off to the side having our own conversation about the latest brewpub he and Presley are opening up.

"It just seems like a lot to give up," I say quietly, out of earshot from Bennett. "The tech stuff, I mean."

"I've had the good fortune of coming up with a couple of great inventions and selling them for a lot more than I ever dreamed of." He shrugs. "I figure it's time to focus on other things. Not having Winston around has been hard on me, but much harder on Presley, especially with the business side of things. We'll still have our staff working on inventions, so it's not like I'm fully giving it up. I'm just willing to let go of the control a little."

"That's a pretty big step."

"Eh. She's worth it." He grins.

"She is worth it." I feel myself grinning back.

My best friend hadn't had the best luck with love before Nathaniel, but the moment they became a couple, things changed for her. She's brighter than she was before . . . calmer, happier. Love did that for her. It's one of the reasons I refuse to stop believing in something I haven't had good luck in myself. I've seen firsthand the way it changes people's lives. Nathaniel and I hug and say goodbye. They have a flight leaving tonight, while Bennett and I will stay until the conference is over on Sunday. The reminder of what I promised him for the next few days makes my stomach flutter.

Bennett and I walk through the lobby in comfortable silence. I can imagine he's probably thinking about the business proposition, while I have my mind in the gutter, picturing him naked under his expensive suit. He pulls out his phone and starts talking, I assume to his father, with the way he's being quiet. I look around, letting the sounds of the casino in the middle of the hotel distract me so that I don't eavesdrop. When Bennett slows down, I walk off to the side, looking inside the glass display of the expensive jewelry store inside the hotel. Because of my mom's profession, I practically grew up in these hotels, usually waiting around for her or one of her girls to finish a job. I watched other people come here and spend an insane amount of money on things: drugs, women, jewelry, gambling, shows, restaurants. Not once did I wish to be one of them. Even now, I wouldn't. If there's one thing I've learned about people who have too much at their disposal, it's that they don't appreciate things half as much as those with none.

"See something you like?" Bennett's voice pulls me from my thoughts.

I turn to him with a smile. "God, no."

"You're a mystery to me, Cupid." He watches me. "You want everyone else to find love but don't believe in it for yourself, you go to meetings with powerful men and somehow make the whole thing feel like a bunch of guys catching up on life, and you stand by the most expensive item in that store and tell me you don't want it, and what's more, is I genuinely believe you don't."

"Well, it sounds like you have me all figured out." I start to move, but he presses me against the glass, his mouth near mine. "I hope you have enough money to replace what's behind me if we break it."

His gaze flicks away from mine briefly, and I know he's thinking about it. His lips tug up on one side as he brings his attention back to me. "Guess we'll just have to find out."

He brings his face down to mine, his eyes twinkling the closer he gets, as if he's testing or waiting for me to push him away. I reach for his tie and pull him closer, faster. He groans as his lips come down on mine, his hand sliding up to cup the left side of my face as his hard body pushes me against the cold glass behind me. A part of me worries that we'll get kicked out, but the fear is quickly replaced by a rush of heat as his hands move down my body, stopping at my waist, his mouth still hot on mine, tongues moving, teeth nipping.

"Is it too early to go back to the room?" I pant against him as he breaks the kiss.

He chuckles, pulling back to meet my eyes. I find a sense of comfort knowing I put that wild look in them. He grabs my hand and pulls me away from the glass, leading me through the lobby without another word.

CHAPTER NINETEEN

ANTICIPATION ROLLS through me as I'm getting ready for dinner. It feels different tonight, maybe because we've come to an agreement of sorts and a part of me knows that tonight he's not going to push me away as he did last night. *As long as I keep my shit together and don't start crying again.* Which, I won't. That was my one good cry of the year. I'm giving myself a last once-over when I hear the knock on the door between our rooms seconds before Bennett appears in the threshold of the bathroom. He's wearing ripped jeans and a suit jacket. It's something I've never seen before and wouldn't have ever thought he'd wear, but it looks damn good on him. His dark hair is neatly brushed to one side, and his eyes are currently on my ass. He moves his gaze slowly up until it meets mine in the mirror.

"Thanks for knocking and waiting for me to invite you in."

The corner of his mouth pulls up. "You left your door open. I figured it was an invitation."

"I could've been sitting on the toilet." I raise an eyebrow as I start putting my makeup away.

"You say that as if there's any chance that I don't think you take a shit."

My eyes widen. "Bennett!"

"What?" He chuckles, gripping his stomach. "Why is this so horrifying for women? Men talk about the size of their shit, the color of their shit, how often they shit. It's human nature."

"It's fucking disgusting." I make a face and brush past him as I step out of the bathroom and walk over to the closet to step into my heels. "You just lost like three points on the hotness scale."

"Three points?" He laughs louder. I can't help but smile, not that he can see it with my back turned to him. "I'll have to work on my bathroom skills."

"Can you stop talking about it?" I groan, turning to face him.

"You look beautiful." He stops smiling suddenly and lets his gaze drift over me once more, not bothering to hide the hunger in his eyes. When his gaze meets mine again, he says, "You *are* beautiful."

I feel myself blush. I've received compliments from a lot of men, but few have made me feel the way his do. Maybe it's because when he says what he thinks, he doesn't allow room for misinterpretation or question. When he says I'm beautiful, I truly feel beautiful. He clears his throat after a beat.

"How upset would you be if I told you I changed our rooms?"

"What do you mean?"

"I got us a suite." He points up, as if to show me where the suite is.

"Oh." I blink. "Like for both of us?"

He cocks his head. "No, for me, my constant hard-on, and my toilet."

"You're ridiculous." I can't help but laugh, but it doesn't last. "I . . ." I lick my lips, glancing away briefly before looking at him again. "What if you don't want to stay the night? What if it goes horribly wrong? What if we're no longer sexually compatible?"

"Trust me, we're still sexually compatible," he says. "What worries you more, the idea of us not being sexually compatible or the idea that I may not want to spend the night?"

"Both." My eyes are wide, a contrast to the amusement I see in his. "What if *I* don't want to spend the night?"

"Do you?"

"I don't know." I chew on my bottom lip, looking at the bed we shared last night—no sex involved.

"Exactly," he says, as if reading my mind. "We were fine last night."

"We didn't hook up last night."

"Last time we hooked up, we spent the night together, Morgan." He raises an eyebrow. "The difference is, we fucked through the night and I left at the crack of dawn and didn't do any pillow talk." He must sense my hesitation, because he squeezes my hand and brings his hand up to my chin, squaring it so that I look at him. "I want the pillow talk this time."

"Oh." My heart stutters. I want to ask *WHY, WHY, WHY?* What is the point of pillow talk if you don't even believe in relationships, but I nod because, damn it, I want this. I want *him*. "Okay. Let's do this. I mean, it's only two nights, right?"

"Only two nights." He closes the distance between us and cups the right side of my face with his hand. "Let me replace all the bad memories you have of this place with good ones," he says, with a warmth in his eyes that makes my knees shaky. "And if you feel overwhelmed, we can sleep in separate rooms."

"Okay."

He leans in and presses his mouth to mine. The kiss is soft, yet demanding, and when he walks forward, the back of my knees crash the bed and I fall back, gripping his shoulders tightly, as if it'll lessen the impact instead of making it worse. Bennett chuckles against my lips as he pulls away. I laugh, pushing him off so he won't continue to crush me.

"You could've killed me," I gasp.

"You pulled me toward you." He's still laughing, shoulders shaking.

"I was falling. It was an immediate response."

"To make me fall with you?"

"Isn't that the way it usually happens?" Our laughter fades, our previous amusement replaced with something else, something real and scary and uncontrollable. Bennett holds my gaze as he picks up my hand and kisses the back of it before pushing himself up. He fixes his jacket as he looks down at me.

"As much as I'd like to continue to explore this right now, we have to be out of our rooms in ten minutes. I'm going to pick up the key while you pack."

I nod, unable to form words, and watch as he walks out of the room.

CHAPTER TWENTY

"WHAT ARE YOU THINKING ABOUT NOW?" Bennett asks. "Second thoughts?"

He'd taken our bags up to the suite while I called Mr. Cruz to talk about a potential client he sent me an email about, so I didn't even get to see it, and now we're on our way to a music show he got us tickets for and I'm trying to push down every insecurity blooming inside of me. I bite the inside of my cheek, trying to figure out how to say something without sounding like an idiot. After a few seconds, I decide honesty is always the answer.

"I don't want to lose my job at SEVEN over this."

"What? I would never . . ." His expression falls. "Morgan, I'm not your boss. I know it may feel like that, but you report to my father. If this makes you uncomfortable because you feel like I can take opportunities away, we won't go there. I never want you to feel like that." His brows pull together. "I would never do anything to hurt you. Hell, every time I look at you, I hear warning bells ringing in my head because of Devon. The last thing I ever want to do is hurt you."

"No. I want this. I mean, I one-hundred-percent want this." I stop walking and tug his hand so he stops with me. I don't care that a sea of people are walking around us in order to get to the show on time. I want to make sure we're on the same page about this. "I know this isn't a relationship, but I don't want whatever happens these next few days to mess anything up between us, especially in the office."

"It won't." His brows are still pulled together though. A part of me wonders if I've brought too many concerns to him at once and he's going to call the whole thing off and agree that this is a bad idea. Maybe it's the worst idea, but I want him more than any idea—good, bad, or mediocre—that I've had in the past year.

I squeeze his hand. "I like that you have warning bells when it comes to me and you find them difficult to ignore."

"Impossible to ignore." He hesitates for a beat, eyes bouncing between mine, but then he steps closer, bringing his lips to mine in a soft yet toe-curling kiss. When he pulls back, I grip his muscular biceps, wishing he would just keep kissing me. He smiles. "We have a show to get to."

HE HOLDS my hand throughout the entire show, while I marvel at everything on the stage and bob my head to The Beatles. I don't know how much of the show he catches, but every time I turn to look at him, I catch him staring at me, and each time, I blush deeper. Thankfully, the lights are dim. Every once in a while, he leans in and sings in my ear, and it's the hottest thing I've ever heard in my life. When it's over, we both give a standing ovation to the performers and walk out singing the final song.

"That was amazing."

"It was worth seeing the smile on your face and the way your eyes get like saucers every time they do a stunt."

I laugh. "Did you even catch any of the show?"

"You were the show." He grins.

"Corny." I roll my eyes, but I swear my face is on fire. "Thank you for bringing me."

"It was my pleasure." He takes hold of my hand again as we walk through the lobby. He nods toward the casino. "You play?"

"Nope."

"Do you want to?"

"Not really." I shrug a shoulder.

"I guess growing up here means you're not impressed by any of it?"

"Yes and no. I didn't really get a chance to experience it the way everyone who comes here does."

"All the more reason to try your luck on a slot machine."

"Oh, what the heck. One time won't kill me."

Bennett chuckles, pulling me toward the biggest machine in the casino. He puts something in it and tells me to pull the lever. I put all my force into it.

"Careful, Cupid. We want to win, not owe the casino a new machine." He winks. I laugh because I know it would take a lot more than my puny arms to break this thing. I stand back and watch beside him as the items on the screen roll into a slow stop. It blinks the lights and says I won five dollars.

"I won." I gasp and jump up, clapping my hands together.

"Five dollars." He chuckles as I do a shimmy.

"Five dollars more than I had when I played that!"

He's still grinning as he wraps his arms around me and kisses me. "You're so fucking cute, Cupid."

"And so rich," I whisper against him.

He laughs harder.

CHAPTER TWENTY-ONE

I'M DYING to go back to the suite, but Bennett insists that we need to go get dinner and drinks first. We won't experience Vegas the way he wants me to unless we do, he says, so I agree even though I feel like we just had lunch with Nate, Ryan and Elias.

"I don't want to experience Vegas," I mutter as we wait to be seated at the restaurant. "I want to experience you."

He raises an eyebrow. "You already have."

"You know what I mean." I slap his chest lightly.

He grabs my hand and keeps it there, staring at me. I swear I can get lost in his eyes, amber with specks of a darker brown. Everything about him feels like I'm immersed in something otherworldly.

"Right this way." The hostess's words snap our attention toward her. We follow behind her and sit in a cozy little corner.

"This is nice." I smile, thanking her for the menu and Bennett does the same.

"Tell me the story of your life," he says as soon as she walks away.

"What?" I laugh. "The story of my life? Which part?"

"Any part. All of the parts."

We're interrupted by the waiter, but Bennett orders a bottle of wine for us and dismisses him quickly, returning his eyes to mine.

"Well, I don't know where to start," I say. "Why don't you tell me the story of your life? That way I know what it is you want me to share."

"My parents came from Cuba on a boat, fleeing from a government that was making it impossible for them to prosper. Dad had connections in Miami and went straight to work. Mom got a job at a restaurant, worked long hours, much to Dad's dismay. When my dad got an opportunity in Jersey, they picked up and left. Mom got pregnant with me, quit the waitressing job she'd gotten there to stay home with me. Dad wanted me to play baseball; I chose football instead. Mom hated it, but she drove me to every game and practice anyway. I did my chores, got straight As, messed around a lot, went to college for football, which my parents thought was absolutely insane." He chuckles. "I ended up becoming fast friends with a really cool guy who turned out to have a really hot, beautiful, smart younger sister." He grins when I roll my eyes. "In college I came up with a concept for a company, started it, hired my dad, and the rest is history."

"You skipped the part about your psychotic ex-wife." I smile at the waiter, who's back with our bottle of wine.

He shoots me a look like he doesn't pity me as he pours it. "You look like you'll be needing more of this than he does, so I'll start here."

I laugh, try the wine and nod my approval. When he walks

away, I look at Bennett. "I don't know shit about wine. It all tastes good to me."

He laughs and lifts his glass. "To this moment."

"To this moment." I smile, take a sip and set it down. "You were getting to the part about your ex-wife."

He sighs heavily. "There's not much to tell. I met Paola our junior year of college. Never imagined getting married, but somehow it seemed like the next step. Everyone else was doing it, so we did. I was starting the company, so I didn't pay as much attention to her as she wanted. She said she wanted kids, we tried for two years, it didn't work, and she ended up getting pregnant anyway." He lifts his glass and an eyebrow. "Not with mine."

"No." I gasp.

"Oh, yeah."

"Wow."

"Yup." He shakes his head. "We separated a little over a year ago. The divorce was quick because—despite all the wrenches she tried to throw—my lawyers were ready. I mean, she was fucking pregnant with another man's kid."

"Jeez, Bennett. I'm sorry." I feel my shoulders sag. "Why do people suck so bad?"

"Human nature, free will, too many options available to us, the Internet, take your pick."

"Well," I take another sip and set my glass down, leaning forward. "My ex-fiancé fucked my mother."

"You're serious?" He stares. Blinks. Stares.

"Dead serious." I nod, pressing my lips together. "It sounds crazy when I say it aloud. I don't think I ever have."

"You've never told anyone that?"

"Nope."

"Not even Dev?" He frowns. I shake my head. "Not even your friends?"

"Only you." I bite my lip. "Well, maybe another person. I can't remember."

"Hopefully not the app guy."

"Maybe the app guy. I can't remember."

He watches me. "Was your ex the reason you were crying the other night?"

"No." I feel myself make a face. "I wouldn't waste my tears on him. I'm mad enough I wasted them on her."

"Will she be at Devon and Nora's wedding?"

"Probably." I sigh.

"Does he know you hate her?"

"Yeah. I mean, he has issues with her too, to a point, but he had more happy years with her than I did. I guess he's able to cling to those easier than I am."

"She visited New York once when we were in college," Bennett says, a thoughtful look on his face. "He wouldn't let her come to our apartment. I always thought it was odd, but it wasn't my place to ask questions. I saw her again once when we were in LA and she was in rehab. He didn't explain and I didn't ask. I just drove him there and waited."

"Yeah, well, if your mother was an addict, a whore, and a madam, I don't think you'd want her around your friends either. Especially when your friends are all well-rounded and have nice, normal families."

"What do you mean a madam?" His eyes widen.

"Right." I pause, taking a sip of my wine. I've never had to explain this to anyone, so I don't even know where to start. I try anyway. "She worked in a bank when my dad was still at home. Regular nine-to-five job. Then Dad left and before we knew it, there were women in and out of the house all the time, and lo and behold, Mom was their boss."

"That's . . . interesting. I'm assuming it bothered you."

I shrug. "Not really. The women were very kind to me. It didn't really start bothering me until a little later."

"Did she want you to get into the business, so to speak?"

"Who knows." I laugh at the absurdity of it all. "How's that for normal?"

"Nobody's normal." Bennett chuckles. "All families have issues, though I have to say yours is definitely at the end of that spectrum. What about your father?"

"Left when I was ten." I blink rapidly, hoping to clear the tears threatening to blur my vision. I clear my throat. "I'm sorry. I swear I'm not usually an emotional mess. It's this place."

"Stop apologizing." He reaches for my hand over the small table and a sense of calm washes over me as he holds it. "You said ex-fiancé. I want to go back to that."

"Of course you do." I smile, taking a sip of my wine and pausing to thank the waiter as he offers a basket of bread. Bennett orders a couple of samplers for us to share, making sure I'm okay with it. I nod and thank him because I'm not even hungry, but I know I have to pick at something if I'm going to continue drinking this wine.

"So, ex-fiancé."

"This part, Dev does know about," I say, remembering the way my brother showed up on Justin's doorstep, dragged me out, and tried to talk me out of the engagement. "Honestly, there's not much to tell. I was with him a couple of years and decided during a drunken night to get engaged. Dev warned me that he was a douchebag." I pause. "This was before I found out he'd fucked my mother. He was cheating on me with all of her . . . employees," I say.

"Wow."

"As much as I hate her for, well, so many things, I've come to terms with that aspect of her life, but only because Dev didn't have to worry about having messed-up cleats when he was playing high school football," I say. "So, despite everything, she really tried. I can see that. At least Devon got out of here, made a name for himself."

"Is that why you got engaged when he was away? To get away from your mother?"

"I guess I wanted to believe love was something other than what I saw day in and day out at home. Justin went to high school with me. He was one of the smart ones, all gifted classes, always treated me like a princess. I never saw the signs."

Bennett squeezes my hand tighter. "He was an idiot."

"He was." I smile.

"And now you're hoping in taking away the veil and having people feel like they can be honest with each other, they'll have a higher chance of finding love?"

"I just don't see why it's not something that can happen for everyone."

"It'll happen for you," he says.

"Careful, Trouble. You don't want me to think you're going soft."

He winks. "I'm hard where it matters."

That makes me laugh loudly. This guy.

CHAPTER TWENTY-TWO

"TELL me another one of your bad memories," he says as we're walking through the lobby.

"Right now? I'm having such a great time though. My stomach is full of food and my veins are overflowing with wine." I sway a little, revealing just how much wine, and giggle when Bennett's hand tightens around my waist. "Sorry."

He pulls me closer so that my head is against his chest and his chin is on my head as we walk.

"I just want one more bad memory so I can replace it with one good one," he murmurs. I stop walking suddenly, looking up at him.

"Bennett." My voice is shaky. "That sounds like more than just hooking up."

"So we're going to have sex and not be friends?"

"I . . . I don't know," I whisper. "I don't want to get attached."

"Do you get attached easily?" He searches my eyes.

"I don't know. I've never done this before. What if I do?"

"Hm. We'll figure it out when we get there." He pushes a strand of hair behind my ear and strokes my jaw with his thumb, his other fingers on the side of my neck. "You're so beautiful, Morgan. One memory."

"I don't want to talk about it," I whisper. "But this moment right here is replacing at least five bad ones."

His lips pull up slightly as he bends toward me and kisses me softly, deeply, with such emotion that it takes my breath away. When he pulls away, I keep my eyes closed, wanting to remember every single moment of the way he looked at me like I was the most precious thing he'd ever held and kissed me in the middle of the casino at the Aria. He's staring at me when I finally open my eyes, his look making my heart skip a beat.

"Maybe you can show me that suite now," I say.

He simply nods but takes a second before fully pulling away from the moment, as if he's also cataloging it for his memory bank.

It's impossible, I think. *He's probably just tipsier than he thought he was.*

A man like Bennett doesn't catalog moments with people like me.

THE SUITE IS everything I imagined it would be—vast, with a full kitchen, large living room, and floor-to-ceiling windows that overlook the Strip. We leave our suitcases in the living room and explore the rooms—there are two—each with king-size beds and massive bathrooms, but one of the bedrooms has a small swimming pool encased in glass that looks like it's hanging out of the suite. My eyes widen as I look at it. There's no way people won't see us if we're in there. Even though we're high up in the tower, there's a clear view from the hotel across the street as well as the other rooms on this floor. I feel Bennett come up behind me before he puts his arms around me and pulls me to his chest, bringing his mouth down to my neck.

"I'd kill to see you naked in there."

"Hm. Maybe you will." I turn my head to give him better access to my neck, and he does, nibbling as much as he can with the blouse I'm wearing. I undo the ribbon in the front and turn around to face him as I slowly work my buttons. He steps back, gaze heated, as he watches me. I toss the blouse and unzip my skirt, letting it pool at my feet before kicking it in the same direction.

"Jesus, Morgan." He bites down on his lip with a groan, taking a step toward me. "Fuck."

He brings his hands up to my shoulders and brings them down the sides of my arms. His touch is soft, but his hands are rough. I shiver at the contrast of it, feeling my nipples harden in the delicate fabric of my ivory bra.

"You're overdressed," I say, my voice a shaky whisper.

The last time I felt this naked before a man was last year with Bennett. I've been entirely bare in front of men in the past and haven't felt this exposed. It's the way he looks at me, like he's trying to read into me, not just stare at my body. I realize, as my heart gets caught in my throat, that this is probably the way he looks at every woman he has sex with, and that should be fine by me, but for some reason jealousy blooms deep inside of me at the thought. It vanishes when he begins to undress, his suit meeting my discarded clothes across the room. As he strips, every movement makes his muscles tighten, making it very apparent that Bennett Cruz did not stop working out when he stopped playing college football. He stands before me like a Greek god, roped in muscles and etched in gold, his black boxer briefs the only item of clothing covering him, and with the size of the bulge in them they are barely covering anything at all. He moves first, offering me a hand, which I take, heart hammering as he tugs me toward the bed. I kick off my heels as I walk, the movement taking four inches off my height and making the distinction between us that much clearer. He's huge where I'm tiny. He's muscled where I'm soft, and as I sit on the bed and he leans over me, with one leg between mine, I realize how much I love the contrast. Bringing my arms around his neck, I reach up to kiss him, losing myself in the moment. He moans against my mouth, holding himself up with one hand and bringing the other down to my breast, exploring over my bra at first, and then reaching beneath it and shoving it up to get a handful and tweak my nipples. I move against the leg between mine, seeking relief for the sensation between my legs.

"Morgan." He bites my lower lip with a little growl. It dawns on me that he's only said my name a handful of times, and this is one of them, and I love the way he sounds raw and out of control as he says it. "Fuck. Keep moving like that, baby."

I moan loudly, breaking the kiss to toss my head back, and his mouth finds my neck, my chest. His hand loops behind my back and he unclasps my bra, dragging the straps down my arms and tossing it aside. He moves his leg and I gasp loudly.

"I was so close." I grip his arm, my eyes hazy as I look up at him.

"I'll get you there." He kisses me again, deeply, thoroughly, before pulling back and dragging his mouth down my chest, to my breasts, taking my nipples into his mouth one at a time. Even the way he does that, circling his tongue around each one and nibbling just slightly, makes me feel out of control.

I feel myself thrash against the mattress, panting. He's not even touching me there yet and I'm ready to come. As if sensing this, he blows on my nipples, and sucks right beneath my breast, then my stomach, my belly button, until he reaches my hips. With one hand, he pulls my panties down slowly, his mouth trailing the slide of the fabric. I feel completely out of control, heartbeat pulsing in my neck, my temple, my core, as he continues to explore me. I squeeze my eyes shut, grabbing the top of his hair when I feel his mouth moving lower and lower on my pelvis, until he reaches my clit. At the first swipe of his tongue, I cry out, arching my back. He brings his other hand between my legs and begins to play with my folds as his tongue continues to lash over me. My legs start to tremble. I start making garbled noises as I try to speak—to tell him to stop, to keep going, to never fucking stop at all. I'm coming before I can even try to stop myself or slow down. I hear the rip of foil and open my eyes to see him covering himself with a condom, his hand stroking as if to make sure it's not going to slide off. His hooded eyes are roaming my body as he does it and I swear it's the sexiest thing I've ever witnessed in my life.

"I'm on the pill." I lick my lips. "And I'm clean."

"It's already on." He smiles softly, shrugging. "I'm clean too though."

I reach for him. "Come here."

"You're so goddamn beautiful, Morgan." He steps between my legs, pressing one hand to the mattress beside my head and the other between us, settling himself between my folds but not pushing in any further.

I start to get impatient, opening my mouth to complain, but his tongue silences me with a swipe against mine. I gasp and begin to grind against the hand he's placed between us, needing the friction to get me off again. Bennett chuckles against my mouth as he pulls away slightly, so I'm no longer grinding against him.

"Ben," I begin to argue, but he thrusts inside of me and all I can do is arch and gasp at the impact. My hands grip his forearms, my nails digging into him as he continues to drive into me, faster and faster, with a tempo destined to make me come undone quickly.

"Look at me, Morgan."

My eyes snap to his and what I find in them sparks a fire inside me that I haven't felt in a long time, if ever. I bring my arms up and wrap them around his neck, moaning every time he pounds into me. It's not just his cock inside me that I feel, but the impact of his thrust against my clit.

"You're so fucking wet," he groans, bringing his mouth to mine. "Your pussy is tighter than I remember it being."

I bite down on his lip, unable to form words to retort to that, and then his lips are crashing down against mine. His kiss becomes hungrier, his gaze gets darker when he pulls back to look down at me, his movements get harder, faster, his grip on my ass gets tighter. Soon, the fire burning inside me seems to burn through me, crawling down my spine and clenching my core so tightly I think I'll explode, and when I do explode, it's with a chant of his name on my lips. "Ben, Ben, Ben, Ben." I swear it's the sound of it that makes him still and groan out my own name as he comes.

CHAPTER TWENTY-THREE

I'M FINISHING my makeup when Bennett walks into the bathroom wearing nothing but his boxers. The sight makes me swipe my mascara right onto the bridge of my nose. He's unbelievably attractive in a way I'm not sure I'll ever get used to. He comes up behind me and wraps his arms around me, kissing my cheek.

"You're distracting." I wipe the dot of mascara off.

"So are you." He squeezes me tighter, looking at me in the mirror. "We look good together."

"We do." I bite my lip to keep from laughing. "So glad you don't have any hang-ups."

"Never have." He kisses me on the cheek again. "You shouldn't either. You're beautiful."

With that, he walks away, past the partition that separates the sink from the rest of the bathroom. I finish up and head to the kitchen, making us coffee while I wait for him to finish getting ready. Today's the last day of the conference and we have two meetings that I'm happy to get over with, but there's also a sense of loss at the thought that once we go home tomorrow, this is over. It doesn't feel like we've had nearly enough time together.

I walk over to the window and look out at the Strip. It looks so innocent during the day, such a contrast to what this place was built on and continues to thrive on. I hear Bennett's dress shoes tap against the marble floor as he walks over to me. He smells so good, I just want to turn my head and inhale, but I continue to look ahead instead.

"It's a lovely day," he says.

"It is." I look up at the sky. "Nice day to jump out of an airplane."

I feel his gaze on me. "Have you ever done that?"

"Hell, no." I meet his gaze. "I value my life, thank you very much."

He laughs loudly, shaking his head. "You're something else, Morgan Tucker."

"Thanks." I bump him with my hip.

"Thanks for the coffee."

"Welcome."

We stand there in silence, just looking at the city, as we drink our coffee. Normally, silence makes me uncomfortable. It strikes me as odd that I have absolutely no urge to fill the air with useless conversation. It just feels right. I take a deep breath and exhale.

"Have you checked your app today?"

"You told me to just be with you while we're here," I say, looking up at him. "I'll check it when I get home and back to reality."

"Hm." He takes a sip of coffee before taking my mug and placing it on the table beside his. When he walks over to me again, he wastes no time in bringing his mouth to mine. "This doesn't feel real to you? My hands on your body like this." He presses me to the glass behind me and brings his hands to my blouse, pressing me with kisses as he unbuttons it and removes it slowly, setting it down carefully over the back of the couch beside us.

"We have to be downstairs in thirty minutes," I murmur against his lips.

"You should probably start undressing me, then." He smiles against me, wrapping his arms around me to unzip my pencil skirt, letting it pool at my feet. I untuck his now-open dress shirt from his pants and help him out of it, his lips coming right back to mine as if holding a magnet. He reaches down and carries me with one arm, pressing me against the glass.

"I wish we could skip the entire conference," he says, reaching between us.

I feel his length, long, hard, and ready between my legs and bite down on my lip, bracing myself for him. He doesn't just thrust inside me though; instead, he teases me, rubbing his tip over my clit over and over, until I'm throwing my head back and moaning.

"Bennett, please."

"Please what, Cupid?"

"Please fuck me," I pant.

"Not until you answer my question." He slips between my folds, once, twice, three times, hitting my clit each time.

"I'll come just from that," I say, but there's a shrill in my voice I can't help because I feel like I'll explode whether he stops or not.

"Hm." He bites my shoulder. "I'd rather you come around my cock." He licks my shoulder. I moan again, my legs starting to shake. "I want to feel you all over me."

"Fuck." I dig my fingers into his shoulder blades. He's not

even fully undressed, but it doesn't matter, I can still feel the way every ridge of muscle beneath his clothes flexes against my touch. "I can't, Bennett. I can't."

"Can't what?" He brings his lips back to mine, kissing me hard once, his eyes on mine. "You can't admit how real this is?"

"Why? You were the one who said this can't happen."

"Maybe I want it to happen." He presses up against my clit again, I swear his girth gets bigger each time he does it. I groan again, shutting my eyes tightly.

"Please, Bennett. Please fuck me," I whisper.

"Open your eyes, baby."

I do. He finally pushes inside of me, slowly, filling me inch by inch. I gasp loudly, nails digging deeper into his shoulders. I'll leave a mark, but I don't care. I wish it would be permanent —let every other woman he's with after me know I was here. The thought is random and alarming. I've never felt the need to claim a man before, why this one? My eyes widen on his as the realization hits me.

"It's real," I whisper. "It feels real."

He grins an alarmingly wolfish grin that has me biting down on my lip as my entire body rattles with an orgasm. His chases shortly after, and as we're there, him holding me up against the glass of our suite, overlooking a city that's brought my life and so much pain, I feel myself fully give into him. Consequences be damned.

CHAPTER TWENTY-FOUR

BENNETT

FOR A WHILE I was convinced I didn't want or need a woman, that I could just go through life acting like a bachelor and be okay with that, taking my pick of women whenever I saw fit. I sure as hell wasn't expecting Morgan. Sure, I thought of our one-night stand from time to time, but it had been riddled with too many outside factors for me to enjoy and accept it for what it had been—incredible sex with a beautiful woman. After this trip though? I can't convince myself not to pursue this thing with Morgan. She's everything I didn't know I wanted. Everything I didn't know I was searching for in a mate. She impressed me with every question she asked the panelist, with every meeting she sat beside me in, and with the strength she showed despite all of the things that had happened in her life that threatened to break her down. We'd agreed that we'd get each other out of our system while we were in Vegas, but I wasn't sure I could make good on that promise. Not when it seemed like she'd gone into my system and coded it with bits of herself, ensuring I wouldn't be able to just move on. I couldn't.

"So I guess this is our last breakfast together," she says, walking into the room with a white robe on.

I know from experience that she's not wearing anything underneath it and that knowledge has my dick hard in a second. I watch her as she walks up to the table, where I've already splayed out our continental breakfast and a few other things I ordered that I know she likes. She's a serious contradiction, with this coy way about her, her flushed cheeks and fluttering eyelids when she's feeling shy, but bombshell seductress when she's in the mood to play that role. And it hits me that maybe that's what she's been doing all her life—playing a role. I'd love to say I've managed to knock her guard down, but who really knows?

"Penny for your thoughts." She reaches for a croissant, raising an eyebrow at me.

"Do you really want this to be over when we head back home?"

"Wasn't that what we agreed on? All the sex while we're here, but back to being coworkers when we're home?"

"Yeah." I nod, taking a gulp of orange juice. "Do you think this can turn into something more?"

"Can it?" she asks. "I guess it can, but I think we should go home and sleep on it."

"Sleep on it."

"Yeah. Like, mull it over when we're not together twenty-four seven and clouded by lust."

That makes me smile. We have been clouded by lust. Happily clouded, might I add. I decide she's right about this. I'll let her sleep on it and think it over, even though I know I don't have to. I absolutely need more time with her, but I keep quiet and play the part that I know she wants me to play.

For now.

CHAPTER TWENTY-FIVE

BENNETT

MONDAY IS AN ABSOLUTE WASTE. For starters, my dad transferred Morgan to the Marketing and Development Department. I knew he was going to. She'd been saying it, he'd been saying it, but it didn't mean I was looking forward to it actually happening. Now, I'm left with an intern for an assistant who can't even answer my questions because he's too busy checking his Fantasy Football League. To top it all off, half of his players are on the bench, his quarterback plays for the Dolphins, and he just traded Todd Gurley. What a waste. I ring him again.

"Edward, may I see you in my office?"

"Sure," he says quickly. I hear him ruffling papers on the speaker and close my eyes with a sigh. When he comes into my office, he has a serious look on his face. "You rang?"

I bite my tongue to keep from hurling insults at him. He's new, he's young . . . he's overly excited. *Let it go, Bennett,* I warn myself. *It's not his fault you're pissed off at the world.*

"You haven't fixed my schedule for the week. I told you I'm no longer meeting with Titanium on Wednesday. Also, I have a meeting with Nathaniel Bradley and Ryan Cooper this afternoon that I'd like you to sit in," I say. "Actually, what is Miss Tucker up to?"

"Morgan?" His brows pull together. "She's . . . I don't know. She's been in Wesley's office all morning."

My jaw grinds. Fucking Wesley. I wait until I'm sure my voice won't have an edge to it before I speak. "Will you please fetch her for me?"

"Sure." He stands up, smile on his face. "I love going to that department. They always have something cool going on."

"Yeah, well, maybe if you can prove you're capable of keeping my schedule on track, one day you'll be in that department."

He walks out without another word. I sit back in my chair, closing my eyes. It's only been two days since I last saw Morgan. She was exhausted when we got back on Saturday so I didn't push to hang out longer, but damn, I wanted to. We'd said whatever we did would stay in Vegas, but I can't help but wonder if she felt as lonely as I did yesterday. The urge to call her was indescribable. The thought of showing up at her apartment was overwhelming.

I need to get a grip. I didn't sign up to become this heavily involved with anyone right now. It is the last thing I need after the fiasco with Paola. Yes, it has been over a year now, but that doesn't change the fact that I don't believe in the things Morgan wishes for herself. She wants a secure relationship, someone who isn't a liar, and I can't give her either of those things. As it is, certain things have been weighing on me and I feel like I need to tell her. I hear my door open, but keep my eyes closed until it shuts.

"Sleeping on the job?"

Her voice makes my heart hammer faster. When I open my

eyes and finally look at her, it stops pumping all together. She really is so fucking beautiful, with the kind of looks that belong on the Victoria's Secret runway, not hiding behind a screen all day, but seeing her excitement when she talks about what she does makes it clear that she's more at home behind a screen.

"Somebody wore me out." I smile at the sight of her blush. She takes a seat across from me.

"We're not supposed to talk about that," she whispers.

"Why not?" I whisper back. "And why are we whispering?"

"I don't know. It seems like something we shouldn't be too vocal about at work."

"Got it." I chuckle. "I want you to come to a meeting with me."

"I'm . . . " Her eyes widen momentarily. "I'm in another department."

"I want you to come anyway."

"Why? You have a new assistant. Have Eddy take notes."

"Eddy is a fucking moron," I say. "He's just . . . on another planet all the time."

"He started the job five seconds ago, Bennett." Her voice is soft, placating, as if trying to soothe a child after the loss of a Little League game. "I'm sure once he gets the hang of it, he'll be fine. Give him a chance. I'm in the middle of putting a website together for a major client."

"With Wesley."

"Yes, with Wesley." She raises an eyebrow. "Whom I happen to work with."

"Locked in an office all morning."

She laughs. "Please don't tell me you pulled me out of there because you're jealous."

"What if I am?"

"What if I remind you we said we would leave that in Vegas and be friends, just friends, when we got here?"

"What if I tell you I changed my mind and I think that's the dumbest thing I've ever agreed to?"

"I'd tell you I have to think about it and get back to you. I am sort of seeing someone, you know."

"The app guy." I tilt my head. "You can't even see him."

"It's an emotional relationship," she says, and I swear it grates at me, the fact that she's willing to be emotionally open with someone on an app and not with me. "I feel like I'd be a hypocrite to not give it a shot."

"I feel like a hypocrite asking you for more time together here, but I can't help myself."

"You said you don't do relationships," she says. "Also, you're my brother's best friend. What do you think Dev is going to think about all of this?"

"I don't know." I clasp my hands behind my neck and lean back in my chair. "He'll probably kick my ass."

"And you're willing to get your ass kicked over meaningless sex?"

"It's not meaningless."

She stares. The thing about Morgan is that she has a hell of a poker face. Maybe she doesn't play it at the tables, but she plays it at life. Normally, people are easy to read, especially when it comes to the laws of attraction. Your eyes widen slightly, you lick your lips, play with your hair, bite your lip, there's always some kind of tell. Morgan doesn't have one. Not that I can read anyway. In the bedroom, she lets go and gives me a connection, but out here she's stone-cold, and damn, if I don't want to break down all of her barriers.

"You said you didn't believe in relationships."

I sigh heavily. "Can I take my words back and try to explain them in a different way?"

"By all means."

"I don't believe in the notion that love is an all-encompassing thing that we cannot live without, but if you want a relationship, I can commit to that."

"Your crazy ex-wife seems to think you can't commit to anything."

I roll my eyes. "Yeah, well, we try not to listen to crazy people."

"I'll think about it."

"You'll think about it?" My eyebrows pull together as I straighten in my seat.

"Not every woman has to jump at the chance of being with you, you know."

"I'm well aware. I just thought we'd be on the same page."

"Because we had such a great time the past few days?"

"I don't know, I'm kind of starting to wonder if I imagined all the laughs and orgasms."

"Bennett." Her face burns bright and it's the last straw. I stand up and walk to the other side of the desk, taking a seat in the empty chair beside her. She shifts toward me, her knees brushing against mine. "What are you doing?"

I reach for her hand, unable to stand this distance between us any longer. "Go on a date with me tonight."

"First you want to drag me to a meeting and now you want to take me on a date?"

"We can do both."

"That's a lot of time spent together." She shoots a pointed look.

I realize she's right. It is a lot of time spent together, but we just spent the last week together in Vegas and I still wanted to wake up beside her yesterday and again this morning, so I don't think that's a problem. I don't say this aloud because I don't even know how I feel about that realization and I don't want to scare her away.

"So no meeting and no date?" I ask, watching as she seemingly thinks about it.

"Yes to both. Give me ten minutes to finish up with Wes though." She stands up, dropping my hand, and starts walking toward the door.

"On a nickname basis now, huh?"

"You are clearly an only child." She looks over her shoulder with a smile. "You have a real problem with sharing."

I stand up and close the distance between us, her sharp intake of breath the only clue I have that she's affected by me at all. I kiss one corner of her mouth and then the other.

"I don't share." I press my forehead against hers. "And I sure as hell wouldn't be okay sharing you."

CHAPTER TWENTY-SIX

MORGAN

ME: Oh my God. Oh my God. Oh my God.

Jamie: You know it's good gossip when she spells out OMG

Presley: ?!? SPILL

Devon: . . .

Oh crap. My heart stops at the sight of my brother's name.

Me: WRONG GROUP TEXT

I switch over to the group text that does not include my brother and start over.

Me: Oh my God. Oh my God. Oh my God. ALSO-DELETE THE OTHER GROUP TEXT BEFORE RESPONDING JUST IN CASE. DEV CANNOT BE IN ON THIS

Jamie: Done. Spill.

Presley: Waiting.

Me: Bennett wants me to be exclusive with him.

Jamie: OMGOMGOMG WHAT

Presley: OMG!!!

Me: I KNOW.

Presley: I thought he said he didn't believe in love?

Me: He did. I mean, Idk that he does, but he says he wants to date me

Jamie: What about Devon?

Me: He says he'll probably kick his ass but he's willing to suffer the consequences

Presley: *shocked face emoji*

Jamie: *shocked face emoji* dude, he's like the hottest bachelor in the city right now

Me: Yeah, him and a billion other guys.

Jamie: True, yet somehow, I can't seem to nail one down

Presley: You had Travis

Jamie: Fuck Travis

Me: Oh. That's new.

Presley: LOL What happened now? He's still dating the Broadway girl?

Jamie: I can't. I can't talk about it over text or right now. I'm literally about to walk into his mother's store. She wants me to help with the remodel. Send wine and Jesus. Thanks.

Presley: What about the app though? Are you going to give up the app?

Me: Idk.

That thought stays on my mind as I put my phone away and walk to the front door of the lobby, where I see Bennett waiting for me. My phone starts to vibrate in my purse the minute I start walking alongside him. Not that he notices, with the commotion around us.

"I'm assuming we're not going very far," I comment. "The heels I'm wearing were not meant for walking."

Bennett laughs. "So why wear them to work?"

"Because I sit at a desk all day. Besides, I switch them out for slides when no one is looking."

"That's interesting." He looks down at my shoes. "They're sexy as fuck. They should be worn all the time."

"I mean, I'd wear them during sex." I shrug.

"You haven't worn those with me." He stops walking, grabbing my arm and effectively stopping me as well. I meet his gaze. "How many people are you having sex with?"

"None at the moment." I raise an eyebrow. "I said I *would* wear them during sex. I mean, I was hooking up with the hottest guy I've ever met last week, but then I got home and—"

He pulls me to him and crashes his mouth down on mine. We're in the middle of Fifth Avenue, during lunch. Nothing about this kiss should be all-consuming, yet when he frames my face with his hands and slides his tongue into my mouth, the only thing I can seem to worry about is how long this could last and teleportation, because I would love to teleport us to my apartment and fuck him right now. He pulls away slowly, tugging my bottom lip.

"We're going to this meeting, then back to work, and tonight, you're letting me take you to dinner."

"Okay."

I'm glad I came to the meeting with Nathaniel and Ryan because I end up learning a little more about what their vision is, which is not what I understood from our original meeting. Nathaniel and Ryan are keeping their company intact, but basically want someone to take over some of their tech accounts, which is where SEVEN would come in. I'm silent throughout the meeting, jotting down notes for Bennett, even though I know from experience his brain is like a sponge and seems to retain everything you throw at him. When we finish, I small-talk with Nate for a little bit before walking out and heading back to the office with Bennett. I look at my phone for the first time since we left SEVEN and see a missed call from my mom. My heart stops. Devon hasn't called though, and if he hasn't called that means nothing serious has happened. I shoot him a text anyway, just in case.

Dev: Spoke to her. She just wants to make sure things are okay since she's coming to the wedding. We need to talk. I'm flying into town tomorrow morning.

Me: You don't have a game this week?

Dev: Bye week.

Me: Okay. See you then.

Shit, he didn't even give me a reasonable heads-up about his trip, but I guess I only need a couple of hours to make sure the guest room looks presentable.

"You seem distracted," Bennett says.

"As are you." I raise an eyebrow at the phone in his hand. He's been texting the entire walk back.

"Yeah." He sighs. "I have to meet with my dad about this. I'll see you tonight though. Seven?"

"Seven is perfect." I smile as we walk through the lobby.

He hasn't held my hand the entire time, but he's definitely not keeping a big distance between us as we walk. A part of me likes it because I feel like it means he's not afraid to be open about us, but a small part of me also wonders if I'm shooting myself in the foot with all of this. I mean, it's sudden, really sudden, despite the history we have. I just started working here and SEVEN is my dream company. If things go south, which they could, will I be okay? Will I still have a secure job? I choose not to bring it up yet. I know he'd reassure me that things will be fine and that his father's the one who makes the call, not him, but it's definitely a conversation we need to have. The last thing I need is something of this magnitude to gnaw at me. I head to my side of the building and he heads to his father's office without a second glance.

My office is small and looks more like a modern cubicle, with glass walls all around it and a desk smack in the middle. This entire wing is like that, save for the communal area with the bean bag chairs and activity tables—coloring, Play-Doh, and other things that would make a kindergarten teacher proud. According to Wesley, studies have shown that when adults take time away from what they're doing and focus on basic creative activities, they're more likely to be productive when they go back to work. I personally haven't felt the need to color, but I appreciate the gesture. Wesley knocks on my office door, as if I can't see him standing on the other side of it. He smiles as he opens it.

"So, I was thinking about next week and how each person will find out who they are matched with. Did you end up picking a really annoying trumpet sound or something for the unveiling? And are the photos we submitted the ones that are going to be shown?"

"Yes, and before you ask, no, I didn't see any of them, so I'm really hoping there are no dick pics."

Wesley laughs. "That would be horrifying."

"For the women, yes. Only men think dick pics are attractive."

"Well, I think tit pics are attractive," he says, shrugging. "Kind of levels out the playing field."

"Not really. Tits actually are attractive."

"Isn't that odd?"

"It's anatomy." I shrug. "Our bodies are also the ones taking the biggest hits." He gets this look on his face I've mostly seen on tween boys. I roll my eyes and add, "I meant childbirth."

He laughs. "Hey, a hit is a hit."

"You're such a guy."

"I am." He stares at me for a couple of seconds. I stare back wondering if there's anything else he needs. "So, I'm just going to ask. Are you seeing anyone?"

"Why?" I'm instantly in defense-mode, my brain going back to my thoughts from earlier about my job and how much I value it and how I need to break this thing off with Bennett before it even starts. It would be the smart thing to do.

"Just wondering if you'd like to go out sometime. You know, grab a drink or dinner or a movie or whatever."

"I'm kind of seeing someone," I say softly. "But if it doesn't work out, I'll let you know."

"I'd like that."

"But who knows, maybe you'll find love on our app."

"Maybe I'll find it with you." He winks as he walks out of my office.

I sigh heavily, leaning back in my seat. This is the reason dating is so difficult. Love is like a bad game of telephone, where everyone's message gets lost in translation along the way. Some woman out there likes Wesley, Wesley likes me, I like Bennett, Bennet likes no one. At the end of the rope, the chances of all of us finding a happily-ever-after are slim because once it doesn't work out with the one we want, we close off. I close my eyes and think about my friend's relationships. Presley and Nate found love together by chance, even though they'd both been sort of pining after each other for years. Jamie's situation with Travis always seemed like the most stable one, but once she reached a certain level of success and no longer spent as much time around him, that became a disaster. My brother and Nora really are the only ones I can think of who have always had a well-rounded relationship, and I think a lot of it has to do with the fact that Devon saw our mother mistreated for so long that he decided if he ever found a woman he'd make sure she knew her worth, and Nora has done the same for him.

There's a knock on my door and my eyes snap open quickly. I nearly fall out of my chair when I see Mr. Cruz standing on the other side.

"Hey," I say, "I swear I was not sleeping. Just thinking."

He chuckles. "Thinking is good. I have a few things I want to speak to you about in my office, if you don't mind."

"Of course." I stand quickly, grabbing my notepad and pen as I go. In the previous company I learned that taking notes on your phone looks very rude, and therefore I stopped doing it, resorting to writing on my notepad instead. It's not like anyone would ever understand my notes even if they got ahold of the pages. I can barely understand them sometimes. I follow Mr. Cruz to his office and shut the door behind us when we get there.

"Ben told me you already know what we'll be doing for Nathaniel Bradley, so I don't have to waste time explaining all of that to you," he says. "They have a client who wants us to develop a dating app for him."

I nod. "Elias. I met him in Vegas."

"Perfect, so you're familiar with the idea."

"I am. I mean, what he told me anyway."

"What do you think of it?"

"Well, two ideas were explained," I say. "The one for the airplane isn't really promising, in my opinion. The other one can be developed."

"You don't think people can find love on an airplane?" he asks, laughing when I pull a face.

"As a nervous flier, I can only speak for myself, but the only thing I'm trying to do on an airplane is survive. The last thing on my mind would be getting on an app to look for a potential boyfriend."

Mr. Cruz chuckles. "You sound like Barbara. She's also a nervous flier."

"The other idea is more of a classic app and I definitely think it has potential," I say.

"Would you be okay to work on that for him?"

"Of course."

"It wouldn't interfere with your own projects?"

I smile. It's crazy to me that this man cares that much about my own endeavors. It's also very uplifting. If he believes in my stuff, I have no excuse not to try my best with everything I do. We square away some things for Elias's potential app and talk about the workplace app and how it's going so far—two people have dropped it, but most of the remaining members have stayed consistent, with the exception of two others. Without seeing names or IP addresses, I know it has to be me and Owl. I haven't exactly been very present, especially after the thing with Bennett. A part of me feels shitty about it. When I leave the meeting, I type a message.

Me: Hey, I know I've been really quiet, but I think I want to take a break from this app. I met someone in real life and I think it has potential to go somewhere.

Owl: We're not exclusive. We can see other people. Wouldn't you rather keep talking as friends and see where this goes first? Or is your thing with that guy serious?

Me: It's not serious.

Owl: If you want to keep chatting, I'm here.

Me: Thanks. I guess it wouldn't hurt.

Owl: You never responded to my last question—beach or pool?

Me: Neither

Owl: WHAT. Pick one.

Me: Fine. Pool. Too many strange creatures lurk in the sea

Owl: LOL yeah, same answer

CHAPTER TWENTY-SEVEN

BENNETT

THE LAST TIME I knocked on this door was to visit my best friend, whom I'd helped move in here after he landed his first contract with the NFL. The fact that I'm now standing here waiting to take his little sister on a date isn't lost on me. I know Devon would kill me if he knew. If he had any inkling of the things I want to do to his sister, of the things I've done already, he'd kill me. I would if I was in his shoes. It's something I thought about the entire ride over here. I need to come clean with him before this becomes something more. I need to come clean about a lot of things with both Devon and Morgan, but it's easier said than done. I push those thoughts away when I hear her unlocking the door.

Tonight, she's wearing tight jeans, a black cable-knit sweater, and tall black boots. It takes me a moment to stop staring at her body, and when I do my eyes land on her pout, covered in red lipstick, and then her wide eyes. I swear every single time I see her, it's like I'm seeing her for the first time, and every time she somehow manages to take my breath away.

It's a scary feeling, one that I can't seem to help. The more time I spend with her, the clearer it becomes that rather than stopping myself from falling, what I'm doing is bracing myself for impact.

"Hey." She smiles, looking up at me through her long lashes.

"Hey." I step toward her, bringing my hand to her face as I turn it upward to kiss her.

She feels so delicate in my grasp, like a branch that I can easily snap between my hands, but she extends further, pushes deeper into me. It occurs to me that this is just the way Morgan is, despite the shit that has been thrown at her, she's managed to keep her heart soft. She's accepted this thing with me as temporary, something that won't lead to anything serious down the road, and yet she gives herself to me so openly that as her mouth molds against mine and her tongue dances alongside mine, I feel myself being consumed by her. With that thought, I pull away, breaking the kiss slowly, not really wanting it to end but with the knowledge that it must. As it is, the only thing I've done every waking hour since we got back from our trip was count down the days, hours, minutes until I could have her again and now that I'm here I wish I could just sweep her off to her bedroom and have my way with her right now.

"I kind of want to stay in," she whispers against my lips.

"Yeah?" I kiss her once more. I can't help it. This time, I withdraw so I won't fall into the trap. "You dressed like that and you don't want me to take you on a date?"

"I dressed like this for you and you already saw me." She shrugs. Her stomach growls loudly enough that I hear it and her face goes bright red. "I guess I am a little hungry."

I chuckle. "Let's get something to eat and then we can come back here and you can let me do wicked things to you."

"Hm." She reaches up and kisses me. "How wicked?"

"Honestly, Morgan, if you don't stop doing this, you're going to starve."

"Fine." She laughs, pulling away and walking toward the kitchen to grab her purse. "Let's go down the street. There's a wine and cheese place that has good tapas." She pauses, looking up at me wide-eyed as she locks the door. "Did you make a reservation somewhere?"

"I did, but I'll take you wherever you want to go." I'd called in a favor and made a reservation at a new restaurant that had a line out the door, but I didn't really mind losing our spot.

"No, let's go where you had planned. I feel bad canceling just because of my overactive libido." Her stomach growls again. This time, we both laugh as she pats it. "And obviously I really am hungry."

"I'M surprised you don't have a car," she comments as we ride to the restaurant.

I'd hired a driver for the night, because the last two times I ordered a company to pick me up they canceled and I was late. I didn't want to take chances tonight.

"I do have a car." I glance over at her. "It's parked at my parents' house."

She laughs. "Do you ever drive it?"

"Sometimes. Usually not in the city. I live within walking distance to everything I do, and when I can't walk there, I'd rather take the train or be dropped off. It's more convenient."

"Hm." She sighs. "I kind of miss having a car. I got rid of mine before college because I knew I wouldn't use it here. I mean, parking itself costs more than a mortgage."

"I'd venture to say you're doing pretty well for yourself." I wink at her.

"Not enough to pay for parking every day." She smiles. "Besides, there's the ordeal of dealing with this." She points at the street around us. "If I'm sitting back here, I'm okay with it, but actually driving in it might give me a heart attack."

"Do you see yourself living here forever?" I reach for her hand and thread my fingers through hers. I hadn't noticed how much I enjoyed holding a woman's hands until I started holding hers. Something about the way her small fingers fit inside of mine feels comforting.

"I guess so. I mean, I'm not sure I want to live here forever. I think I'd want a house with a yard to raise my kids in," she says. "Nothing big, but definitely a place for them to play outside."

Her words hit me right in the chest. I hadn't expected her to talk about kids, but I guess I can see it. I can picture her living in that house and watching a couple of kids as they go crazy in their yard. Maybe this is the part where I tell her I can't have kids? Maybe this is my out, where it all ends, where she sees that even if I wanted to make this official and stick around forever, I could never give her the dream she's built in her head.

"Anyway, who knows what the future will bring? I always thought I'd have kids by now and I don't even have a boyfriend." She lets out a soft chuckle.

"Twenty-four-year-olds don't often talk about having kids these days."

"Twenty-five. I had a birthday after we met, you know," she says. "And I guess if that's the case, twenty-five-year-olds don't often talk about being engaged at twenty."

"Ah, the drunken engagement." I bring her hand up and kiss it. "Do you regret it?"

"I mean, the guy turned out to be a real asshole." She laughs as she says it, but I find no humor in it. A real asshole who slept with her mother was what he turned out to be. Based on that alone, I want to kick his ass. The car slows and stops in front of the restaurant. She gasps as she looks outside. "This is where we're going? There are like a billion people in line. Also, we could've totally walked here."

"It's a good thing I made a reservation." I wink. "And if you want, we can walk back and burn off all the things we're about to eat, but you'll be burning a lot more calories tonight."

She laughs as we step onto the sidewalk. I walk over to the driver and let him know I'll text him twenty minutes before we're ready, but that we may just walk back. Once we're inside, the hostess escorts us to a table in the back of the restaurant. Not wasting any time, we order wine and bread the minute we're in our seats and peruse the menu quickly.

"Let's just share things," Morgan suggests. She glances up at me. "Is that okay? Do you share food? I just realized I kept taking food from your plate in Vegas and I didn't even ask."

I chuckle because it's true. "I wouldn't have had sex with you if I wasn't okay sharing food after that display."

"Sorry." She covers her blush with her menu. I reach forward and lower it. She's still blushing when she meets my gaze.

"I would love to share food with you."

Her face lights up in a way that has me sucking in for air. I sit back in my seat and thank God when the waiter comes back with the bread and wine. Morgan doesn't even let the basket hit the table before she pulls out a sourdough roll and starts tearing it.

"When was the last time you ate?"

"Honestly? I've been trying to figure that out all day. I think breakfast." She frowns, popping a piece of bread into her mouth. "I think I skipped lunch."

"Not very responsible," I say.

"I know." She takes a breath. "I feel better already."

During dinner, the conversations seem endless. We talk about everything from my upbringing to hers and how unlikely, yet unsurprising it is that Devon made it to the NFL. She tells me where they were when they found out he was being drafted. I tell her how I was on my honeymoon at the time. I feel like I can talk to her about anything and I'm pretty sure she feels the same way because she hasn't stopped and doesn't shy away from things that would make another person embarrassed.

"Long story short, my mother made me do some very shady things growing up," she says. "But honestly, now that I'm an adult, I guess I kind of understand her a little better. I would never make the choices she made, but I can see where things went wrong and how she became this ghost of herself so quickly." She smiles, a sad look in her eyes. "I wish you could've met her when she was in her prime, before the drugs and everything else. She was such a badass."

"I think you're pretty badass yourself, so it's not difficult to believe you're a product of another badass woman."

Her smile stays intact, but her expression, if possible, turns sadder. I find myself wishing I could take all of that sadness away. We change the subject and finish eating and drinking our wine. Once the check is paid, we get up and make our way to the front of the restaurant hand in hand. A rush of wind smacks us as I pull the door open.

"It got even colder," she comments, wrapping her arms around herself.

Instinctively, I drape an arm around her and pull her toward me. The ease of it all gives me pause. When did this become instinctual? When did having her in my arms begin to feel second nature? As we walk past the line of people waiting outside the restaurant, a figure steps in front of us. It takes me a second to realize it's Paola. I feel my footsteps get heavier as I walk in her direction. She's smiling, but it doesn't reach her eyes. The look in them is murderous. I grip Morgan a little tighter.

"Bennett Cruz," Paola says, narrowed eyes taking me in before moving to Morgan. "And who would this be? You're more presentable than the last whore. I'll give you that."

I open my mouth to defend Morgan, to tell Paola to shut the fuck up, mind her business, and go continue to spend all of her divorce settlement money. Instead, Morgan's laugh breaks through the night before I get a chance to say a word.

"You must be the crazy ex-wife," Morgan says, tsking. "I'm sure it's hard for you to see him move on, but remember that the reason I'm in his arms tonight and you're standing in line, pissed off at the world, is because you landed the perfect man and you stupidly threw him away."

Paola blinks. She can't seem to think of anything to say to that. I can't either. Amusement bubbles up inside me and escapes in the form of a loud, barked-out laugh. The sound makes Paola pissed, judging from the way her expression morphs from horrified to pissed off as she takes turns glaring at me, then Morgan.

"Enjoy him," Paola says. "You'll get sick of him the minute you realize his job is the love of his life."

"I'll take my chances," Morgan says, tugging my hand so that we begin to brush past Paola. She looks over her shoulder one last time. "If they do let you into the restaurant, order the scallops. They're to die for." That makes me laugh hard again. I squeeze Morgan's hand. She glances up, biting her lip. "Sorry. I kind of get carried away when I feel attacked."

"No, that was . . . that was great," I say, still laughing. "Paola's allergic to shellfish though. She wouldn't die if she eats them, but I know to her that sounded like you threatened the fuck out of her."

"Oh, my God." Morgan's eyes widen. "I would go back and apologize, but I don't appreciate being called a whore."

I lean down and kiss her as we walk. "You're scrappy."

"You learn a thing or two from escorts." She smiles.

"Do you think your relationship with your mother is salvageable, after what she did?"

"I don't know." She sighs heavily. "My first instinct is always no, and when I saw her I thought definitely not because I'm still pissed off, but honestly? I don't know. She's my mom. I guess there will always be a part of me who wishes things could be different. I'm not holding my breath though. It's not like I'll ever count on her for babysitting or anything." She lets out a quiet laugh that breaks my heart.

"I can't have kids."

She blinks up at me. "What do you mean?"

"A couple of months after we got married, Paola decided she wanted to start having kids right away. I was hesitant, but it was what she wanted and she was my wife. I was never home. I think in her mind, having a kid gave her a sense of belonging. Anyway, she was never able to get pregnant with me. The minute she started cheating, she ended up pregnant. Put two and two together." I shrug.

"Have you been to a doctor?"

"No."

"So you're just assuming you can't have kids. You haven't actually had your sperm counted." She shoots me a small smile that almost makes her look shy. "Maybe one day you'll meet a woman who knocks you off your feet and you'll want to start a family. I personally want to adopt."

We're almost at her building, but I feel the need to stop for a second and put a placeholder on this moment, because it feels important. She turns toward me and tilts her head to meet my eyes as I face her.

"This thing between us, it doesn't feel casual."

"Is this the part where you break things off?"

"This is the part where I tell you how much I enjoy having you in my life and want you to stick around."

"Okay." She smiles softly. "I just need to be sure that this won't affect my job and what I'm doing at SEVEN."

"It won't."

"Then, I'm not going anywhere." She lets go of my hand and reaches around my neck, pulling me closer. When I press my lips against hers and feel her sigh against me, I'm sure this is the kind of happiness people spend their lives chasing.

CHAPTER TWENTY-EIGHT

MORGAN

I SIT UP IN BED, eyes wide when I look at the time and glance beside me to see Bennett sleeping like a baby—if babies were grown men who happen to be hot as hell and have an unattainable air about them. I begin to shake him.

"You need to wake up."

He grunts. "Why? It's Saturday."

"Exactly. My brother's coming into town today, remember?"

"Does that motherfucker ever play football?"

I laugh. "It's a bye week."

"Fuck." He sighs heavily as he blinks his eyes open, and when he catches sight of me, he smiles. "You're so beautiful."

"Bennett. This is not the time to have sex, unless you want my brother to kill you today."

He groans, sitting up in bed and swinging his legs over to stand up. "I can kick his ass easily."

"Yeah, right." I snort.

He looks over at me as he stands to his full height. "You don't think so?"

"I mean, maybe?" I squint, as if I'm trying really hard to look at his incredible physique.

He grins, shaking his head as he heads to the bathroom. I sit back in bed, sighing. When he comes back out, he's already half-dressed.

"I don't know why it's such a big deal for your brother to find out. I'm sure he'll understand."

I raise an eyebrow. "You're not scared he'll flip out and start a fight?"

"I can handle it." He shrugs a shoulder and starts buttoning up his shirt. I watch, enthralled, as each inch of his sculpted torso is hidden button by button.

"I don't want him to give me a whole speech about how stupid it is for me to get involved with the owner of my dream company." I stand up and head to the bathroom. "He wouldn't be wrong, either. It's probably amongst the stupidest decisions I've ever made."

He's so quiet, that I have to peek out of the bathroom, toothbrush hanging out of my mouth, to make sure he's still there.

"Hold on, give me a moment. I'm trying to process the fact that you're calling me a stupid decision."

I laugh, spitting the toothpaste into the sink and rinsing. "I didn't mean it like that."

"How do you mean it, then?"

I walk back out of the bathroom and search his expression for some kind of tell that he's just pulling my leg, but his brows are drawn in as if he's trying to figure something out. I close the distance between us and grab the front of his now fully buttoned shirt.

"Hey, what's wrong?" I tug his shirt.

"Nothing." He shakes his head and flashes a brilliant smile. "I just have some things on my mind."

His answer doesn't really satisfy me, but I let it go because he really needs to get out of here before my brother gets here.

CHAPTER TWENTY-NINE

"NORA WANTS me to start looking for a tux," Devon says from the couch.

"I don't know how you're going to achieve your goal if you just sit here, fixated on ESPN." I look at the time on the microwave. "You've seriously been glued to that thing for two straight hours. Do all of your friends do this?"

"I'm not fixating on it," he mutters.

"Yeah, okay." I pick up the plastic plates with our PB&J sandwiches and walk over, handing his over as I fold a leg underneath myself and take the seat beside him.

"We need to talk about Mom."

My chewing slows. "Why?"

"Because she's coming to the wedding and Nora keeps talking about having kids, which means Mom would be around more often."

That makes me laugh. "If you're expecting Mom to be a model grandmother, I think you're in for a rude awakening."

"What's your deal?" He lowers his now empty plate. I still

have a sandwich and a half to finish. I focus on that, avoiding his gaze. "She had a really bad moment in her life, but she's cleaned up her act. She's been clean for almost two years now."

"She said one."

"Well, I pay a staff of people to check on her and it's definitely closer to two years since I started doing that."

"That's good. I'm happy for her."

"You told her you didn't want her in your life."

"That's true."

"Morgan."

"What?" I sigh, looking at him.

"Why?"

"I'm surprised you didn't ask her."

"I did. She wouldn't tell me so I'm asking you." He raises his eyebrows. The SportsCenter theme song interrupts our conversation. He looks away from me and back to the television, and my attention follows. News about a new quarterback for his team flashes on the screen. Devon stands up quickly. "What the fuck?"

"I'm assuming you didn't know about this." I continue eating my sandwich.

I've been going to games my entire life, so I understand and respect what happens on the field, but the locker rooms from Little League to the professional teams are always a shit-show. I text Nora, because I'm sure she's expecting him to get things done today but I know he'll be more than a little distracted. He's going to be on the phone all day now, and even once he's done talking about it until his voice is hoarse, he's going to continue to obsess over it.

Nora: Great.

Me: I can help. I mean, idk what you want the tuxes to look like but I can help

Nora: That would be amazing. I'll email you the links. Bennett is supposed to meet him at a place at three *worried face emoji*

Me: I'll try to get him there. If not, I'll go.

Nora: THANK YOU. LOVE YOU. Remember, dress shopping next weekend!

Me: CAN'T. WAIT.

I clean up, go to my room and change quickly, wondering what I should do now. Should I text Bennett about the appointment? Should I wait and see where Devon's moping and worrying leads? As I tie my Converses, I decide to do both.

Me: Some guy got traded to my brother's team and he's freaking out. Nora said he's supposed to meet you somewhere at 3. I'm going to try to get him there, but if not, I'll go

Bennett: I know. I texted him as soon as I heard. Keep me posted.

I stare at my phone. Keep me posted? That's it? I don't know what I was expecting, but that certainly wasn't it. Devon is still on the phone, pacing the living room, when I shut the door behind me. He runs a hand through his blond hair. It's long and messy and if I was Nora I would've had him cut it a month ago. Last time I said this to him, he said Nora liked it because he looks like Thor now. I wait until he's done with the phone call before stepping closer to him.

"Is everything okay?"

"Our season is basically over because of this shit. No big deal though." He shrugs as he looks up. "We've been keeping an eye on Carson's shoulder for a few months since he's been recovering, so we thought he was golden. We definitely didn't expect something like this in the middle of the goddamn season."

"Will they trade him away?"

"No, but he's seriously injured and instead of using our backup, they decided to bring in a free agent. It's fucking bogus."

"Oh." I look at the television, where the news about this is on loop. I swear these people discuss these things more than the owners of the damn teams. And then you have people like my brother, who listen to every single word as if they could be on to something. "How do they think they know what they're talking about? Like, how do they expect us to believe they know more than what the team is saying to you guys?"

"Because Cole Murphy actually knows what he's talking about." Devon scoffs. "And the coaches didn't tell any of us anything about this."

"What?"

"Why do you think I'm mad?"

"I don't know." I throw my hands up. "You freak out over everything."

"No, I don't." He shakes his head again. "Fuck. Where's the sage I brought?"

I tilt my face toward the ceiling. Seriously with the sage? I don't say anything about it because he's clearly stressed out and I'd rather him light some sage and walk around the apartment thinking it's going to take his problems away than hear him bitch about it for the next half hour.

"You know you have to meet Bennett at the suit place at three o'clock, right?"

"Yeah." He lights his sage and replies to a text message with his other hand as he walks around.

"It's two-fifteen."

"So we have forty-five minutes to get there."

"Uh, do you forget where you are? We'll never make it in time. I told Nora I'd make sure you get there."

"So let's go." He tosses the sage in the sink.

"You're not wearing shoes."

"I'll go get shoes, then." He walks toward his room, eyes on his phone, and crashes into the side of the couch. "Fuck."

"Okay. That's it." I stomp over to him and snatch the phone from his hand. "Get your shoes on. Change your fucking shirt and do something about your hair, for God's sake. You look like you just rolled out of bed."

"Some women find that alluring."

"Well, I find that you look like a hot mess." I shove his phone into my purse. "Get your shit together."

"I need my phone. Jerome is about to call any minute."

"Yeah, well, I'm sure Jerome can fucking wait. We're dealing with a crisis."

"This is a crisis," Devon shouts from his room. "My friend and quarterback is in the middle of getting replaced."

"It's business, Devon," I shout back from the kitchen as I try to get rid of the stuff in the sink.

"Is this acceptable?" He reappears with a different shirt, shoes, and his hair hidden beneath a baseball cap. I lift an eyebrow.

"Are you trying to get your ass kicked?"

"Ah, come on, a little rivalry never hurt anyone."

I laugh. "Famous last words from someone going to the Bronx wearing a Red Sox hat."

As we walk downstairs, I text Bennett a heads-up.

Me: My brother's wearing a Red Sox hat.

Bennett: WTF? Does he have a death wish? He doesn't even like baseball

Me: Exactly.

I glance up at Devon. "Bennett wants to know if you have a death wish."

"Hilarious." He rolls his eyes. "Since when are you texting buddies?"

"I don't know. It kind of just happened." I put my phone away quickly.

Maybe I should come clean about this whole thing with Bennett. I chance a peek at my brother, who's still brooding since he saw the news about his team and decide against it. There's no way I'm telling him this right now. He's older than me and for a long time his friends seemed like an extension of him. That is, until I saw Bennett in their shared college apartment that time. That was the first time it hit me that the guys my brother hung out around were living, breathing, super-hot guys and I kind of wished the age gap wasn't that wide. These days I don't feel the distance between us. It's not like he's gotten younger, but we have so much in common and I feel so close to Nora, that being around them is seamless. That is, until the moment I mention I'm sort-of dating his best friend. I know that would be the moment when all bets are off. Even though he's never warned me away from his friends, he's definitely made it clear to them to stay away from me. It's all been in jest, with a laugh and a pat on the back, but I know him well enough to know he's serious.

"Bennett's a good guy," Devon says, and I swear I feel my heart drop into the pit of my stomach. I hold my breath for the rest of the statement. "But he's been through a lot of crap and I'm not sure he's ready to give any woman what they need. Not what you need." He shoots me a pointed look that I avoid by clicking the *L* for lobby in the elevator steadily, as if the elevator is going to move any faster because of that. "You've been through too much too."

"I don't know where you're going with this conversation, but I'm feeling really awkward and uncomfortable right now."

Devon chuckles. It's not an amused sound. "Yeah, well, I'm not feeling very comfortable either, but something tells me I need to warn you to stay away from my best friend."

The elevator doors open. Thank God. I rush out of there like I'm on fire. We need to stop talking. He needs to stop talking. I definitely underestimated my brother's intuition, thinking he would never in a billion years figure this out, but if he's talking about this and he hasn't even hung out with us, I don't even know what the hell I'm going to do when I see Bennett at the store. Steadily avoid him, I guess. Thankfully, Dev starts talking about his quarterback again and that takes up the entire ride to Queens and he's still going as we get out of the car and walk up to the store.

"This is where you're getting your suit for your wedding?" I look up and down the street dubiously. "I mean, if you need to borrow money, Dev—"

"Shut up. According to Bennett, this guy is the best in the east." He laughs, holding the door open for me.

"Hm." I'm taken aback, first by the smell of leather, and then by the appearance of the place. It looks like Barneys threw up its entire men's designer suit collection smack in the middle of the projects. "This is definitely unexpected."

"Told you," my brother says. Two men come up to us dressed in nice suits—one navy, the other in black. They're clearly father and son, even though the son has long dreads and the father is clean-cut. They both have kind eyes and warm smiles as they greet us.

"It's a pleasure having you here, Mr. Tucker," the older man says, shaking my brother's hand before turning toward me. "I assume you're the future Mrs. Tucker?"

"Oh, no." I laugh. "She's back home. I'm his sister."

"Ah." The man's eyes light up. "My name is Michael

Hannah. I go by Mike though."

"Nice to meet you, Mike."

"I'm also Mike," the younger one says, greeting us. "Some people call him Mike Senior to differentiate. Most of my friends call me Jamaican Mike."

"Jamaican Mike," I say, smiling. "I like that."

He shrugs a shoulder. "It's easy to remember."

"Nora's Jamaican," I say, nodding over to Devon. "His fiancée."

"Oh, yeah?" He turns his attention over to Devon again.

They start talking about Nora's grandmother's cooking skills, but the door opens behind us again and when I turn and see Bennett walking toward us, their words mute in my ears. He's wearing a sharp blue suit and white button-down shirt. I lick my lips as he closes the distance between us, his gaze still on mine. I remind myself that I'm supposed to not make this obvious. I'm supposed to look away and pretend we're just friends, just coworkers, just brought together by a mutual loved one—who happens to be my overly protective older brother and someone neither of us should want to upset especially today—but it's easier said than done. He smiles at me; it's a warm, yet sexy smile, a secret smile that speaks volumes, as he walks up to me, picks up my hand and places a kiss onto it. I swear I feel like I may just melt right there. He releases me, breaking our connection, and walks over to one of the Mikes—Senior, I realize as I turn around fully.

"My boy," Mike Senior says. "Haven't seen you in a while."

"You should've never left," Bennett says, saying hello to the other Mike with the same hug and handshake while still looking at his father. "Ever since you let Mikey take over, this shop hasn't been the same."

The son scoffs and says something in Jamaican that I know

is a curse, but I don't understand. Evidently, Bennett does, with the way he throws his head back in laughter and punches him in the shoulder. He says hi to my brother next, the same hug and handshake, turning to face both Mikes.

"This is my best friend. He wanted to go to the department store but I told him I take my duty as best man seriously and wouldn't have lived with myself if he didn't come here first."

"You did good," the older Mike says with a laugh.

They walk over to a rack that's been separated from the rest of the clothes and start to show Devon different tuxedos and suits. I focus on messaging Nora and letting her know we're at the store and fill her in on the details. She tells me our bridesmaid dresses are powder-pink, so as long as he keeps that in mind, he's free to pick whatever he wants. Bennett dresses impeccably, so I walk over to where there are two chairs and take a seat in one of them. They can figure it out amongst themselves and if they need me, they'll let me know. I pull up the dating app and scroll through to see if I have any unread messages from Owl, and there's one from this morning.

Owl: You've been quiet

Me: My brother's going through a work crisis. I'm helping him pick out his tux for his wedding now

It takes a few minutes for him to respond.

Owl: Sounds fun

Me: Eh. I'd rather be at work

Owl: Pretty sure you're the first person to ever say that

Me: It's because I love what I do and I do what I love

Owl: Lucky girl

Me: You don't love what you do?

Owl: Most days. Sometimes I wish I could do something else

Me: Why can't you?

Owl: It's complicated

"Morgan." My brother's voice booms from what I assume is the fitting room area. I push a button on my phone and put it in my purse as I stand up and head over there. When I do, I find the younger Mike and Bennett standing around Devon as the older Mike pins the sleeve of the jacket. I look at my brother in the mirror and smile.

"You actually look presentable."

"Gee, thanks." He chuckles. "Do you like this one?"

"A lot." I give him a once-over. It's a classic tuxedo with a bright pink handkerchief peeking out of the pocket. "That's not the right pink, but that's an easy fix."

"Nora said pink."

"Yeah, powder-pink, not fuchsia."

"Here. Pick one out," Young Mike says, bringing a box of handkerchiefs over. I pluck out the powder-pink one.

"Are all of the guys wearing tuxedos?"

Devon looks at Bennett. "What do you think?"

"It depends. If you want you can wear a tux and the rest of us can wear suits." Bennett shrugs. "What does Nora want?"

"She's too focused on making sure everything else is perfect. I told her I'd handle this."

"And she trusted you to do that?" Bennett frowns.

"No. She trusted you to," Devon says.

I laugh. "The wedding is outdoors. Maybe suits for the rest of the guys would be a good contrast? They can wear pink ties or something."

"I like that." Bennett smiles at me. "What do you think, Dev?"

"I think you two should make yourselves useful while I finish up here and show me whatever you pick when you're finished."

"Benny, you know where the regular suits are," Young Mike says. "I would go with you but my hands are tied." He lifts his hands to show us all the pins he's holding for his dad.

"I think I know my way around this place better than you do."

"Offer the girl water while you're at it," Mike Senior says.

"And look at the shoes," Devon says.

"I guess it's safe to say Bennett can get a part-time job here if things don't work out at SEVEN," I say.

They all laugh, but it's Bennett's deep chuckle beside me that makes my heart stutter. I ignore it as I turn around and follow him out of the dressing room, through the main area, to the other side of the store.

"This place is massive. You'd never know from looking at it from the outside."

"They have big clients," Bennett says.

"I can imagine." I start to go through the suits. "How'd you find out about it?"

"A friend of mine, Lorenzo. He's Italian and always wears the sharpest suits. I used to think he was spending a fortune at high-end stores until I asked and he told me to come here."

"Where you don't spend a fortune," I say, slash ask, because the price on the sleeve of the suit I'm looking at states otherwise.

"The rack you're looking at is the crème de la crème." Bennett chuckles. "Mike's prices range, but ten out of ten you're going to find better quality here than you will anywhere else. I'd take one of his eighty-dollar suits over an eight-hundred-dollar Armani any day."

"Big praise coming from you." I let my gaze run down his body slowly. His suits really do fit him like they were made for him, and now I know why.

"If you keep looking at me like that, people are going to get ideas, Cupid."

"I can't help it," I whisper, meeting his eyes again. "And Devon is being weird like he knows something, by the way. I dodged his questions earlier about why we were texting and he told me to stay away from you."

"He told *you* to stay away from *me*?" He raises an eyebrow as he walks over to me. "I should be flattered that my best friend is trying to keep my heart safe."

"Your heart safe?" My eyes widen. He brings a hand up to my face as he continues to look at me like I'm the most precious thing he's ever seen.

"I'm fragile, you know."

I snort out a laugh. "You're so full of crap."

"Am I?" He comes even closer still. "I've been through a lot of heartache."

"So have I."

"I would never break your heart though."

"I would never break yours."

"I have my doubts about that, Cupid."

"Rule number one, never doubt me, Trouble."

His lips come down so softly that I barely feel them on mine, but I swear I feel them everywhere else and I think, not for the first time, that this thing between us runs a lot deeper than the stolen moments we've shared. He breaks the kiss just as slowly as it started and presses his forehead against mine, exhaling.

"I missed you this morning."

"I missed you," I admit. "I thought you were going to come over and help with Dev."

"I'm here now."

I smile, because he is, and that's the only thing that matters.

CHAPTER THIRTY

BENNETT

EVEN IF MORGAN hadn't told me that Devon suspected something was going on between us, I would've guessed from the way he's been watching our every move. On one hand, I'm dying to scream it out so we can just be open about this. On the other hand, I need to respect Morgan's wishes to not tell her brother. It sucks because we're sitting across from each other at a restaurant and the urge to reach out and touch her hand is driving me fucking crazy.

"How's the dating app going?" Devon asks.

I cover my face with the menu as Morgan answers, "It's going."

"So you still haven't met him in person?" he asks.

"Maybe, maybe not."

"You've met him?" I lower my menu. "Isn't that against the rules?"

"What do you know about the rules?" Devon lifts an eyebrow. "Did you join?"

"Maybe, maybe not."

Morgan's eyes narrow. "Did you?"

I shrug and go back to my menu.

"Would it matter if he did?" Devon asks.

"Obviously not," Morgan mutters. "He can do whatever he wants."

"You seem bothered."

What the hell is happening and why does it sound like he's amused by this entire thing and not pissed off at the possibility that something is going on between me and his sister? I set down my menu and look at him. He's the kind of person who likes to measure things by everyone's reaction to what comes out of his mouth.

"How are you liking the app, Ben?" Devon asks. He's such a shit, but I take the bait and run with it.

"Honestly? I think the interface needs a little updating. Other than that, it's pretty good."

"Have you been sexting with the person it paired you with?"

I laugh because I can't help it. Morgan scoots her chair back and stands.

"I need to use the restroom." She throws her napkin on the table. I stop laughing. She has this murderous glare in her eyes just before she turns around that makes me want to run after her.

"How long has this been going on?" Devon points between me and Morgan's empty chair.

I close my eyes momentarily. "I swear I'm not going to hurt her."

"I never said you were." He frowns. "But if you do, I'll have to kill you."

"I wouldn't."

"How long have you been . . . God, what are you even doing? Fucking my sister?"

I flinch. "Dating."

"Dating my sister." He says it as if he's testing out the idea. "How long?"

"A couple of weeks."

"She just started working at SEVEN."

"It's a long story, but we kind of ran into each other while I was still with Paola," I explain. "Well, once everything went to shit."

"I'm assuming she knows you were married."

"Yes. She knows everything."

"And you know she was supposed to get married the month she broke off her engagement?"

"I want to find her ex and beat his ass up for what he did to her."

Devon's eyes narrow. "What exactly did he do?"

"He hurt her." I stick to that. Morgan said her brother didn't know what went down between them. I can only imagine that if he did, he wouldn't allow their mother to attend the wedding.

"Hm." He takes a sip of his sweet tea, still watching me. "I don't know the specifics, but I always hated that guy."

"What does he do now?"

"Hell if I know." He shrugs. "He was always a problematic little shit. They got engaged while we were in college. The moment I found out, I flew home and tried to convince her to reconsider, but they stayed together."

"I bet she wished she'd listened to you."

"Who knows. She never said. Besides, teams had already started showing interest in me by then, so I promised her I'd pay for her college if she left him."

"Damn. That's harsh."

"She didn't listen to me, obviously, but when they broke up she cried for months. Not days, not weeks . . . months."

His words feel like an unsettling dose of reality. He must

have really been the love of her life. The reason she decided to play Cupid but not actively search for love herself. For some reason, I don't like any of those thoughts or the way they cloud around all of the good moments we've shared together. I catch a glimpse of Morgan making her way back toward us. She really is the most beautiful thing I've ever laid eyes on.

"You really like her, don't you?" Devon asks.

"Like I never imagined liking another person." I look at him. "I swear I would never do anything to hurt her."

"I know." He smiles, small and sad. "It's not her I'm worried about."

I stare at him a moment longer. I know him well enough to know he's dead serious. When Morgan returns to the table, her mood is brighter, but I can tell something is off. Devon must sense it too because he stops joking around about dating and keeps the conversation about football, his future in the sport and the team, and the wedding.

"Is Mom going to walk you to the altar?" Morgan asks.

"Who else would do it?"

I glance away. I'd rather talk about the dating app than have to listen to him harp on about how great their mother is after knowing what I know.

"I don't know, someone who's not constantly in rehab?" Morgan asks. "Someone who won't have to cover her arms with makeup?"

"Morgan." Devon's voice is a warning.

"I don't care. We shouldn't have to hide this from the world just because she's a screwup. We shouldn't have to be the ones constantly embarrassed. She's the one who should carry that burden, yet somehow, here we are, walking on eggshells again."

"It's obvious you're in a bad mood, and I'm sorry if I put you there, but this isn't the time to talk about Mom."

"You know when a good time to talk about Mom is?" she asks. "Never." She stands up again. "I'm sorry. This was a mistake."

My heart pounds as she walks toward the front of the restaurant. I look at Devon, back at the door, back at Devon.

"I—" I grab my napkin and toss it on the table.

"Just go. I'll see you both at her place later." He waves me away. "Fair warning, when she gets like this, the best thing to do is give her space, but I know your overprotective ass won't allow that."

I shake my head as I make my way to the front of the restaurant. He's right. I would never allow her to just walk away like this without going after her to make sure she's okay.

CHAPTER THIRTY-ONE

MORGAN

I'M HALFWAY to the subway station when I hear Bennett shout my name behind me. It's so unexpected that I actually stop and turn to face him.

"What?"

"You're taking the train?"

"Obviously." I turn and continue my walk. He'll go back to my brother. I mean, he'll have to, right? It would be weird for him to follow me and take the train with me. If he does, we wouldn't have any excuses about this to give Devon. When I realize he's still at my heels, I sigh heavily and stop again in the middle of the stairwell. "Please note that the only reason I'm letting you chase after me like this right now is because I hate causing scenes."

"Noted."

"I hate being the center of attention."

"Noted."

"I hate it when people talk about my personal life in front of me like it's just a series of events to gossip about and not my actual life."

He blinks. "You lost me."

"The app. The dating thing." I point in the direction we came from. "That whole scene back there was awful."

"I'm sorry." He looks like he might seriously be sorry. I don't let my guard down.

"Did you or did you not sign up for the app?"

"I did."

Shock ripples through me. I count ten heartbeats before I pivot and continue my way down the stairs. Fuck him. He made fun of me about the app, made fun of me about joining, made fun of me about potentially matching with Wesley, and didn't once think of mentioning he was on it? And if he's on it, who has he been talking to? And is he sexting with her? Anger builds until I feel sullied with it. My head remains high as I wait for the train and God, I hope it's the right one because I haven't even stopped to check my route app. At this point, I don't care where it takes me as long as it's away from here.

"Morgan. I should've told you." His voice breaks through my thoughts. I close my eyes at the nearness of it, the rawness. "I'm not involved with whoever I've been paired with. We decided to remain friends."

"You decided to remain friends?" My gaze flashes to his because how many people could've possibly agreed to remain friends?

"Yeah. I had a feeling you might be Robin." He shoots me a sheepish smile, but if anything, it further fuels my anger.

"You knew it was me all along."

"Not all along."

"You're such . . . " I growl. "You are the worst kind of asshole."

"First you call me a classic douchebag, and now you're calling me an asshole," he says with a chuckle. "No, not just an asshole, but the worst kind."

I lift a hand. "I seriously do not have time for this right now."

"For what?"

"You're causing a scene and I don't have time to be embarrassed about it."

"I'm causing a scene?" He grabs my elbow and stops me from reaching the yellow line on the tarmac. I turn to face him.

"What else would you call this?"

"Trying to have a conversation. I'm trying to talk to you."

"Well, I don't speak to liars, so take your conversation elsewhere. Go back to the restaurant and talk to your friend. He's who you're supposed to be consoling."

"I'm talking to you and I'm not a liar." He lets go of my elbow but keeps his gaze on mine. "I'm not a liar."

"You lied about the app."

"I didn't lie. I just didn't tell you."

I roll my eyes. "Same difference."

"If I was on the app and it had become something more, I would've told you about it," he says. "But you started dropping hints from the beginning and I kind of pieced together that it was you I was talking to, so I suggested we remain friends."

"That is not what you suggested." I raise my eyebrows. "And you called it stupid. A stupid app. God, I'm such an idiot. I should've known it was you."

He reaches for my hand. "I'm sorry I didn't come clean sooner."

"It just makes me think, if you lied about this, or kept it from me, what else are you lying about or keeping from me?"

"Nothing." He squeezes my hand. "Your brother knows about us."

My mouth drops. "Are you fucking kidding me right now?"

Bennett sighs, throwing his head back and looking up at the ceiling as if he's saying a prayer. Maybe he is. Maybe he should pray for his damn life right now. The train gets here. He straightens. I let go of his hand and get inside the car as soon as the first batch of people step out. Bennett follows, holding on to the pole beside me.

"I wish you wouldn't follow me."

"I need to make sure we're okay."

"We're not." I look up at him. "I need time to digest all of this."

"I want us to be okay."

"It's not up to you."

"Which is why it's important for me to stay with you right now while you process all of this."

"I already texted my best friends. I'm meeting them at a brewery, so unless you're okay with them drilling you with questions, I suggest you step off now."

"Too late," he says as the train doors close. I exhale. Bennet grins. "I could go for a beer right now anyway."

I turn around and face the other side of the car. If he's going to follow me around the city, fine by me, but it doesn't mean I have to look at him.

———

I TAKE out my phone and call Presley to make sure she's here as we reach the front of the brewery.

"I'm unlocking the door right now." She opens the front door, eyes wide when she spots Bennett beside me.

"I hope you don't mind that some asshole tagged along," I say, hanging up the phone and dropping it into my purse.

"It's cool," she says. "Jamie can't make it. She got caught up with Travis's mom." She turns to Bennett. "You must be Bennett. I'm Presley, the girl who will kick your ass if you mess with my little sister."

He shoots me a look.

"Sorority sisters," I explain. "And best friends."

"Oh." He smiles, leaning in to give Presley a kiss on the cheek. "Nice to meet you. Save your ass-kicking skills for a real asshole." He looks at her a little closely. "You're Nathaniel's fiancée."

"I am." She smiles, holding the door open wider. "Please, come in."

We do. I shrug off my jacket and set it on one of the picnic tables along with my cross-body bag. I inhale the smell of cedarwood and smile.

"It looks just about ready to open," I say.

"It is. Ezra is actually letting us try some of the new brews today, so I'm kind of glad you brought an outsider." She places three coasters on the table and starts walking toward the back. "Be right back."

I sit down. Bennett sits beside me. His leg brushes mine and I instantly stiffen. I busy myself with looking at everything in the brewery—the bar taps, the thirty long picnic tables, the art on the wall—barley, hops, amber liquid, all beer related. Presley comes back with two beers in her hand and Ezra in tow holding another. I smile at him. I never met either of my grandfathers, but from the moment I met Ezra years back, I wished he'd been one of them. He's the hippest old man I've ever known.

"Beer for ma girl," he says, placing a beer in front of me and a kiss on my head. "Haven't seen you around in a few months. How's the job?"

"It's good." I smile and point my thumb toward Bennett. "This is one of the owners of SEVEN."

"Ah, you're the boss?"

"I'm a boss, but not hers," Bennett says, shaking Ezra's hand. "You're the beer maker?"

"Depends on whether or not you like this hop." He nods toward our glasses. "If you like it, I brewed it. If you don't, Presley did it."

Presley laughs loudly. Bennett and I follow suit.

"Thanks for the help, Ez." She winks at him as he walks off.

"If you need me, I'll be back here."

I lift my beer toward my lips and take a sip. "Hm. Good."

Presley does the same, nodding. "A little too hoppy, but good. It needs a few more days."

"I think it's pretty good." Bennett sets his down. "Do you actually help with the brewing process?"

"Sometimes," Pres says. "I've come up with some cool concepts for some of the beers, but some haven't worked out. Nathaniel and I are trying to fuse bourbon into one right now. I'm really hoping it works."

"That sounds dangerous," I say. "Beer and bourbon."

"Because you're a lightweight." Pres winks, smiling. "So I guess we're not going to talk about guy trouble today."

I cough into my beer. Damn her.

"Am I the source of the guy trouble?" Bennett asks, tapping my knee with his. I keep my eyes on Presley. I will not look at him.

"I don't know," Presley says, "Are you? I heard you joined her dating app and lied about it."

"News travels fast," he mutters.

"My fist travels faster." She raises an eyebrow. "So, did you lie or not?"

"I didn't lie. I just didn't flat-out tell her about it. I wasn't even joining because I thought I would match with anyone. I just wanted to see how it worked."

"Did you purposely match your accounts together?" Presley asks.

This time, I do look over at him. I didn't even think that was a possibility, but I don't know what his sneaky self can do. For all I know he's a bona fide hacker. He meets my gaze.

"I didn't purposely match our accounts. Your platform did that. You can blame me for a lot of things, call me a liar, whatever, but don't pin that on me."

"Okay." I look back at my friend because I believe him, but I don't want to look at him. Every time I do, I swear my chest feels like it caves a little deeper. I realize that I can't handle this. I thought I could. I thought I was ready to date, to find love, but I'm not ready. How can anyone ever be ready to let their heart live outside of their chest? It's a difficult idea to fathom. In the grand scheme of things, this is a small, tiny situation and somehow, it's made me feel like a complete idiot for trusting him as much as I have. The thought of giving him the power to let him crush me with a single action makes me want to take it all back and crawl back inside of my shell.

"Morg says you don't believe in love," Presley says.

I hear her words, she's sitting right across from me, but my thoughts are clouding my hearing and I don't catch the full statement or question.

I hear Bennett respond beside me, and she responds back. They're having a full conversation now about God knows what because I'm too lost in thought, trying to find a way to get back to not caring about him, or us, or whatever was happening, to pay attention. The more I think about it, the more I realize it's a losing battle because I'm in love with him. It's that simple. I can fight it, I can argue, I can kick and scream, but it won't change how I feel.

CHAPTER THIRTY-TWO

BENNETT

"YOUR FRIEND IS NICE."

We're just steps away from her apartment building and she hasn't said a word to me. I've let her brood long enough—let her pretend I wasn't sitting beside her at the brewery or standing beside her on the subway. I gave her as much space as I could allow, but I can't just end the day with this weird discomfort that feels big enough to swallow me whole.

"Thanks," she says. "She liked you. Maybe if you'd joined the last dating app I made and kicked off at her first brewery you would've hit it off and you'd be engaged to her right now and not Nathaniel."

I sigh. It must be a woman thing to take one small circumstance and blow it up in a major way. This is not the kind of situation I've been equipped to deal with. Whenever Paola would say shit like this, I would just ignore her and let her think what she wanted, but look where that led us—to her believing rumors and acting on them rather than staying and trying to work things out with me. Looking back on all of it, I know I didn't try hard enough to keep her. In fact, I didn't try at all. In my mind, our relationship had run its course and it was time to move on. I'd always treated my relationships that way, but after a pricey divorce, I realized it was a mistake on my part. With Morgan things feel different—easy, like water—and I sure as hell don't want to lose her. I take a chance, reach for her hand, and breathe a little easier when she doesn't fight me on it.

"Any app I would've joined would have led me to you."

"I wasn't on that one." She looks up at me. Her eyes are a little clearer, less troubled than they were a few hours ago.

"Do you believe in destiny? In the idea that every single action you take leads to a particular outcome?"

Her brows pull in slightly. "Yeah, I guess."

"I think every action I've ever taken led me to you."

She stops walking and looks up at me with a strange expression on her face, and for a moment I feel like this is it. She's going to tell me to go fuck myself and leave me standing here on this sidewalk without a chance in hell of getting her back. Instead, she reaches for my other hand and threads her fingers through mine.

"I really, really like you, Bennett."

I smile. "I really, really like you too."

"Like, I think I'm really falling for you." She drops her head when she says it, as if it's something she's ashamed to feel, or admit, or both. "I didn't want to, but I am, and I know you don't believe in any of that but I learned that lying, even by omission, is something I can't afford to do anymore." Her head snaps up and she meets my gaze again. "It's something I don't want you to do either."

"I won't. Not again." I step closer, dropping her hands to cup either side of her face. "And I do believe. I think I fell for you a while back."

The way her eyes light up makes me wish I'd said something sooner, because damn, it's a beautiful sight. We're both smiling as I lean in to kiss her.

DEVON is already inside when we get into the apartment. He looks up from where he's sitting on the couch and nods.

"Have you kissed and made up?"

I chuckle, glancing over at Morgan, whose face is completely red.

"You're not going to be mad or give us a whole speech about how stupid this is?" she asks.

"No." He shrugs. "You're both adults. I trust and love both of you. As long as you know I'm not getting caught in the middle of it, I'm fine with it. If it doesn't work out, I don't want to hear it."

Hearing him say that should relieve me, but what it does is raise questions. What if things don't work out? Morgan had reasons she didn't want to start this and they seemed so small back when she mentioned them, but now that we're here and it feels more real than ever, I have to wonder if she was right about it all. We'd see each other at work and we'd see each other at any functions having to do with Devon and Nora. I let those thoughts simmer for a bit. I wouldn't mind seeing her around at work.

Sure, it would suck if she ended up getting together with someone else there, like Wesley, but I'd deal with it. I'll have to make sure if things do go south, I won't make her feel uncomfortable at work or at Nora and Devon's events. I glance over at Morgan and smile. She smiles back. And just like that, we're together.

CHAPTER THIRTY-THREE

BENNETT

CONGRATULATIONS, Owl, it's been three weeks! Click below to reveal Robin's identity. I click it even though I already know, and see a picture of Morgan smiling back at me. Beneath it reads: *Morgan Tucker, app and website developer at SEVEN, creator of the workplace app.* Even though we already discussed this and she knows I'm Owl, I would kill to see her face when she gets the notification and sees my picture and description. Instead, what I get is a phone call from her.

"I still can't believe you didn't tell me you were Owl."

I sigh. "I thought you were over that?"

"I am, but seeing your face on the app thing kind of threw me back into that loop. Now I'm replaying every single conversation we had on there, trying to figure out if there any possible way I could've figured out it was you."

"I guess you need to get to know me better." I smile. "Maybe let me take you to lunch every day, spend every waking moment with me."

She snorts into the phone line. "You'd get sick of me quickly."

"Never," I say. "I could never get sick of you."

"That's what everyone says in the beginning of a relationship. Just you wait, Bennett Trouble Cruz. Just you wait."

I laugh. "I'm sure my mom would've given me that middle name if she'd heard how good it sounded."

"She would've given you that middle name if she'd been able to spend time with you before naming you."

"Hm." I walk to my kitchen and start brewing coffee. "You should come over and make my breakfast."

"You should come over and make *me* breakfast," she retorts.

I look at the time on the microwave. "Give me an hour."

"I'll be dead in an hour."

I chuckle. "Give me thirty minutes and I'll pick something up on the way."

"See you soon."

With that, we hang up, and I can't stop smiling the entire time I'm getting ready or am on my way over there.

CHAPTER THIRTY-FOUR

MORGAN

"REMIND me why we're going to this event."

I'm wearing the most expensive dress I've ever worn in my life, courtesy of Gucci, who loaned it to Bennett for me to wear. The entire thing is absolutely ridiculous, but as it turns out, whenever there's going to be a major event like this, designers actually reach out to Bennett so that he'll wear their tuxedoes and as a courtesy, they offer a dress for his date. Tonight, I'm the date.

"Because we were invited and these people only invite the crème de la crème." Bennett walks over as he buttons his cufflinks. He pauses behind me in the mirror and assesses me, his gaze heating with each inch of me he takes in. "You look fucking delectable."

"Delectable?" I laugh despite the blush that spreads over my features.

"Yes." He leans in and bites my exposed shoulder blade before sucking the spot. "Hm."

"I can't believe you just did that."

"Believe it, baby." He winks before walking back to his closet. I exhale, putting my hands on my hips.

"It's kind of showy, don't you think?"

"It is, and I like it." He peeks out from the closet.

"My ex-fiancé would've never let me out in this." I look at the slash over my breasts that shows just enough cleavage to make you wonder whether or not my nipple may be making an appearance. Yeah, Justin would have never let me wear this.

"Your ex is a fucking moron." Bennett scoffs. "Don't you love to categorize things like that? How many categories of morons are there and which was he?"

"The ultimate moron."

Bennett laughs as he walks back into his closet. I find myself laughing with him. I can't remember ever being with a man confident enough with himself that he was okay with me talking about my previous relationships. I didn't even think it was possible to have this kind of openness with someone.

"Did your ex live here with you?" I ask.

I know her name, but I'd rather not say it aloud. Unlike Bennett, I am kind of insecure about all of this and not as comfortable talking about his past conquests, which, judging by how good he is in bed and what I heard about him in college I know must be a lot. A part of me feels stupid for even caring, with my background and the things I had to do when I was younger, but for some reason it bothers me.

"No. I got this after the divorce," he says, stepping out and switching off the closet light.

He's wearing a black tuxedo with a dark red outlining that matches my dress perfectly. I've seen this man naked, in suits, in jeans, in sweatpants, but the sight of him in this tux makes my mouth go dry. His dark hair is slicked back and the five o'clock shadow he's eternally rocking looks like it's part of the outfit.

"I take it you like what you see," he says with a twinkle in his eyes.

"Classic douchebag." I smile. "You look great."

"You look better than great." He grins, walking up to me. "Let's go. The faster we get there, the sooner I can get you out of that dress."

THE ART GALLERY is riddled with people I've only seen on the cover of magazines. It's like a who's-who of the city's elites and I don't even know where to look in order to avoid them.

"You having fun?"

"No, I'm freaking out," I whisper.

Bennett smiles. "They're just people."

"Yeah, easy for you to say. You're used to attending these things."

"Fair point." He nods. "The first time I went to an event like this I was stunned, but I quickly realized that despite what the tabloids write, these people are totally normal. And the craziest thing," he says in a dramatic whisper, "is that they don't even bite."

"You're kidding." I place my hand on my chest. "That is crazy."

"I know." He chuckles as he leans in and kisses me softly. "You're so beautiful."

"Thank you." I run my hand over my dress. "This thing I'm wearing would make anyone look beautiful."

"Trust me, you don't need a dress to make you beautiful."

We're interrupted by a photographer who asks to take a couple of pictures of us.

"What if they publish these photos?" I ask once the photographer moves to the couple beside us.

"Not 'what if,'" Bennett says. "They'll probably be in tomorrow's paper."

"Oh."

"Does that bother you?"

"Not really. I mean, I guess? It's not like anyone knows we're dating." I bite my lip, glancing up at him. "That is what we're doing, right?"

"I think it's safe to say we're dating."

"Does your father know?"

"He knows I'm serious about someone. I haven't given a name."

"Bennett." My eyes widen. "He's going to read about it in the paper."

"Who cares?"

"I care. He's my boss and your father and we work together. Oh, my God. All of our coworkers will know."

"Is that a problem?" He raises an eyebrow and I swear I know what he's thinking. I roll my eyes.

"Not because of Wesley, if that's what you're getting at."

"That was exactly where I was going actually."

"I thought you weren't a jealous person?"

"Who said I wasn't a jealous person?" He frowns, setting down his empty champagne flute.

"I don't know. You're cool when we talk about my ex."

"Because he's your ex, as in past. Wesley is constantly throwing hints at you. I'm surprised he hasn't cut up a little heart and written you a love note."

"You exaggerate. He likes me, but it's not like that."

"It is so like that."

"I kind of like that you're jealous. Is that weird?"

He laughs, shrugging. "It is what it is."

"You don't feel threatened by him though. Do you?"

"No, of course not. I know you're with me." He puts an arm around my shoulder and tucks me into his side. "I just don't like the idea of another man thinking he has a shot with you."

"Ah." I nod my head, smiling. "That's why you're cool with him seeing the pictures. It's a pissing contest."

"More like a confirmation that you're mine."

"Am I?" I tilt my face to meet his eyes.

"I hope you are."

"And what would that make you?"

"Yours, obviously."

Obviously. I love the sound of that.

CHAPTER THIRTY-FIVE

I GLANCE OVER AT BENNETT. "Does your mother know we're dating?"

"She has this theory that my car only moves out of their driveway for two reasons: when I'm going to our vacation home in the Hamptons and when I'm dating someone."

"Interesting." I glance out the window. "How many times have you picked it up this year?"

"Three times."

I continue looking out the window, gnawing on my lip as the thought gnaws at me. I jump slightly at the feel of his hand reaching over and his fingers splaying on my leg. He squeezes my thigh. I count to three before looking over at him.

"I've been to our vacation house three times this year." He grabs my hand and threads our fingers together. "You look cute when you're jealous."

"I guess there's no use in trying to convince you that I'm not jealous." I shrug. "I usually am not a jealous person though."

"Jealousy isn't a bad emotion to have unless it's keeping the other person from living their life the way they want to live it. I like that you're jealous at the thought of me having dated other women." He brings my hand up and kisses the back of it. "As long as you know I won't even remotely show interest in another woman while we're together."

I smile, shifting to lift my legs and place them on his lap. He sets his hand on my ankle. "Careful, Trouble. I may start thinking you believe in love after all."

"Careful, Cupid. You may be the one I end up falling hard for after all the smack I talked."

"Would that be such a bad thing?"

"You tell me," he says, lips twitching.

"Obviously I don't think that would be a bad thing."

"That's obvious, huh?" He smiles as he pulls into his parents' driveway and parks at the side of the house, in front of the attached three-car garage.

I readjust and set my legs back in the passenger side as he grabs the keys and pushes the button that switches off the car. He gets out of the car, so I start doing the same, but before I'm fully out of my seat he's holding the door open for me and offering me his free hand to take. I've never been with a chivalrous guy before. I've never been with a man though, not one like Bennett. It's a thought that excites me as much as it scares me. Once we're standing by the front door, I'm grateful for the wine bottle I brought along because I don't even know what to do with my hands. It wasn't even that long ago that I was standing in this very spot with my brother beside me. This feels entirely different from that, but when his mother pulls the door open, she greets me with the same warm smile and tight hug, and all of my discomfort withers away.

"It is so great to have you back." She pulls away and hugs

Bennett beside me, taking the box of food in his hands. "I told you not to bring anything but your beautiful girlfriend."

I bite the inside of my cheek to try to control my blush, but it's impossible. Thankfully, she turns around and leads us toward the kitchen without another word. Bennett sees it though and chuckles as he takes hold of my hand again. We spend the entire afternoon lounging in the backyard, drinking wine, eating and talking about every single topic imaginable—from politics, to religion, to technology. I imagine myself growing up in a house like this, with two parents who love me unconditionally and speak openly about things. It's obvious that he was raised to speak his mind and bring a debate to the table. They don't even back the same political parties, yet they talk about it with absolutely no contempt. These are the exact kinds of people we need in the world—nonjudgmental, loving, compassionate. It makes the environment I grew up in seem that much more toxic.

"Penny for your thoughts," Bennett says as his dad cleans the grill and his mom makes some room on the table for dessert.

"Just thinking about how different this is from how I grew up."

"Your father wasn't around, right?" his dad asks, looking over his shoulder.

"No. He left when I was pretty young. I remember him, but not much."

"That must have been hard."

"Harder for Devon." I set my wine down. "He had nobody to look up to once he left. It's not like our mother had inspiring men around. She was pretty messed up."

"I'm sorry to hear that." Mr. Cruz frowns, setting down the brush and walking back over to sit across from us again. "Are you still close to your mom? Devon doesn't talk about her much."

"No. I decided to dissolve that particular relationship. She wasn't very interested in being a mother." I shrug. "It happens. I mean, it happens to some of us. Obviously, you guys have the family thing figured out." I smile.

"My father wasn't around much either," Mr. Cruz says. "He was a real bastard when he was though. Barbara's childhood wasn't ideal either. We knew early on that we wanted to have a child and that we would do everything in our power to raise him with respect and love."

"You've done a great job of that." I glance over at Bennett, who's watching me as he sips his wine. The expression on his face makes my heart skip a beat. He smiles as if he knows and I force myself to look back at Mr. Cruz and Barbara, who's walking over with a plate of brownies. "Thank you for inviting me over again."

"Hey, you're family," Barbara says. "You come over with or without Ben whenever you want."

"Thank you."

"I mean that," she says.

And because of the way she looks at me when she says those words, and because of how welcome I feel here, I completely believe she does.

On our way home, I'm still contemplating her words and how serious she is about them.

"Were your parents this nice to your ex-wife?"

Bennett looks over at me. "They're nice to everyone."

"But this nice?" I ask. "How was it after you divorced?"

"Well, I should probably preface this by saying my mother never liked her. She always warned me that there was something off about her. I didn't really pay attention or lose sleep over it until it was too late." He shrugs. "I filed for divorce and she followed suit. It was as if she couldn't get rid of me fast enough, but then something changed and she started to take it all back. She went to my parents' house, crying, begging them to help me see reason. My mother said she would speak to me, and she did. She tried playing devil's advocate for a little while, but then the lies grew and Paola's new boyfriend got involved, and it was just too much for my parents and they stopped welcoming her."

"Damn," I whisper. "How long were you in that process?"

He chuckles, reaching for my hand. "Honestly? The day you walked into my father's office was my official last day of dealing with her shit."

"Good timing, I suppose." I bite down on my lip and smile at him.

"Great timing." He brings our entwined hands and kisses the back of mine. "The perfect timing."

CHAPTER THIRTY-SIX

"HOW LONG WERE you with your ex-girlfriend before you got married?"

"That's a random question." I glance over at Morgan, who's sitting beside me on the couch.

Lately she's been asking more and more questions about Paola, and while I'm okay with answering, I'm a little wary about where this may be going. I keep expecting her to get mad and start picking a fight over any little thing I say. She hasn't though. She seems genuinely curious. We both have our laptops on our lap. I'm answering emails, and she's coding some new app she's trying to develop while fixing some others my dad gave her to look at. She pushes her laptop away slightly and meets my gaze.

"I was thinking about my friends and their relationships. Presley has a pretty solid relationship, but she and Nate have known each other forever, even though they got together fairly recently. I don't even think they were together a full year before he proposed. Then there's Jamie, who was on and off with

Travis longer than Presley has been with Nate, and they can't seem to get their shit together."

"Are they together now?"

"No. He has a girlfriend." She sets the laptop down on the coffee table and turns to me as if she's about to spill some major gossip. "The girl looks exactly like Jamie. It's the most insane thing. Like he definitely has a type. Obviously James is mad because the girl is a younger version of her."

"Would you be mad if I left you for a younger version of you?"

She laughs. "No, because you'd go to jail if you went for someone younger than me."

"True story." I reach for her hand and bring it up to my mouth, kissing it lightly. "You're pretty irreplaceable, Morgan Elizabeth."

She takes her hand back and reaches for my computer and places it beside hers on the table before climbing over my lap and straddling me. Bringing both hands up, she runs her fingers through my hair, keeping her eyes on mine.

"Pretty sure I just fell for you, Bennett Cruz," she whispers as she brings her lips down on mine.

I smile against her mouth as she begins to kiss me. I love this about her. She's not afraid to be open about her feelings. Maybe it's because she knows I already fell for her and she doesn't feel the need to hide her own feelings toward me. I haven't actually told *how hard* I've fallen, but it's pretty obvious. We've been spending every waking moment together lately and I'm the one who keeps initiating it and complaining when she says she needs to go home. Our phones start to vibrate on the table at the same time and we break apart.

"That's weird." She frowns, getting off of my lap to reach

for our phones. She hands mine to me. *Workplace has matched you! See who you got.*

"Well, this is awkward," Morgan says as she clicks on her phone. "Another glitch for sure. I'll have to figure this one out."

"We didn't match?" I frown, clicking on the app quickly, because if the glitch means she matched with Wesley, I would seriously consider throwing her phone away right now. *Say hello to your match: Morgan Tucker.* There's a photo of her and one of me beside her. I chuckle at the ridiculousness of all of this, but also because I'm relieved that it's our faces beside each other.

"It's not supposed to alert us twice about this, especially after such a long time in between." She frowns, smiling a little. "I still can't believe you joined after all the crap you talked."

"I can't believe it either." I toss my phone aside and smile at her. "I can't believe it paired us up."

"I honestly still have my doubts." She puts her phone down on the table. "I keep trying to figure out how you could've gone into the database and matched with me purposely."

I laugh. "You think I'm a professional hacker or something?"

"No." She rolls her eyes. "Besides, Wes made sure that the firewall was solid, so I know it's not a possibility, but still, what are the odds?"

I shrug. "I don't know, but I'll take those odds."

"I wonder who Wesley matched with," she muses.

It's stupid, especially since we're together, but the thought that she may have wanted to actually be paired up with someone else bothers the fuck out of me. Morgan seems to read the expression on my face for what it is, because she smiles at me, shaking her head.

"I kind of like that you're the jealous type, Trouble."

She climbs back on my lap. I grip her thighs, pulling her closer still and leaning into her with a kiss. I bite her lower lip and tug it, sucking it as I pull away from the kiss.

"I'd erase every motherfucker in that database if you'd have matched with someone else."

"You can't do that." She laughs, then gasps when I tuck my hands underneath her shirt and caress my way up her stomach to her breasts, cupping them softly as I brush my thumbs over her nipples.

"You think I'm going to let a piece of technology take my woman from me?"

"No." She arches into me, her hands flying to my hair as I drop my face to her neck and start raining kisses along it. She lets go of my hair and reaches down to take her shirt off and toss it so that her chest is bared to me. I lick her clavicle and continue making my way down her chest, stopping as she lifts my shirt and tosses it to join hers. She presses the tips of her fingers down my chest, my arms. "I love your body."

"I love yours," I murmur against her nipple, swirling my tongue around it. Her grip tightens on my hair again. "I want to explore it until you get tired of my mouth, my fingers, my cock inside of you."

"I'll never get tired of you." She begins to grind against me as I continue kissing and sucking.

She's wearing these tiny shorts with her sorority letters on the back of them that I'm sure I can just slide to one side and fit into, so I lower my sweatpants and let her settle herself on me again, grinding the cotton over my cock and moaning as I hook a finger to set the fabric aside, brushing against her clit with the movement. I slide myself into her wet folds, gripping her ass when I feel her tight pussy close around me. I hold her there for a couple of beats, relishing the warm feel of her and the way her breathing seems to quicken so much that she's gasping for air and we're not even fully fucking yet.

"Bennett," she pleads, trying to grind against me. I hold her steady, not letting her move. "Ben. Please."

"Please what, baby?"

"Please, please let me move." Her nails dig into my biceps. "Let me fuck you."

I throw my head back at the words coming from her mouth and loosen my grip because, fuck, if your beautiful girlfriend asks you to let her fuck you, you'd be a fucking idiot not to let her.

CHAPTER THIRTY-SEVEN

MORGAN

I HAVE an eleven o'clock scheduled with Mr. Cruz to discuss some accounts he wants me to take over. Even though I've been doing this here for over a month and worked elsewhere doing the same kinds of things, having my own accounts to deal with feels official, like I've finally made it. I'm smiling as I think about this when Wesley comes barging out of the general direction of our offices with a panicked look on his face. I stop walking. God, I hope he didn't get fired or something. Not when I'm about to be assigned next level type work and will probably need all the help I can get.

"What's wrong?"

"You can't go in there." His chest rises and falls as he takes gulps of breaths.

I glance over his shoulder. "Why not?"

"You just . . . can't."

"Wes, you're being really weird. I have a meeting at—"

"Yes, I know. Bennett told me to tell you that Charlie is waiting for you in his office."

"But my meeting is at—"

"It got moved up."

I stare at him for a couple of beats and let out a small laugh. "Okay. I guess I'll see you in a bit, then."

Walking in the opposite direction, I take my phone out and text Bennett.

Me: People are being weird. Wesley won't let me go into my office.

I watch the screen as I await a response, but it doesn't come quickly enough. Mr. Cruz's secretary signals for me to go into his office, so I put my phone away and walk inside.

"Morgan." He smiles, but he has the telephone receiver in his hand. He puts a finger into the air and quiets his voice as he speaks into it. "Yes, I know. I already told you how I think you should handle this. I expect you to get it done. See you later." He hangs up. "I'm sorry. Family drama."

"Ah, I know all about that." I smile and sit across from him. "I wasn't sure what to expect, so I didn't really bring anything."

"Oh. No need. I just want to go over some things with you." He leafs through the papers on his desk. "Barbara keeps getting on me about going paperless and I'm really beginning to think she may be on to something."

I laugh because it's such an obvious thing to do. "Don't you drive an energy efficient car?"

He stops fiddling with the papers on his desk and glances up at me. "I see your point."

"I mean, to each his own." I shrug. "I personally love doing everything on a computer, but I can't seem to kick the habit of buying paperbacks."

"Oh, but that's the grandeur of it. Paperbacks are not a habit to kick. They're an art to embrace."

"I like that." I smile. "I'll have to remember to say that to Dev the next time he makes fun of me for spending hours at the bookstore."

"I found it." Mr. Cruz chuckles as he waves a sheet of paper. "The first thing I want to discuss is the workplace app."

I press my hand over my stomach. I should've had breakfast this morning. I'm not sure I can take this kind of news on an empty stomach. As if sensing my trepidation, Mr. Cruz tilts his head with a kind smile.

"Hey, the numbers are great. Nobody dropped it. Only a few people stopped using it before time was up, and according to Ben, you and him were two of them, so I think we can overlook that number." He raises an eyebrow. I blush. He continues to read from the paper, "The majority of the people were pleasantly surprised when they saw the person they'd been chatting with, and get this, ninety percent of them have gone on more than one date."

My mouth drops. "Oh, my God."

"I know." He smiles. "Pretty impressive, huh?"

"I can't even," I whisper. "That's really impressive."

"You did good, Morgan. Now, we want to buy it from you."

I blink. "What?"

"I mean, assuming you'd want to sell us the concept, of course, and we'd love your input on it going forward, but we feel that this is something that definitely has potential on a wider market, and we already have some companies that would be willing to give it a try."

I uncover my mouth. "You really want to buy it?"

"We do."

"Oh, my God."

"You haven't even heard how much we want to pay you for

it." He laughs, sliding a sheet of paper over with a dollar amount I'd only ever dreamed of ever having in my own bank account.

I blink. "For one app?"

"Yes." He smiles. "We would love to talk to you about future concepts though."

"Definitely." I nod slowly, still staring at the paper in front of me.

"I'm glad you're open to the idea." He laughs. "We'll have to have another meeting to go over specifics and bring in our attorney and finance guy. You're more than welcome to get your own lawyer to come in and look over the contract, but we'd really love to get this done sooner rather than later. We'd like to set up a strategy to aim for a launch before the next holiday season."

"Sure. Of course. Oh, my God." I glance up at him. I've sold apps before, but never for this much, and never anything I did ninety-percent on my own. "This is real life?"

"This is real life." He chuckles. His office phone rings, breaking his amusement as he lifts it to his ear. "Okay. Good. Yes." He hangs up. "Sorry about that. Now that this is out of the way, I would love your attention on Elias's concepts. He's handed over his account and wants us to develop it further. That means, of course, you'd have to meet with him."

"That's fine."

"I'll send you his contact information so you can set something up," he says, going over his notes. "Ah, this is one I'm not sure you're going to like, but we have this dating app that needs to be revamped. They had a huge security breach last year and even though it's been handled, the number of subscribers dropped drastically. The owners of the app want to give it a new name and interface in hopes of salvaging it."

"That sounds like fun. Why wouldn't I like it?"

"It's the cheating app. Some people are okay with it, others aren't. The way I see it, just because you're working on the app doesn't mean you condone what they're using it for."

"Oh." I slump back in my chair. "I've never been one to judge, but this is definitely a sore subject for me."

"For a lot of us," he agrees.

"Can I think about it?"

"Sure. Let me know by the end of the week."

"Okay."

"How do you feel about game apps?"

"I know they're really popular, but my knowledge on them is pretty limited."

"I'm sure you're aware that we run one of the most successful game apps already, and we'd really like to venture deeper into that world. We have a few people on those accounts, including Wesley. I met with him last week and he mentioned that he'd like to have you as part of their team if you're open to it."

"Oh. Wow." My eyebrows raise. I have so much respect for Wesley's team and all the stuff they develop, but I've never really considered what it would be like to work with them on anything. "I mean, I would love to, but like I said, I don't have much knowledge on the matter. I'm afraid they'd kick me out."

Mr. Cruz laughs. "I'm sure they won't. If you're interested in learning, I would love to send you to a boot camp on game development. The next one is starting next week and will run for two weeks. You can report there instead of here for the next two weeks and we can have another meeting about this once you're done. All expenses paid, of course," he adds.

"Seriously?" I whisper. My mouth falls open. I knew working for SEVEN would change my life, but I didn't realize just how much. Unable to form words, I start to nod like an idiot. "Yes. I would love that."

"Perfect. I'll send you all of the information so you can register."

We move on to another account he wants me to take over, and then another. By the time we're done with the meeting, I have three accounts to handle, including SEVEN's, and an app sold.

"Please remember, I want you to use this company to grow your own concepts," he says. "I don't want you only catering to our current clients, but if you ever find yourself doing a little too much for them, remember you're also a current client." He winks from his desk, and it reminds me so much of when Bennett does it that I just stand there staring for a beat before getting myself together and walking out.

I feel like I've been holding in a scream for an hour, so when I see Bennett leaning against the wall across from his father's office, holding a bouquet of flowers, it's the first thing I do. He laughs as he straightens, opening his arms for me to jump into.

"Oh, my God. You knew? You knew!" I laugh as he squeezes me tighter.

"We had a meeting about it a couple of weeks ago, and again last week," he says. "Are you happy?"

"Happy? I'm . . . I don't know what I am, but happy doesn't seem to cover it." I smile wide, taking the flowers from his hands and reaching up to kiss him quickly. I look around to make sure nobody saw that.

"Paola was here earlier," he says, his expression suddenly serious. "She kind of told everyone we're together."

I drop my arms, letting the flowers hit my leg. "What do

you mean? What did she say? Is that why Wes didn't let me go to the office?"

"Yeah." Bennett sighs heavily. "She just came in here screaming. Security had to escort her out. I'm sorry."

"What did she say?" I frown, examining his face and suit for scratches or a spill. I'm not sure what to expect from this lady. "Did she do anything to you?"

"No, we got her out before things escalated, but she started screaming that she was looking for Morgan Tucker, Bennett's new girlfriend." He reaches for my hand and squeezes it. "I guess she saw our pictures together."

"Why would she do that? What does she want?"

"Attention." He exhales heavily. "Things didn't work out with the guy she cheated with, she miscarried the baby. Even though I didn't have to force the divorce because at the time she was still with him, shortly after she started trying to get me back and when she couldn't she started doing stupid things to sabotage any potential relationship I may have had, which I didn't." He shoots me a pointed look. "Not until you."

I shrug. "I don't care. I'm not going to let her rain on my parade and I'm definitely not going to let her dictate our relationship. Fuck her."

He grins. "Do these new responsibilities come with the opportunity to work remotely?"

"Remote . . . oh, you want to take me home before lunch?" I raise an eyebrow.

"I sure do." He leans in and kisses my forehead, my cheek, the side of my mouth. By the time he reaches my neck I feel a little breathless. "You think your boss will mind?"

"I don't know. Why don't you ask?" I whisper.

"He's your boss, not mine."

"He's your dad, not mine."

"Hm." He nips my earlobe. "Maybe he won't notice."

I laugh. "I'm not taking my chances. I just got a promotion. I don't want to risk getting fired over sex with his son."

"It's kind of crazy because technically I'm his boss."

"Don't even joke, Bennett." I pull back.

He presses the back of his hand to my forehead. "You feel warm."

"Oh, my God." I lift the flowers and smack his arm. "You're seriously going to get us both in trouble. Let's stay till lunch."

"That's like a million hours away," he groans.

"Three." I start walking toward our offices.

"You should've stayed over last night," he says.

"I can't stay over every night."

"Why not?"

"Because that sounds a lot like moving in with you." I shoot him a pointed look.

"That doesn't sound like a terrible concept."

I shake my head, smiling, as we walk through the doors. This time, nobody stops me and everyone is working. I brace myself for them to notice me and give me strange looks, but if anything, the few people who look up from their desks and spot me only smile at me and get back to it. I let out a deep breath.

"I'm going to find somewhere to put these," I say, walking toward the break room. "You get to work. I'll see you at twelve."

"Eleven fifty-five."

"Twelve, Bennett."

"Fine." He leans in but thinks better of it and just walks away with a wink.

I, on the other hand, cannot stop smiling. Wesley is in the

break room with Ashley from accounting. I recognize her only because he's shown me, like, thirty-five pictures of her. They met on the app and apparently really hit it off. I smile at them.

"Hey," he says.

"I'll catch you later," she says to him, smiling and waving as she walks by me.

"She's really pretty," I say once she's out of the room.

"She is." His smile drops after a moment. "I don't know what you heard—"

"Bennett told me his ex came by. What did she say?"

"Nothing much. She knew your full name though. She said you're dating Bennett and that if any of us are friends with you we should warn you that he's bad news and a cheater."

"Wow. She called him a cheater?" I blink, shaking my head. "She really is crazy."

"Absolutely. She had this look in her eyes that I've only seen on really crazy people," Wesley says.

"So that was it?"

"Well, she started kicking at everything when security tried to escort her out."

"Paola did?" My eyes widen. "I can't picture her doing that."

"You've met her?"

"Yeah, and I didn't know she was crazy. I just thought she was a royal bitch." I adjust the plastic cup I put my flowers in to make sure it doesn't spill over before facing Wesley. "She called me a whore, so I went off on her in front of a group of people she was with."

Wesley laughs. "Well, now the outburst makes a little more sense."

"She's a loser." I shrug. "Anyway, tell me about Ashley."

He blushes. "She's a keeper."

"Oh, my God you found love on my app." I smile. "I feel like a fairy godmother."

"Or Cupid."

"Stop." I groan. He laughs. We walk out of the break room. Just as we reach my office, I turn to him again. "I'm selling the workplace app to SEVEN."

His mouth falls open. "That's amazing."

"I know."

"Are you taking your money and quitting?"

"Not unless I want to live out of my car in a few years," I say. "It's good money, but not enough to survive on in this city."

"You can always get a couple of roommates."

"No, thank you. I'd rather stay here and continue learning."

"I'll give you private lessons, for a fee."

I laugh. "Now it sounds like you're offering me other kinds of services."

"I can offer those too," he says, then frowns. "Actually, no way in hell am I offering those. Bennett has been looking for a reason to kill me."

I laugh. "And you have Ashley."

"And I have Ashley." He nods. "Lunch today?"

"I'll have to take a rain check."

"Got it." Wesley looks around for a beat before meeting my gaze again. "Has Charlie mentioned anything about maybe working with us on a couple of things?"

"He just did actually. I'm going to be out for the next two weeks taking some classes on gaming."

He smiles. "You're doing it."

"I am." I smile back. "Thanks for mentioning my name."

"Are you kidding? We make a good team." He taps the glass

outside of my door. "'Kay. I'll let you get to it. Let me know if you need help. Your job is a lot more interesting than mine as of late."

With that, he walks away and I walk into my office.

CHAPTER THIRTY-EIGHT

I DECIDE that because it's only Tuesday and I won't start the game development class until next week, I need to take advantage of being in the office today. Bennett is out all day with meetings, so he dropped me off this morning with the promise that I'd meet him back at his place tonight. He keeps bringing up the "moving in together" thing and I'm seriously torn. On one hand, I would love to do it, but I also fear it may be too soon. Jamie moved in with Travis a month after she met him and look where that led them—destruction and dysfunction. I can't say the thought doesn't excite me though. And he's right, we really have been spending every waking moment together. With Devon's team not making the playoffs, I imagine he'll want to come back here and stay in the apartment, which was fine last year when I wasn't living there, but that could get awkward fast now. If it happens, I can get my own place . . . or I can take Bennett up on his offer and move in with him. I'm still mulling this over as I walk out of the building, taking out my phone to text him and let him know that I'm going home to get clothes before heading to his place, when I run into someone.

"Sorry," I say absentmindedly. I run into people every day walking in and out of this building, and I've stopped looking up when I do so.

"Not as sorry as you're going to be."

I snap my attention in the direction of the voice because I know it's Paola. I'd know her voice anywhere after all of the phone calls and running into her that one time.

"What are you doing here?"

"A little birdy told me things are getting serious between you and my husband."

"Ex-husband." I raise an eyebrow. "Don't be petty."

"Ex-husband," she says, shrugging. "I told you I'd be watching you."

"You already wreaked havoc in there last week. I'm pretty sure you made your point." I take a step back because I truly don't know what this woman is capable of, though she doesn't seem like the type to get physical. My eyes drop to her hands, but she only seems to be holding papers, or pictures, something glossy.

"And what point would that be?" She raises an eyebrow.

"I don't know. You tell me. You're the one who's clearly disturbed by the idea of Bennett being happy."

"I'm disturbed by the idea of him being happy with you," she shouts. "You, who waltzed into our lives and destroyed it in a single night, after we'd been married for nearly four years."

I blink. "You're delusional. You cheated on him. You got pregnant with another man's baby, for God's sake!"

"He cheated on me with you," she shouts, tossing the contents in her hands at me. On instinct, I press a hand to my chest, securing the pictures. "I made mistakes, yes, but the baby was his. We were working on our marriage until you came along."

Her words make me freeze. The baby was his? Is she lying? Is he lying? I groan. I shouldn't even be giving her the time of day. "Get out of my face."

"Not until you see the photos," she says. "I had him followed, you know. We were working out our differences, but I knew if things went south I needed proof of his deception. I knew you looked familiar when I saw you at that restaurant, but it didn't hit me until I saw your photo in the paper together."

Bringing one of the pictures up slowly, I look at it, trying to keep my expression neutral as my hands start to shake. It's a picture of Bennett and me the first night we met, at the bar, on my birthday nearly two years ago. I shake my head and glare at Paola.

"You're full of shit."

"Am I?" She raises an eyebrow. "Is that not you? Look at the date. My PI had it dated."

"I know the fucking date."

"We were still married. We were going to see a therapist the following day and then he decided to give up on me, on us, on our baby." Her voice breaks, her brown eyes filling with tears. "I lost my baby because of you, because I couldn't handle the betrayal," she wails. "I couldn't handle it and I lost everything. My husband, my pregnancy, everything."

"You're lying," I whisper, shaking my head. "You're a liar. You were cheating on him."

"And so was he," she yells, "with you."

"I . . ."

"Nothing more to say," she says, wiping her face. "What's done is done. Have a nice life, but remember, if he cheated with you, he'll cheat on you."

She walks away, leaving me standing in the middle of the sidewalk just outside of my workplace, with a dozen photos at my feet. They keep picking up wind and flying off, but I can't seem to lift my feet to chase them. I fold the one in my hand and try to pick up as many as I can, shoving them in my purse, before finally walking away.

If he cheated with you, he'll cheat on you.

How many times have I said that? How many times have I thought it? Too many, and if what she's saying is true . . . no, what she's saying is definitely true. The proof is in everything she's just given me. I continue to scan the rest of the pictures. She's documented everything, from the alleged affair Bennett had with me to her positive pregnancy test, ultrasound, and miscarriage date. I think back on everything he's said. Even as Owl he'd confessed cheating on his wife. I just hadn't realized it was with me. Bile rises in my throat as I take the stairs down to the train. I broke up a marriage. Even if the marriage was on the rocks when I met him, I still contributed. I'm the exact person I've always hated. I've turned into my mother.

CHAPTER THIRTY-NINE

GROWING up in a conflicted household has taught me to shy away from arguments, but my anger propels me forward and drives me to Bennett's place. I stand on the stoop and pound on the door. He gave me a key but I can't bring myself to use it, not when my reason for being here is to confront him and get to the bottom of this. His dimpled smile is wide as he opens the door, but it loses its luster as he scans my face. The entire ride here I felt ready for this, but now that I'm standing before him, the task seems impossible. Calling him out for being a liar, a cheat, a no-good asshole, when he's looking at me with such affection.

"What's wrong?"

"You lied to me."

"What?" He frowns. "When? What are you talking about?"

"When we spoke on the workplace app, you said you cheated on your wife." I swallow, hoping the knot in my throat dissipates. "At the time, I wrote you off. We decided to be friends, just friends, but that was before." I pause again, taking a shaky breath. God, why does it feel like my chest is being ripped open? "You . . . did you cheat on her with me?"

He blinks, staring at me for one beat, then two. He licks his lips before speaking. "Why don't you come inside?"

"Answer the question, Bennett."

He rips his gaze from mine and looks around, probably not wanting me to cause a scene in front of his stupid, rich neighbors. Fuck him. Fuck them all. I grip the photos in my hand and throw them at his face with all my might, which is enough for some of them to hit him. He steps back.

"What the hell, Morgan?"

"What the hell *you*," I shout. "You know how I feel about cheating. You know it's a deal breaker for me. You know this, yet you lied to me. You used me!"

"I didn't know you back then," he shouts back.

"So you admit it." I reach out to hold the handrail beside me.

"We weren't supposed to see each other again," he says. "It was a one-night stand. It wasn't supposed to . . . you weren't supposed to walk into my father's office. You weren't supposed to turn out to be my best friend's little sister. You weren't—" He stops talking suddenly, as if catching himself, but I already know where he's going with this.

"Supposed to find out?" I cross my arms. "I wasn't supposed to find out and call you out on your shit? I wasn't supposed to discover just what a liar and an asshole and a cheater you truly are?" I uncross my arms and turn around to walk away. "You disgust me."

"It was over," he says to my back. "It was over between me and Paola when we hooked up."

I stop at the bottom of the steps and face him. He's barefoot and it's freezing out here, the forecast set to snow, but he's on the second step now looking like he may just chase me down the block. Let him try and lose all his toes for all I care.

"Were you married?"

"Yes, but it was—"

"Was she trying to work things out? Salvage your marriage?"

His frown deepens. "Yeah, but—"

"Was she pregnant?"

"With another man's—"

"Do you know for certain it was another man's baby or did you just assume?"

"She told me it was." He throws his arms up. "What the hell, Morgan? What happened to not paying attention to crazy people?"

"I'm beginning to think I was listening to a crazy person when I agreed to that." I turn again and start walking away from his house. He follows.

"God damn it, please come inside. Let me explain. Let's talk about this." He grabs my arm.

"You go inside. There's nothing to talk about. This is over." I jerk away. "Go inside before you blame me for the hypothermia you're about to catch."

He doesn't continue following me.

Somehow, I manage to keep my head held high and my expression neutral until I reach the subway, the adrenaline pumping in my veins holding me together as a million things run through my mind. Paola's words come back to haunt me and keep me hostage as I walk to my apartment. I can't seem to shake them off. I can't seem to forget the way Bennett looked when I confronted him, as if he'd been attacked. I guess that's what a liar looks like when he's slapped with the truth. Walking into my apartment, I feel like a zombie. Thankfully, I don't have to go into work at all next week, since I have the game development classes to attend. Instead of calling my friends, or worrying about dinner, I head to the shower, strip myself of this day's clothing, and go to bed early.

It's midnight when I wake up, and after my initial cloudy state, I remember what happened today and start to cry, really cry, even though I'm still in disbelief. I can't believe he lied to me, after everything we shared. I can rationalize the one-night stand for what it was, but why didn't he tell me up front? Why keep it from me? The only explanation I can come up with is that he knew I'd leave him. He knew I'd call this entire thing off, even if it meant breaking my own heart, because I cannot stand the thought of being with a cheater, and a liar. I just hate that he turned out to be both. I hate that I fell as hard as I did for him. I hate that I'm obviously in love with him and didn't fully admit it to myself until this moment, during the worst imaginable time. The worst part is I don't feel like I hate him. I'm not sure I can. I hate what he did, and when I think about him I want to claw his eyes out, but I don't hate him. I will myself back to sleep, but it's no use. I glance at my phone and switch it back on. I'd put it on airplane mode when I left his place because I didn't want to deal with his calls or texts. As suspected, it vibrates uncontrollably the second it finds service. His name floods my phone screen. I clear it and ignore it. I may be confused and not know what'll happen next, but I know I never want to feel like this again.

CHAPTER FORTY

BENNETT

I BROUGHT FLOWERS. I didn't really stop to think that maybe these tropical-looking flowers aren't the right kind for this occasion, but what type of flowers say I'm sorry in a million different ways? I'm not sure. I'm also not sure it even fucking matters. If I'm lucky, she opens the door, but she may take them and stomp on them, for all I know. When she finally comes to the door, she doesn't open it fully, just enough to let me see a part of her. That alone rips me apart a little bit. I put the flowers a bit higher, so she can see them better. She stares at them, stares at me, and sighs.

"Flowers don't fix everything, you know."

"I know." I lower the flowers. Fuck, I shouldn't have brought them. "I'm sorry. Please let me explain everything."

She shrugs. "Go ahead."

"The day I saw you, that night at the bar, I'd just found out Paola was pregnant with that guy's baby. I kind of . . . I don't know. I went out to get my mind off things."

"To get your mind off things," she whispers at first before

her words get louder. "And then you decided that I looked naïve enough and stupid enough that you could just use me to cheat on your wife with and I'd never find out. I mean, how could I, right? You left me at that hotel room without another word."

"Morgan." I close my eyes briefly, hoping to gather myself because I swear I've never cried before but the pain in her eyes right now makes me feel like I just might. "Please don't say that. I didn't use you. I—"

"You used me. You used me to feel better about yourself," she says. "You used me in order to prove to yourself that you could still get a woman that wasn't your wife. Tell me that wasn't the case, Bennett. Tell me you were there just to have a drink."

"I was there just to have a drink and then I met you and that changed."

"You weren't even wearing a wedding ring." She watches me for a moment before shaking her head. "You disgust me. If this is the kind of thing you do whenever you feel wronged by someone, I want no part of this. I refuse to be the other woman or the rebound. I just . . . I can't. Please leave."

Before I can plead with her, she slams the door in my face. I stand stock-still for a moment, looking at the door as if maybe staring at it will call her to open it again. When she doesn't, I look at the flowers in my hand and sigh. Instead of taking them with me, I lay them over the little welcome mat she has outside her door. She'll probably toss them, but I don't care. I didn't come here with any expectations.

CHAPTER FORTY-ONE

BENNETT

"OH, fun, another person heartbroken and moping. These are exactly the kinds of people we should be hanging out with a few weeks before our wedding."

I look up to see Devon and Nora as they walk into my parents' living room.

"You really do look like shit," Nora says.

"How's Morgan doing?" I ask, despite myself. I promised myself I'd give her space, despite the urge to go after her and grovel.

"Good," Devon says. "Better than you."

"She's out and about," Nora says. "Putting together my bachelorette and stuff, but she has been moping in between."

"Fuck." I groan, covering my face. "I forgot about the bachelor party."

"It's being taken care of," Devon says. "We decided on a joint party."

"What? And Morgan's doing everything?" I stand up. "I should be helping out."

"You really want to spend your Sunday hanging out with your ex-girlfriend?" Devon raises an eyebrow.

"More than anything."

He chuckles. "You're the exact opposite of just about everyone in the universe."

"She hasn't called me. I thought she'd call by now."

"I told you I didn't want to hear any of it." Dev raises his hands. "We're here to have lunch with your parents and thank them for letting us borrow their vacation home next week."

"Even though it'll be freezing and we won't be able to enjoy the amenities," I say. "Who decided on a winter wedding anyway?"

"I did." Nora raises an eyebrow, daring me to say something else.

I sigh. "I guess we can still use the bowling alley and movie theatre."

"And indoor, heated pool," Devon adds, frowning. "I swear I think I go there more than you do."

"You do."

"That's because your parents hated your ex-wife and never invited you when we went over," Nora quips.

"Pretty sure it was the other way around. It was her who had her differences with them," I respond. Not that it fucking matters. The fact that she's still brought up in conversation is absolutely ridiculous. She's ruining my life and she's not even in it.

"Besides, the bipolar weather is saying it'll be in the seventies next weekend."

"In December?" I blink. "What is happening?"

"The world is ending," Dev says, smiling. "Better get your shit together so you don't die alone."

"Fuck you."

"Between you and me, I think you should let Morgan handle the bachelor/bachelorette party. Jamie and Presley are helping her with all of it. Give her space."

"I've already given her space."

"She'll come to you when she's ready."

Devon walks away, toward the kitchen, where Mom is making *croquetas* and *empanadas*.

"What is she never comes back to me?"

"Then I guess it wasn't meant to be." Nora shrugs, smiling sadly.

"It was though. It *is* meant to be."

"So, you wait."

"I didn't use her to cheat on my ex-wife, Nor," I say. "I mean, technically I did, but it's complicated."

"I'm not here to judge, but you have to understand that Morgan's been through a lot. A lot more than you can imagine."

"Devon doesn't even know the half of it." I scowl.

"He does. His mom confessed a lot of things to him recently. To say he's pissed off on his sister's behalf is an understatement. She doesn't know he knows, so don't mention it to her. They both had fucked-up childhoods," she says, "The only thing you and I can do is chill and wait for them to come around. They'll let us know when they need us."

"Fuck." I run my fingers through my messy hair. "I hate waiting around like an idiot. I feel helpless."

"What happened with Paola?"

"I put her in her place. Threatened to sue. Told her I'd get a restraining order if that's what it'll take to get her to back off."

Her eyebrows raise. "I don't remember her being this crazy in college."

"I don't either." I bark out a laugh. "I mean, I married the girl. Obviously, I didn't think she'd go through these lengths to get back at me. And for what? She cheated on me, got pregnant with another man's child, and then told Morgan it was mine all along. She's a damn liar. Why try to fuck with my life after all this time?"

"Maybe she's bored. Women do crazy things when they're bored."

Her boredom is not my problem. I need to focus my attention on getting Morgan back.

CHAPTER FORTY-TWO

MORGAN

"YOU REALLY DON'T THINK this dress is too short?" Jamie asks, plucking invisible lint off the electric-blue dress she's wearing.

"Thank God the weather is amazing right now," I say, looking at my own short dress in the mirror. "If the length of these dresses had a name, it would be called The Perfect Slut."

Nora and her best friend, Tina, laugh. "If you ever need to switch gears from app development, I think you have a future in labels."

"I never had an issue with short dresses before," Jamie adds. "I seriously think the closer I get to thirty, the blander I become. It's no wonder Travis is dating a younger version of me."

"Oh, my God." I groan. "Can we not talk about men and how much they suck tonight?"

"Well, yours will be there." Presley raises an eyebrow.

"Thanks for the reminder," I say. "But he's not mine anymore."

"Oh, sweetheart." Tina squeezes my shoulder. "You'll be all right. We'll make sure of it."

"Thanks."

"I told you we could split the party and let them do their own thing," Nora says.

"Nope. This was the original plan and we're sticking to it. Fuck him and fuck men."

"Oh, God. Tonight is going to be great," Nora quips.

"It'll be epic," Jamie says, then cringes. "See? I even say words like epic now. Who even am I?"

THIRTY MINUTES LATER, we're on a party bus. I sandwich myself between Jamie and Tina, while Presley sits on Nate's lap across from us and Nora sits on my brother's beside them. Tina's husband is meeting us later on in the evening, so at least from now until then, I'm safe. Devon's friends are all sitting in the back, Bennett included. I made it very obvious that I don't want to look at him at all and he seemed to get the memo, because he didn't even try to say hi to me when I got on.

I promised myself I would be cordial.

I can totally do cordial.

I need at least two drinks in me before I get to that point, but I can totally do cordial.

With that thought, I take the vodka tonic that Jamie hands me and start bobbing my head to the beat as Tina bumps me and falls into the rhythm of "Tribe" by Bas and J. Cole. Soon, between the trifecta of my drink, my girls, and the music, I completely forget that he's there at all.

The night is laid out like this: bar hopping, because that's what Devon wanted to do, followed by a dance club, because that's what Nora wanted to do. I reserved private areas in all the locations because of Devon and his friends. The last thing we need is for people to start snapping questionable pictures out of context that'll end up on ESPN tomorrow.

"You've got to be kidding," Jamie says, typing furiously on her phone. "They're just now finishing up the set up at the first place."

"That's fine." I shrug.

She meets my gaze. "We'll be on their tails."

"Who cares? I'm sure it looks perfect." I look at the phone in her hand and see the pictures they're sending as they come in. "That looks insane."

"I should've just met you guys there."

"Then you wouldn't have any fun, James."

"I'm worrying right now anyway. Might as well be worrying while I'm doing things."

"Do me a favor, drink and shut up."

I do the same and continue dancing in my seat. The guys sitting in the back are hollering and rapping along. One of them stands up and starts working the pole, which makes us all laugh.

"Jermaine doesn't even drink," Devon says loudly as he laughs and snaps a picture of his friend.

"Jermaine is hot as eff," Jamie says quietly, to me. Not so quietly, being that Tina hears her and laughs.

"Jermaine is trouble," she says.

"Aren't they all," I quip.

Tina laughs. Jamie sighs. The three of us take another sip.

Jamie and I lead the line to the bar and confirm with the guy up front that we do indeed have a space reserved in a private area. He pushes a button on his earpiece, relays the message, and tells us to take the side door. We head that way and are greeted by a staff of three, who lead us to a large room that's decorated to the nines with rose-colored balloons, beer buckets, and Champagne. There's a bar in the middle with a guy behind it. I turn to one of the women who works here.

"This is only for us, right?"

"Yes. The bar is included in the price."

I lift my eyebrows and look at Jamie. "This is not amateur shit."

Jamie laughs and gives me a fist bump.

"This is incredible," Nora says as she walks up to us.

"Really? Do you love it?" Jamie asks.

"We figured we'd start off with a softer theme," I add.

"I absolutely love it and can't wait to see what else you have in store, but honestly? I'd stay here all night." She winks at us and walks back to the rest of the group.

"Wouldn't that have made our lives easier," I say.

Jamie nods. "Let's go get drinks."

I DON'T KNOW how it happens, but I end up directly behind Bennett as we walk into the last bar before finally going to the club. I've been able to avoid him all night, save for a few stolen glances here and there, but suddenly here he is, a brick wall in jeans and a nice suit jacket walking in front of me. He smells so fucking good, it takes everything in me to not lean forward and inhale him. *He's a liar and a cheater*, I remind myself, and that's all it takes to sour my mood all over again, but only for a second. I quickly remind myself where I am and what I'm celebrating and hold my head high as I walk through the door.

"Morgan," Jamie calls out from the front of the line.

"Excuse me," I say, trying to brush past Bennett.

"You were behind me the whole time?"

I nod once, hold my head high and walk forward to where Jamie is. She holds my hand as we walk into the private area that looks similar to the first, with its own bar and plenty of seating. The group has gotten bigger now, more of Devon's friends and colleagues joining in. He introduces me to a new one every so often and continuously checks up on me, which makes me wonder if my discomfort is beginning to show or if he's just being the overprotective brother he usually is in these settings. It's when he's holding my hand in one of his and Nora's in the other as he's thanking everyone for coming that it starts to really hit me that he's getting married.

I absolutely adore Nora. She's become my sister and family, but hearing him say how thankful he is to be starting a new family with the love of his life hits me square in the chest. A new family. It's one-hundred-percent the alcohol getting to my head that makes me look up at him and wonder what'll happen to me. What'll happen when they start having children and create their own little nucleus? Will we still see each other this often? Will we still talk every day? Will they have time? One thing taking my mother to the rehab center showed me was that I really don't have many people in this world. Devon and Nora are the extent of my family. Somehow, I make it through Devon's speech with a smile on my face, but the minute people start clapping and he lets go of my hand to kiss Nora, I feel like I'm going to lose it. I wait until he gives me a hug, and then Nora gives me one before shooting like a bat out of hell in search of the bathroom.

Once I find one, I lock myself in a stall and take a deep breath. I need water. Like a gallon or two. The main bathroom door opens and closes. I look down and see men's dress shoes— dark caramel-brown and a hem of dark-washed jeans.

"Go away, Ben."

"I'm done giving you space."

"Oh, that's funny, I don't remember asking you." I unlock the stall door and open it. "Seriously, go away."

"What's wrong?" His brows pull together as he steps forward. I move to close the door again and he stops walking toward me. "This is killing me, Morgan."

"Which part?"

"All of it. I hate not seeing you. I hate not talking to you. I hate not hearing your laugh or the ease in which you insult the fuck out of people without a care in the world."

I laugh. "I don't insult people."

"Maybe just me, then?" He smiles. "But it's okay. I like it."

"This isn't going to work. You lied to me in the worst way."

"I didn't lie to you."

I shoot him a look. "So you weren't married the first time we hooked up?"

"I was."

"Okay, so you lied."

"If you want to get technical, I lied."

I blink. "A lie is a lie. Jesus Christ. Do you just go around lying to people and then coming up with ways to justify it?"

"No."

"Only me, then?" I cross my arms over my chest. "Either way, it doesn't matter. It's over. I'm done. The last time a guy started lying to me, he ended up fucking my mother."

"Don't put me in a box with that asshole."

"You put yourself there." I uncross my arms and walk over to the sink, washing my hands and drying them quickly.

"I already told you this, but it bears repeating. She'd already been cheating on me. I met you the night she told me about the pregnancy. We were done. I was done. There was nothing she could've said or done at that point to get me back. And then I met you and it was your birthday and you were all alone, yet you said I was lonely."

"You were." I toss the paper towel into the trash can as I pivot to face him. "You still are."

"I haven't been lonely since the day you walked into my father's office."

I roll my eyes. "Okay, Romeo."

"I'm serious, Morgan. When you're with me, I feel light. I haven't felt light in years," he says. The way he says it, with the serious tone and those sincere eyes, almost makes me want to believe him. "Years."

"I guess you'll need to find your light elsewhere, because I'm not going to let you drain mine."

With that, I walk out. My chest physically hurts as I head back over to the party, but I keep a smile on my face through it. I've been hurt before and I survived.

THE CLUB IS LOUD. That's a good thing because it means no one can talk to me. It's a bad thing because it means I can't talk to anyone either. Tina's husband got here, so my partner in dancing is gone. Jamie has been talking to one of my brother's friends for the past thirty minutes. Everyone else seems to be dancing, drinking, and generally having a good time. Bennett is drinking and watching me with every sip he takes. I'm not going to lie, if things hadn't gone south between us, I'd be standing between his muscular legs right now. Alas, men fucking suck. I'm about to pull my phone out when my brother comes up to me.

"You're moping. No fucking moping at my bachelor party."

"I'm at Nora's bachelorette." I grin up at him.

"I'm not kidding." He hands me the drink in his hand. "Come dance. Or go find a random guy to dance with. That's your usual move."

I laugh and stand carefully, making sure not to flash anyone. Maybe Jamie was on to something with the short dress thing. I join him, Nora, and some other guys on the dance floor. Jamie and the guy she's been talking to walk over and join in beside me. We're moving and laughing and singing along to the music, throwing our hands up, and for a split second I wish so badly Bennett's arms were around me, moving along with me. I glance over to where he's standing and see one of Nora's friends, April, talking to him. She's been tipsy most of the night, and with the way she's looking at him I can only imagine what she's offering.

Bennett, on the other hand, keeps his expression passive, acting like he's not really paying attention to her. As if sensing me, he looks over and locks eyes with me. Despite the way my heart jumps, I manage to keep dancing. April doesn't seem to get a clue, she stands directly in front of him and starts moving against him to the music as he stares at me. That's the moment I decide I can't do this. I can't stand here and watch him with another woman. I also refuse to cause a scene at my brother and Nora's bachelor party, so I turn around instead and bump straight into one of Devon's teammates. I can't remember this one's name, but the force of the bump makes me take a quick step back, and I'm grateful when he grabs my arm to keep me from slipping and shoots me a grin. Before I realize what's happening, I have a new dance partner. He leans in.

"Your Devil's sister."

I laugh at the nickname my brother has acquired. "That would be me."

"I'm Darian." He extends his hand for me to shake, which I

do. He doesn't give it back right away and I don't even mind. We dance holding that one hand for a couple of beats until he finally drops it. "You don't come to our games very often."

"I haven't been to any this year." I cringe. "I'm a bad sister. I know. I don't like your team though."

"Really?" Darian throws his head back with a howl of a laugh. When he straightens, he wraps an arm around me and pulls him closer as we dance. "I have a confession. I didn't like them either. I'm a Dolphin, born and raised in the three-oh-five, so none of my family likes the team either. They root for me though."

"That's all that matters, isn't it?" I smile.

"For me it is."

When the song finishes and loops into another, I slow down and offer Darian a smile. "Thanks for the dance."

"Sure. Thank you," he says quickly. "I'll see you at the wedding."

I walk away and go back to the table I'd been in before, taking a seat there before taking my phone out. I glance up quickly and look at the dance floor, where everyone is still dancing. I tell myself I'm not going to look in Bennett's direction, but it's impossible. I have to know if he gave into April's obvious attempts. Neither one of them are there when I look. A knot settles in the pit of my stomach. Did he leave with her? No. He wouldn't just leave. Did they go somewhere more private? Is he kissing her, touching her, fucking her? My thoughts only seem to get less appealing and the knot seems to grow bigger. I decide to scroll social media because I can't handle reality right now, but a notification from the workplace app pops up and I click it, pulse thrumming in my ears.

Owl: I miss you

Owl: You look beautiful

Owl: I want to touch you, even if it's just to hold your hand

Owl: You smell so good

Owl: I love watching you laugh

Owl: I hate seeing you dance with other men

Owl: You get this look on your face when your sad about something, like you transport yourself to another reality just so you won't feel all of the emotions that come with whatever it is that makes you sad.

That last one gets me. It was sent right before I went to the bathroom at that bar and he chased me down. I look around the room in search for him and finally spot him leaning against the empty bar, no April in sight. I type in my response as I hold his attention and see when his phone alerts him of the text.

Me: You're*

I watch as he takes it out and reads it. Watch the way his lips twitch with amusement and continue looking at him as he looks back at me. It's dark in here, but I can imagine that twinkle in his eyes I've seen so often before and I wish I wasn't so keen on leaving him. I wish I was one of those people who could be wronged and brush it off like nothing happened, but it hurts. I've never envisioned myself as the other woman and the picture Paola painted for me rests heavy on my mind. There are three sides to every story. I'm not completely irrational. I know Bennett truly doesn't feel he did anything wrong because he's been able to justify, the way I'm sure his ex-wife can give a million reasons as to why she resorted to cheating, but it doesn't matter. I'm not the kind of woman who stands for this kind of thing. You can't champion women and turn a blind eye when you're the one who potentially screwed one over. I'm definitely not on my mother's level with the betrayal, but it doesn't make me feel any less disgusted with myself. My phone vibrates. I glance down and see a new text from Bennett, this time not in the app.

Bennett: Let me take you to breakfast tomorrow

Me: No way

Bennett: I know you booked a room with your friend, but stay at the house tonight.

Me: HELL NO

Bennett: You can stay in one of the guest rooms, not with me. I just want more time with you.

I set my phone on my lap and mull it over. Another text comes in.

Bennett: Please?

Me: Fine

I look at him as I type it and watch as his shoulders sag in relief when he reads the text. The sight of it makes me want to smile, but I don't.

CHAPTER FORTY-THREE

MY HEAD IS KILLING ME. I don't even remember getting here last night, so when I open my eyes and find myself in a four-poster bed in an unknown room, it takes me a second to remember that I agreed to stay in Bennett's parents' vacation house. I sit up quickly and look around, then pat myself down once I realize I'm wearing the pajamas I'd packed. Who even changed me? Oh, my God. This is beyond mortifying. I swing my legs over the bed and head to the en suite bathroom I see open and notice all of my toiletries are out and displayed as if I'll be staying here all week and not just a drunken night. I brush my teeth quickly, shower because I swear I have alcohol coming out of my pores, and change into the easiest thing I can find—sweats and an oversized T-shirt that Devon wore when he was in college. I walk out of the room and roam the hallway, taking the stairs slowly as I keep my ears to the ground, in hopes to hear voices, preferably Nora and Devon's. Unfortunately, they sleep like the dead and probably won't be awake until this afternoon, and according to my watch it's only ten o'clock. Fuck my internal clock and its unwillingness to let me rest.

Once I'm on the first floor, I look around and follow my nose, the smell of bacon leading me to the kitchen. I freeze upon entering. Bennett's back is facing me. He's wearing a gray T-shirt that probably matches my own, though while mine fits me like a dress, his molds over his back and shoulder muscles. I clear my throat. He looks over his shoulder, one side of his lip tugging into a smile.

"I'm surprised you're awake."

"Did you sleep with me?"

"Seriously?" He chuckles, switching off the stove and moving the pan that's sizzling with bacon aside. He faces me fully, crossing his arms on his chest, the amusement never leaving his face. "How much of last night do you remember?"

"I remember telling you to get lost when you tracked me down in the bathroom like a creeper," I say. "Speaking of which, did you dress me in my pajamas and take out my freaking toiletries for me? Who does that, creeper?"

He starts to chuckle and it soon turns into a full-on belly laugh that I haven't heard very often, but man, it makes me want to turn into a comedian for a living. No. He's an asshole, I remind myself. A grade-A asshole, classic douchebag, total creeper.

"You unpacked your things," he says, still laughing. "You made a whole show of changing into your pajamas. You did a little striptease for me, which I would have fully appreciated, by the way, if you'd been sober and not started screaming at me and trying to throw punches when the zipper got tangled in your hair and I tried to help you."

"Oh." I frown. "I don't remember that."

"Pity." He turns around again and starts stacking the bacon

on a plate. "If you need something for your headache, I put a few bottles over on that counter." He nods with his head, not looking in my direction and suddenly all I want is for him to look in my direction.

"Thanks." I walk over, shake some pills onto my palm, and take a water bottle from the counter.

Instead of going back to the room I came from, I decide to sit down. Once you smell bacon, there's no way to ignore it. My stomach hasn't stopped growling since I came in here. As if reading my mind, he brings the plate over and sets it in front of me.

"I'm making toast and eggs. You want?"

"Yes, please." I lick my lips, watching him cook the rest of the meal in silence, enthralled with the way his arms move, the way he moves around the kitchen with such ease.

I always did like it when he made us breakfast, or lunch, or dinner, but I figured it was because he was taking on a task I didn't want. Now I realize it's more than that. It's the way he does things that I like, and the fact that he's doing them for me, without hesitation. I don't think I've really had that before. Even now, when he should absolutely be upset at me, he's making me breakfast. If the tables were turned, I'd let him starve. He returns with scrambled egg whites and toast on two separates plates, placing one in front of me and the other on the place setting a couple of chairs down from me. Definitely far enough that I know without a doubt he won't reach out and hold my hand, but still, he made me food.

"Why are you being nice to me?"

"You want me to be mean?"

"You said I tried to hit you last night and insulted you."

"You insulted me when you walked in here and insinuated I was a creep and potentially took advantage of you." He meets my gaze. "I understand you're mad and you think I'm a liar, but I'm not a bastard, Morgan. I would never do that to you or anyone."

"I know." I set my fork down, suddenly not as hungry as I was when I walked in here. "I'm sorry."

"So am I," he says, sighing. "Look, I've been thinking and maybe it's best we remain friends until after Devon and Nora's wedding."

I blink. "Oh. Okay."

"I just want to keep the peace, especially around their big day. They don't deserve to have to deal with our drama and we shouldn't bring that kind of vibe around them."

"I agree," I whisper, even though I'm not sure I do.

I was fully prepared to argue with him today, or maybe just talk things through. More than anything, I wanted him to prove me wrong about him. Friends is good though.

"You do?" he asks, his eyebrows pulling in.

For a second, I think he may retract his statement. I await it on bated breath. It was just last night that he told me he missed me, that he couldn't stand being away from me, but maybe that was a lie too. I force myself to eat half of the contents on my plate and clean up the rest quickly, washing the dishes and setting them on the drying rack. I dry my hands and toss the towel down as I make my way out of the kitchen again.

"Thanks for breakfast."

"Any time," he says, his jaw clenched.

He looks uncomfortable, but why? I shake the thought away as I walk out of the kitchen, glancing back one last time just as I round the corner to take the stairs, and catch him hanging his head between his arms.

CHAPTER FORTY-FOUR

BENNETT

AFTER A ROCKY NIGHT WITH MORGAN, I promised Devon I'd steer clear from her path until after the wedding.

"If you want to go after her, fine," he said, "but wait until after. I don't want my wedding to become a *Jerry Springer* episode. Nora doesn't deserve that."

He's right, of course. Not that I would ever let things escalate like that. Before last night I would have said Morgan wouldn't either, but now I'm not so sure. One second, she was fine and the next she was acting like she was in the middle of a war zone, with hundreds of people attacking her, when in fact, it was just me trying to help her get ready for bed. She'd slapped me, called me an asshole, a cheater, a liar. She'd told me she'd never trust me again and that nothing I told her would change her mind. I hated it. I hated the distance, the way she looked at me with distrust, the way she didn't argue when I said we should just remain friends for now.

It boggles my mind that she acted like she didn't care at all, when inside I am dying because I don't want to lose her. I've fallen in love with her and I don't want to let her go, but letting her go is the only thing I can do.

For now.

CHAPTER FORTY-FIVE

MORGAN

BENNETT: How's the class going?

My pulse quickens at the sight of his name on my screen. My brother and Nora's wedding is looming and I'm a few days away from finishing the gaming course. I haven't seen Bennett in a week and a half and the only indication as to how he's doing has been through the random text messages he's sent, like this one, which isn't saying much. The texts have been platonic and not very insightful as to how he's actually feeling, or more accurately, how he's feeling about us. Part of me is kind of grateful for that. The other part of me wishes like hell he'd say more, do more, because the more days that pass, the less I want this to end. I gather myself and text back.

Me: It's surprisingly fun

Bennett: I miss seeing you around SEVEN

I bite my lip, smiling, as I think of what to type.

Me: You only miss me because you don't have any friends there

Bennett: For this exact reason

My mood sours when I think about what Paola said during one of the first calls she made to SEVEN. She'd claimed Bennett had slept with all of his previous assistants and that it was the reason they were no longer there. Wesley claimed it was most likely a lie, but I never asked Bennett directly, and after the whole cheating thing I wish I had. It's not ideal, though, to have to ask someone direct questions in order to get answers they should be offering up regardless. Finally, my curiosity gets the best of me.

Me: Did you really sleep with your previous assistants?

Bennett: Absolutely not and you can ask every single one of them if it'll make you feel better

Me: That's the thing. I shouldn't have to.

I put my phone down and keep working on the homework assigned in today's class. When my phone rings again, it's a number I don't recognize, but an area code that automatically sends my heart racing.

"Hello?"

"Morgan. It's Mom."

"Mom?" My heart drops. "What's wrong? How did you get my number?"

"I'm . . . I need help."

"What kind of help? What happened? Where are you?"

"Rodney's house. I moved in last week."

"Okay," I say warily because she sounds off. "Are you . . . using?"

"Not. Not yet. I haven't, I swear, but I want to. I really want to, Morgie." She starts to audibly cry and I swear the sound feels like a sharp object to my heart. "I called my sponsor. I called Devon but he's not answering. I'm out of options."

"I'm thousands of miles away." I close my eyes. "I . . . what am I supposed to do?"

Not to mention, I swore her out of my life. I don't say that because it feels like a trigger and I wouldn't forgive myself if I was the reason she went over the edge again, especially with Devon's wedding looming over us.

"I don't know," she whispers after a moment.

"Where's Rodney?"

"Out of the country for work."

"I . . . " I bury my face in my hands. Even if I do go, I'd miss the next two classes and I don't know what that would mean for the class in its entirety, but if I don't go, she'll call Devon and he has too much on his plate as it is. I'll just have to do this the way I did all those times growing up—by myself. "I can be over there tonight. Will you be okay until tonight? I'll drive you to the place we took you to last time. You liked that place. It had pretty gardens and yoga."

"Yeah."

"It'll be like a spa weekend."

"I'd like that."

"But you cannot use, Mom. You can't. No matter how tempting it is, you can't use before I get there."

"Okay. I won't."

Despite myself, I feel tears prick my eyes. We both know what I'm asking is impossible, but if she makes it, if she's able to keep from using until I get there it will make all of the difference.

"I'm going to hang up now. I'll be there tonight."

"Tonight," she repeats.

I hang up quickly because I can't stand the despondence in her voice. It's still early enough that I can pass by SEVEN and catch Mr. Cruz there. I hate that I have to do this, but I don't see any other option, so I pack a few quick things in an overnight bag and head over there, with my mother on my mind. If she goes into rehab tomorrow, there's no way she's making it to Devon's wedding. It's cutting it too close. The last time she went to rehab we couldn't even speak to her until she had detoxed and was in there a couple of weeks. I bite the tip of my thumb to keep from crying. Devon will be so disappointed. Despite all of her flaws, he really loves her and wants her by his side through it all.

Thankfully, Mr. Cruz is still at work when I finally get there. I knock on the door after Patty tells me he's in there, and he calls out for me to step inside. I do, freezing when I see Bennett sitting down across from him, much like that first day I arrived here, but this time I catch them both off guard.

"I'm so sorry to interrupt your meeting," I say, keeping my eyes on Mr. Cruz. "I need to speak to you."

"Of course. Please, come in. Ben, I'll see you later?" He frowns, looking at his son, his expression clearly dismissing him.

Bennett stands slowly and walks over to where I am by the door. I keep my eyes on the floor as he nears, unable to meet his gaze. If I do, I'll break down. I know myself. Despite everything, right now, I want nothing more than to have his arms around me, shielding me from the cruelty of the world, from its harsh realities that seem to drop without warning.

"You okay?" he whispers.

I nod, still not looking at him. He seems to get the point and finally walks out and closes the door behind him, leaving emptiness in his wake.

"Please, sit down," Mr. Cruz says.

"Thank you." I lick my lips, walking up and taking the chair Bennett just cleared. "I'm so sorry to barge in here like this."

"Stop apologizing. What do you need? Is it the class?"

"No. The class is perfect. It's awesome." I close my eyes

and will myself not to cry. "I know this is awful timing, but I need a few days off. My mom just called and . . ." I gasp for air, but instead of holding back tears, I start to cry with absolutely no warning at all. "She's an addict. Was an addict. *Is* an addict," I say. "I guess once an addict, always an addict, but she's had her shit together for two years and she just called me and she's spiraling. I can hear it in her voice and Devon's wedding is coming up and he has all this crap going on and I don't want him to worry about this on top of all of that—" I bury my face in my hands. "I know you ask Devon about her but he's embarrassed to say any of this to people, especially you and Barbara and Bennett, who seem to have the perfect family."

"You do what you need to do, Morgan." Mr. Cruz gets up from his chair and walks around his desk. He places a hand on my shoulder. "Does Bennett know any of this?"

"He knows some, but not the part about her spiraling. It just happened and I just . . . I need time."

"I understand." Mr. Cruz steps back and looks at me with the most compassionate expression I've ever seen. "Listen, you go do what you need to do. I would appreciate it if you let Bennett know about all of this because I know he'll be worried sick, but I understand if you need a breather before doing that."

"Thank you. I'll take my computer and work remotely for now. I promise I won't drop the ball."

"Morgan, we've all been there. Maybe not what you're dealing with specifically, but we all have families and families bring complications. Take the time you need. If you need anything from me or Barbara, please let us know."

"I will. Thank you so much." I start to cry again. "I'm sorry. It's just, I've never had people who seem to genuinely care like this. I mean, aside from Devon."

"Well, you do now. I'll tell you the same thing I told your

brother when I first met him: you're family now. No matter what. No matter what happens between you and my son, you'll always be family. I mean that."

Somehow, I manage to smile, and I force myself to walk out of his office before I completely lose it and start bawling again. I grab my laptop, my purse, and walk out.

CHAPTER FORTY-SIX

I HAVE the driver drop me off at the address my mom sent me and stand outside of the gate for a full minute before ringing the bell. It's the kind of mansion that looks like it could be featured on *Million Dollar Homes*, with iron gates, a circular driveway, and a fountain with an angel shooting water out of his trumpet. This is definitely not the kind of man Mom usually goes for. I assume he's old and boring, because if he's not, I don't think he'd be with Mom. I take a deep breath and push the doorbell. A light flickers above the bell, a camera. I do a little wave and the gates go into motion, creaking gently as they open up toward the house. Hiking my bag on my shoulder, I make the trek to the front door, which I can tell from here is massive and much like the gate, covered in ornate gold that weaves into what looks like two doves. Either this Rodney guy bought the house from the pope or he's extremely religious. By the time I reach the front door, it's opened for me. A man stands on the other side with a kind smile and kind eyes, but he's definitely too old for Mom, and dressed in a butler's outfit.

"Your mother is in her bedroom," he says as he holds the door open. "I'm Ramses."

"Nice to meet you." I walk inside and stand in the middle of the lavish entryway. Devon and Nora have a pretty nice house in Boston, but this is unlike anything I've ever seen in person, with a double staircase that curves on either side of where I stand.

"This way," Ramses says. I follow along quickly, taking the stairs behind him. We come to a stop in front of a large glossy wooden door, and he knocks. "Ms. Tucker, your daughter is here." He turns back to me. "She won't open the door for any of us. She has asked only for you or Sir Rodney, but he won't be back in until tomorrow evening."

"I'll be needing to take her away," I say quietly. "I don't have a car, but—"

"Sir Rodney would like you to take one of his. I'll have it out front when you're ready. The missus doesn't want to accept his money, but he will have nothing of it. He insists on paying for any treatment she may need for as long as she needs it," he says, lowering his voice. "Sir Rodney lost his wife five years ago to addiction. As a recovering addict himself, he knows how difficult this is and he genuinely cares for your mother."

I nod slowly, everything becoming a little clearer now. I glance back at the door and wait for Ramses to leave before turning the knob and pushing it open slightly. The room is cloaked in darkness, despite it still being daylight outside. I walk forward.

"Mom?"

"Morgan." Her voice breaks upon saying my name. "You came."

"I told you I would." I walk over to the foot of the bed in the center. Even this looks like it belongs in Versailles. "You . . . how did you . . . how have you been holding up?"

"I'm okay," she says, her voice soft. "I haven't used. My sponsor was on the phone with me for two hours. I feel a little settled."

I walk over to the windows and pull the curtains open, squinting at the blinding light that floods the room. Turning around, I catch the first real glimpse of my mother and can't help but gasp. She looks like hell. Her eyes are puffy and red, her hair is messy, she has no makeup on, which wouldn't normally matter if it weren't for the state she's in. Despite the hell she's put me through, it breaks my heart to see her this way. I expect my anger to kick in, the way it often does, but it never comes. Maybe it's because I've grown up. When I was a teenager and she hit rock-bottom, as she calls it, I was scared and alone and confused and angry because parents weren't supposed to leave their children to fend for themselves. Now that I've lived a little more, met different people, experienced life a little deeper, I see this entire situation differently. My mother looks small and fragile, like a child. Her eyes are wary as I make my way to her, sitting down beside her on the edge of the bed. While I was still living at home, Mom tried to seek help three times and wasn't able to remain sober. Each time she fell back into it was linked to some kind of trigger—her on-and-off boyfriend leaving a final time, Devon leaving for school, and me being accepted into an out-of-state university. When I finally did leave, I visited often so she'd see that I wasn't abandoning her, and that was when I found out she'd been sleeping with the only guy I allowed myself to open up to. Being back here now, under these circumstances, brings back all of those memories. I try to push them away, to not give into the pain building inside me, but it's impossible.

"Do you want to talk about it?" I whisper. "You were doing well."

"After I saw you that night, I started thinking about what you said, and I don't know." She shrugs a slim shoulder. "You wrote me off. Your own mother. I started thinking about all of the things I've done throughout the years—the things I remember anyway—the things I've been told I've said and done, and I'm not okay." Her voice breaks. She blinks, letting tears trickle down her cheeks. "I'm not okay, Morgan. I thought I was. I met this amazing man who's willing to stand by me, who's welcomed me into his house without second thought, but I lost my family. I lost my baby girl. I'm losing my son soon."

It occurs to me that everything I felt during Devon's bachelor party wasn't dissimilar to what my mother may be feeling right now. I put my hand over hers. It's the first time I've had any physical contact with my mother in as long as I can remember. Vada Adams was never a physical person, not in love nor in discipline. It's a wonder my brother has always been so affectionate. It's a wonder I welcome it as well as I do. She lets out a strangled sob, her shoulders shaking as she holds my hand back in a tight grip.

"I'm so sorry for everything," she whispers.

I look down at our hands, because what else can I do? Despite my being here, I'm not sure I'm any closer to forgiving her than I was the last time I saw her. I'd like to say I'm a big person who can forgive and move on, but I'm not. I think about Bennett and how much it still hurts when I imagine playing a part in the demise of his marriage and my lip begins to quiver.

"Let's pack your bags. We'll leave first thing in the morning." I let go of her hand and stand up. "Where are your clothes? The closet?"

"Yes," she says. I walk in that direction and switch the lights on.

"Holy shit." My mouth drops as I take in the entirety of the closet. "This is the size of my bedroom."

"Rodney designed it."

"He's very . . . extra." I cringe the minute the words leave my mouth. What if he records the conversations in his house? "What does he do anyway?"

"He owns a successful production company."

"Oh. Wow. Must be really successful," I muse as I go through her things. She has more clothes here than I could ever dream of owning. I search for loungewear, which for my mother means gym clothes. She doesn't really believe in lounging comfortably.

"He's also a philanthropist. He's in Venezuela right now helping people get out."

"How did you guys meet?" I ask, because let's be honest, how would a successful producer who happens to also be a philanthropist end up with a woman who runs her own prostitution company?

"Philanthropic producers also like to fuck, you know."

"I know, but I wouldn't think he'd keep you around." I glance up to see her walking into the closet. "No offense."

"None taken." She smiles, though it doesn't reach her eyes. She looks so tired, so sad. "Truth is, sometimes two people from entirely different worlds meet and just click, and that's what happened with us. We met in a casino and started talking and much to my dismay, he didn't try to take me back to his room. He bought me dinner instead."

"Why didn't you go with him on his trip?"

"No passport." She shrugs.

That doesn't surprise me. The only reason I have a passport is because my friends and I went to Mexico for spring break in college. Otherwise, I still wouldn't have one. Mom helps me pack the rest of her things in silence. She falls asleep easily and

I decide to slip out of her room when I feel like it's safe to. I feel exhausted, but I know there's no way I'll get any rest tonight. Instead of sleeping, I open my computer and start working on some of the things Mr. Cruz and I spoke about during our meeting, mostly jotting down ideas for apps and things social media should take a look at once we start this campaign.

The following morning, Ramses helps us put our things in the car. As I get into the driver's seat, it hits me that this is definitely the most luxurious car I have ever driven. I'll probably only be comfortable driving it at turtle-speed because a scratch on this baby will probably cost what I make in a year. Ramses comes around to the driver's seat. I lower my window.

"Sir Rodney will fly directly to Los Angeles."

"So I leave the car there? At the facility?"

"That'll do," he says. "Sir Rodney knows the owner. It won't be a problem."

"Okay," I say. "Thanks, Ramses. It was nice to meet you."

He smiles. "Likewise. Maybe we'll see you again around here."

I smile back but don't respond. I can't imagine ever coming back here. When I start the car, the radio is set to a Christian station.

"He's very religious," I say as I drive out of the gates.

"He's not religious. He believes in the Word. There's a difference."

"If you say so."

I'm not going to sit here and argue religion when I'm driving my mother to rehab. Besides, the music is catchy and soothing.

"You didn't tell your brother you were coming," Mom says.

"He's getting married in less than a week. I didn't think it would be fair to drag him into this. As it is, he doesn't even want my boyfriend to try to get back together with me until after the wedding because he doesn't want the vibe to be less than perfect."

Mom snorts. "He should start burning sage in the morning."

I glance over. "Are you kidding? Nora does that every morning, and now he does too."

Mom laughs, shaking her head, then stops laughing suddenly and starts crying. The amount of emotions she experiences within the minute is jarring. I turn the music a little louder in hopes that it soothes her, but all it seems to do is make her cry harder.

"I'm a total screwup," she says. "How did I go from having a good bank teller job to this?"

"Mom, I know you're having a moment right now, but we're literally driving a two-hundred-thousand-dollar car right now. You live in a mansion and your boyfriend wants to be there for you. He wants you to count on him. I think you're doing okay."

"I don't have you. Your brother is starting his own family now. He already doesn't call much. Once they start having kids I'll probably never hear from him."

"I'm trying to be nice, but honestly, we didn't exactly grow up in a great family environment."

"I know," she wails. "And that's my fault."

I bite my lip. I can't really argue that.

"Do you think you'll ever forgive me? For Justin?"

I take a deep breath and let it out. "I don't know."

After that, she's quiet. Somewhere in the four-hour drive, she falls asleep and stays asleep. My phone starts to buzz, but I ignore it. I'm too paranoid, driving this expensive car, to even attempt a phone conversation right now. Especially if it's Devon.

CHAPTER FORTY-SEVEN

I STOP to put in gas, end up having to Google how to do it, and book a hotel in Los Angeles on my phone while I'm at it. I also look at my missed calls and see one from Bennett. My first thought is: Great, his dad told him what happened. My second is: Oh, shit, I hope he didn't call Devon. Either way, he called two hours ago, which means it's too late to worry about either.

By the time we reach Los Angeles, it's past lunch and I'm starving, but I refuse to stop until I get to the treatment facility. When I do, I wake up my mom and grab her bag. She starts crying again and maybe it's because I'm tired or because I've heard her crying on and off since I got her phone call, but I can't wait to get inside and drop her off. She sits beside me as I fill out papers, her knee bouncing the entire time.

"You did the right thing," I tell her. "You didn't cave."

"But I would have."

"But you didn't." I glance over and meet her gaze. Her eyes look haunted, as if she's barely there.

"I still want to."

"Well, it's a good thing we're here, then."

I go back to the papers in front of me. They call her name. We both stand up. I grab her bag and walk alongside her toward the nurse, who leads us to an office and tells us the doctor will be right in. We take a seat. Mom is still shaking. I stop writing notes on the admittance papers and look at her.

"Mom, are you sure you did not take anything?"

She shakes her head, but I'm starting to doubt my own ability to read whether or not she's high. Maybe I've been away from this too long and somehow forgot? The door opens and a lady about Mom's age, wearing a comforting smile and lab coat, walks inside.

"I'm Dr. Pierce. You must be Vada Adams," she says, looking at Mom. "We got a call from Rodney earlier about your arrival."

Mom shoots her a distrusting look. "How do you know Rodney?"

"He's been here once or twice."

"Did you fuck him?"

"Mom." My eyes widen. I hold back on reminding her she slept with her own daughter's boyfriend even though it's on the tip of my tongue.

She looks at me. "He's a very handsome man."

"I was his doctor, Ms. Adams," Dr. Pierce says, taking a seat behind her desk. "I can assure you we keep things professional in this facility."

"She's been here before," I say.

"Oh." Dr. Pierce raises her eyebrows. She opens up the chart in her hand. "How long has it been? Two years?"

"One year and nine months," Mom says.

"And you have not used," Dr. Pierce says, glancing at me for confirmation.

"She says she hasn't. She called me yesterday, but this is the soonest I was able to bring her," I explain. "I don't know if she used."

"I didn't," Mom says loudly. "I told you I didn't."

I sigh.

"Since she's been here before, I'm assuming you're familiar with our schedule and visitation," Dr. Pierce says. "We like to wait a week before allowing visitors to come back. During that week, she'll be in therapy and detox."

"I live three thousand miles away. It's kind of difficult for me to visit."

"You're not coming back?" Mom asks, her eyes filling with tears. "You're just going to leave me here?"

"You need to get better."

"I'll miss the wedding. Devon's counting on me to walk him down the aisle. I'll look like a deadbeat mother. He'll never forgive me," she says quickly.

"Devon will be happy to hear you acted responsibly and asked for help before doing anything stupid," I assure her.

"And you? Where will you be?"

"I need to go home. I need to get back to work."

"You won't come visit me. You won't forgive me." She reaches for my hand and squeezes it. "You'll never forgive me."

"Let's focus on getting you better, okay?"

"I want my family back. I want my children back."

"We'll all be in touch," Dr. Pierce says. "I'll keep your kids updated as well as Rodney."

"What have I done?" Mom yanks her hand away from mine and buries her face in both hands.

I put my hand on her shoulder. "It's never too late to get your shit together."

She nods but keeps her face buried. Dr. Pierce and I discuss her treatments a little longer. When we finish, we all stand up, and the same nurse comes to escort her away. Mom throws her arms around me and holds me tightly, burying her face in my neck.

"I don't want this to be the last time I see you. I'm sorry for what I did. I'm sorry for not knowing the right way to be a mother. I'm sorry for not being there. Please don't leave me."

"I'll be around." I swallow the lump in my throat. "I'll come back."

She pulls away. "You promise?"

"Sure. You can introduce me to your new boyfriend so I can make sure he's not Batman."

She smiles, laughing a little. "Okay."

"Okay."

"Thank you for coming for me."

"You're my blood, remember?" I swallow.

She blinks rapidly and turns to walk away. I wait until she disappears down the hall before walking back to the lobby and out to the parking lot. My heart feels heavier with each step I take. I glance over my shoulder at the building one last time, biting my lip to keep from breaking down, though I'm sure I wouldn't be the first or last person to do so here. I'm about to cross the street to the parking lot when a black car pulls up and stops beside me. The back door opens and I watch as Bennett gets out with a bag in his hand. I'm so shocked that I have to do a triple take.

"Bennett?"

He walks over as the car drives away. "I came as soon as I heard."

"How did you even find me?"

"My dad told me what happened and I remembered the

place," he says. "I came here with Devon once when he had a game out here."

"But . . . " My mouth drops. "Did you call him? Does he know you're here?"

"I didn't call him. Not yet."

"I can't . . . " I bring my hands up to my face, where I feel tears wetting my cheeks. "I'm sorry, I can't process this right now."

He wraps his arms around me and holds me tightly as I cry onto his chest. I focus on breathing him in, on the fact that he's actually here, that I'm no longer alone in this, but I can't seem to stop crying long enough to focus on those things.

"You shouldn't have to go through this alone," he says. "Do you already have a place to stay?"

"Yes." I cry harder. "I got a shitty hotel down the street. If I'd known you were coming I would've picked something nicer."

"I don't care where we stay." He chuckles, kissing the top of my head. "As long as I'm with you."

CHAPTER FORTY-EIGHT

"THIS IS DEFINITELY the shittiest hotel I've ever stayed in," Bennett says later.

We're lying in the middle of an uncomfortable bed, where I feel every single spring stabbing me every time I move. We haven't even undressed, haven't kissed, haven't done anything beyond hold each other and talk about the whole thing with my mom. A part of me wonders if he was serious about us just being friends and that's why he hasn't even tried to kiss me, but then he looks at me in a way that makes my heart flip and I know that's not the case. He readjusts and reaches for his cell phone.

"How mad will you be if you lose the forty dollars you spent on this room?"

"Honestly? Not that mad." I laugh. "You can just buy me dinner and we'll call it even."

"Good." He clicks and clicks and tosses his phone aside. "Let's get out of this shithole."

WE END up in the Chateau Marmont and as he checks in with the front desk, I'm watching everyone like a hawk in case I see any famous people. I tell Bennett this as we walk to our room.

"Did you see anyone?"

"I don't think so." I frown. "It occurred to me as I looked around the lobby that I don't know what anyone looks like in their regular clothes."

"I'll be sure to let you know if I see anyone." He laughs, bringing an arm around me and pulling me into his side. "Are you too tired to go get dinner?"

"Definitely not. I haven't been here since I was a kid and I kind of want to take advantage."

When he drops his arm to open the door, I try not to dwell on how much I want to be in his arms again. The room isn't a fancy suite like the one we had in Vegas, but it's a billion times better than the one we just came from. We get ready in silence. He gives me my space in the bathroom and I give him his. I appreciate it because it gives me a chance to process everything that's happened in the past twenty-four hours. I decide to lie down while I wait for him to finish getting ready and evidently fall asleep because when I open my eyes again, it's completely dark out. I sit up quickly, checking the time and realize it's only eight-thirty. Bennett is sitting at the desk, typing on his laptop. I watch him for a silent moment. He has the perfect facial features and the most intense expression on his face as he reads whatever is on his screen. I decide to stop doing the creeper thing and clear my throat before I speak up.

"You should've woken me up."

"You were tired." He glances over his shoulder momentarily before closing the computer and walking over to the bed. He sits on the edge, and reaches out to brush my hair out of my face. "You sure you want to go somewhere? We can order room service."

My shoulders sag. "I'm leaving tomorrow afternoon and I haven't really seen anything."

"So we get up early," he says.

"You look hot though."

He chuckles. "I'll look just as hot tomorrow."

"So arrogant." I grin, reaching up to tap the tip of his nose. He takes my hand and our smiles drop. The air shifts between us, our amusement replaced by something else. I squeeze his hand. "Thank you for coming. I really did not expect that."

"You don't have to thank me, Morgan. I wanted to be here." He tilts his head. "I want to be where you are all the time."

"We need to talk." I feel myself smile. I sit up, Indian style, in front of him.

"Let's talk."

"I was really upset with you for lying to me," I start, "But I'm over it. I mean, I don't want you to lie to me again, but I don't believe any of what she told me. I knew deep down that she was lying about the baby and about you guys working things out if it weren't for me."

"I swear that when I met you, my marriage was one-hundred-percent over," he says, "I wasn't divorced, but we were finished and she knew that."

"I believe you. I just wish you'd told me sooner."

"I wish I had too." He scoots closer to me. "I'm sorry I didn't."

"I've never had anyone go out of their way to be here for me on a day like today."

"If you'd told me, I would've dropped everything and come

sooner. Even as your friend I would've done that." He searches my eyes. "I mean that."

"Is that what you want? For us to stay friends?" I whisper.

"No, but if you don't want to pursue this with me and you just want us to stay friends, I'd deal with it because I just want to spend time with you."

"Even without having sex?"

He squeezes his eyes shut momentarily. "I mean, I would think about it a lot, but yeah, even without having sex."

I laugh. "What if I start dating someone else? Would you want to go on double dates?"

"Would you?" He raises an eyebrow.

"No." I scowl. "I would hate that."

"Yeah?" He scoots closer, until his nose is almost touching mine. "Why is that?"

"I don't like the idea of you being with another woman."

"I don't like the idea of you being with another man." He taps his nose against mine in an Eskimo kiss. "Quite the dilemma we're in."

"Only if you don't want to be with me."

"Are you kidding?" He chuckles, pulling away slightly, and bringing a hand to cup the side of my face. "In case I need to spell it out, I'm completely in love with you, Morgan Elizabeth."

For a solid moment, my heart feels like it might just burst. Somehow, I manage to keep from externally screaming and jumping on the bed, and continue holding his gaze. He leans in close again, his lips almost touching mine.

"Hey, Ben," I whisper.

"Hm."

"I love you too."

He finally brings his lips to mine. The kiss is slow and delicate, his tongue sliding slowly into my mouth to meet mine as his hand caresses the side of my face. The growl of my stomach reminding me I haven't had anything to eat breaks our kiss. He smiles against my mouth.

"Let's get you something to eat."

CHAPTER FORTY-NINE

BENNETT

NEITHER ONE OF us eats much even though the food is great. The wine is even better. Morgan is sitting across from me, staring at me as she drinks, as if she can't really believe I'm actually here. I guess the feeling is sort of mutual. The minute my father called me and told me what was happening, I dropped everything and took the first flight available. Had she told me what was happening instead of telling my father, I would've traveled with her. The thought of her alone on that flight and taking care of her mother once she got there was heartbreaking. I understand why she wouldn't want to tell Devon right now, since his wedding is approaching quickly, but I hate that she thinks she has to carry the burden alone. More than anything, I hate that she's had to all these years.

"Penny for your thoughts," she says.

"I was just thinking about how amazing you are. How strong. And how I want you to share your burdens with me so they won't feel so heavy on your shoulders."

"Oh." She blinks, setting her glass down and pushing her

chair back to walk over to where I'm sitting. She stands between my legs, brings a hand up and runs her fingers through my hair, tilting my head back with a tug at the end. "And here I was thinking that you were thinking about fucking me."

"I'm always thinking about fucking you." I reach up, cupping the back of her neck and bringing her face to mine. Instead of kissing her, I press my lips to her jaw and work my way down her neck, sucking on the spot where her pulse is quickening. "Let's get you out of these clothes."

I tug the tie of her dress, feeling my own pulse kick when the dress curtains open in front of her body, revealing her bare breasts and her tiny red lace underwear. I flatten my palms on her abdomen and make my way up to her breasts, squeezing them as I lean forward and cover her left nipple with my mouth, sucking and biting, before moving onto the other. Her grip on my hair tightens as she gasps. I do it again, and again, and again. Her tugs get harder, her gasps louder.

"I've missed you so much," I say against her flesh, tugging her underwear slowly down her legs. She kicks them away. I bring my attention back to her lips, kissing her slowly, pushing my tongue inside her mouth. A groan escapes me as we kiss and suddenly I need to taste her everywhere. The need to make up for lost time blinds me with lust. I break the kiss and make my way down her body as she reaches to unbutton my shirt. I reach around her and push the empty plate in front of me to the other side of the table before lifting her onto it and burying my face between her legs. I don't waste time teasing because I'm sure how long I'd last tonight. I've spent too many days without her. "I love the taste of you on my tongue," I say as I lick her. "Love the way you move against my mouth."

"Bennett," she sighs, throwing her head back as she grinds against my mouth, chasing her orgasm.

I suck her clit and am rewarded with the convulsion that's only made better by the chant of my name. I stand up, carrying her to the bed and tossing her onto it. She places her elbows on it and sits up to watch as I unfasten my jeans, lowering them along with my boxer-briefs. I push her legs apart and kneel between them, running the tips of my fingers along her legs and stopping at her clit. Her eyes widen, another gasp escaping her lips as I reach her clit and rub with my thumb, dipping two fingers inside of her. She brings a hand between us and closes it around my cock, moving it up and down in a rhythm that makes a burn run down my spine and straight to my balls. She cries out, her hand increasing the movement as she comes again, and it takes everything in me to unwrap her hand. Before she can fully come down from her orgasm, I thrust inside her, grabbing her hips tightly and holding her there as my cock pulses inside her.

"Bennett," she pleads, trying to grind against me. I hold her steady, not letting her move. "Ben. Please."

"Give me a moment, baby. It's been too long since I last had you and I need time to convince myself this is real."

"It's real. It's so real," she whispers. "I love you."

I bite down on my lip, shutting my eyes briefly, relishing this moment. When I open them, I meet her gaze. "Say it again."

"I love you," she says. "I love you."

Then, I start to fuck her, driving into her hard and fast, spreading her legs wide, opening her as much as her body will allow her. With each stroke, she screams my name. Each scream making my balls tighten. She's so wet and I'm so out of control that I can barely focus on her face. I reach up and pinch her nipples, and she arches into my touch, the movement giving me deeper access to her.

"Bennett, Bennett, please," she pants. "Please. Oh my . . . I'm going to . . . I'm so . . . "

I pound in harder, digging my nails into her waist, groaning her name as she explodes all over me and I follow shortly after. Yeah, there's no fucking way I'm giving this up again.

CHAPTER FIFTY

MORGAN

I WALK into my apartment with a huge smile on my face and drop the bag on the floor by the door, tossing the keys on the kitchen counter. The television is set on ESPN, of course, so I know Devon is already here.

"Oh, look who's finally home," Devon calls out.

I roll my eyes. "I'm too exhausted to argue right now."

"Too bad." He stands up from the couch and walks over to me, arms crossed. "What the fuck were you thinking?"

"I was thinking that I've done this before and you're getting married in less than a week—the last thing I want to do is stress you out with anything. Besides, they don't let you take sage on airplanes, so you wouldn't have survived the trip."

He stares at me for a beat before breaking out in laughter. "Fuck you. Sage is great for your energy. I should've brought extra to burn it in Bennett's apartment while I'm here."

"He will lose it." I smile thinking about it.

"I can't believe you didn't call me, Morg."

"I was fine. It was fine." I shrug. "Bennett showed up on his own. He said he'd been there with you once when you played a game out there."

"Yeah." He shakes his head. "Damn, that guy has the memory of an elephant."

"Anyway, Mom's fine. She said she hadn't used when I got there, but she was acting weird so there's really no telling," I say. "And her boyfriend is loaded. Like more loaded than you are."

Devon scoffs. "Yeah, right."

"I'm serious. I drove a Bentley from Vegas to LA and that was like a side car. His house is insane, like gold everywhere."

He frowns. "What's he doing with Mom?"

"That's exactly what I said." I shrug. "She said they click."

"Yeah, she clicks with that bank account."

I laugh. "Whatever. She seems happy despite this episode."

Dev looks like he doesn't believe me. "Obviously she's not coming to the wedding."

"I don't think so." I offer a small smile. "I can walk you down the aisle if you want. I mean, you'll have to return the favor if I ever marry Bennett."

His eyebrows hike up. "You guys went from not talking at all to talking marriage?"

"We worked things out."

"Shit, I hope so after he chased you to the other side of the country to hold your hand through this shit." He blinks. "I still can't believe you didn't call me."

"I'm sorry I didn't call you, okay? But look at the way you're acting. If you'd gone, you would've been screaming at Rodney's butler and stuff."

"He has a butler?"

"I swear he's like Batman or something."

He chuckles. "I hope he's not your type. How awkward would that be?"

"Oh, please." I roll my eyes. "I'm not Mom."

He cringes. I shrug. I'm over it. Well, as over it as I can be.

"So you and Bennett, huh," he says. "I guess that's good. Saves us from having to pay an extra setting at the wedding."

I snort. "Right, because you're so tight on cash."

"Nah, you're right, especially with my bangin' new contract."

"What do you mean?" I frown, trying to catch a glimpse of the television to see if he's telling the truth. If he is, I know they'd be talking about it.

"You know how I was a free agent?"

"Yeah, not that I really know what that means, but what about it?"

"I signed a new contract with a new team."

"Oh, God." My heart sinks. "Where are you going now?"

"Here, dummy. I'm coming home."

"What?" I shout. "No way. You're lying."

"Not lying." He laughs. "I'm seriously coming home."

"Oh, my God." I launch myself at him, throwing my arms around his neck. "I'm so, so, so, so happy. Now I don't have to pretend to like your stupid team."

He laughs. "You never pretended to like them."

"You're right." I squeal, letting go of him. "Oh, my gosh, I'm so excited. What number will you be? Do you get to pick? Wait, are you moving back in here?"

"That's one of the things I wanted to talk to you about. I don't mind us all living here for a little while, but I was thinking I could get you your own place. There's a unit in this building—"

"Nope." I put a hand up. "First of all, I love you, but no, thank you. I can afford my own place. Second of all, I'm moving in with Bennett."

He stares at me. "What do you mean?"

"We're moving in together."

"You . . . you're serious."

"Of course I'm serious. Why wouldn't I be serious?"

He frowns, taking his phone out and typing something. He puts it up to his ear. "Hey, yeah, thanks. I know. I'm glad to be back. Eh, Nora likes it here. She'll get used to it. Right. Actually, I wanted to talk to you about Morgan." He looks at me.

My mouth drops. "Devon."

"Yeah, no, she's standing right here talking about moving in with you—"

"Devon, I swear to God." I launch myself at him, reaching for the phone, but he dodges every attempt and continues talking as if nothing is happening.

"I love you, you're my brother, but I swear if I see my baby sister cry again, I'll kill you," he says in the most nonchalant tone. I stop fighting him and stare at him again. I'm going to kill him for this. "Yep. See you tomorrow."

I take a step back and cover my mouth. "I can't believe you just said that."

"I had to warn him."

"Yeah, but we haven't talked about moving in together again after we got back together. Oh, my God I'm going to kill you in your sleep."

"Sure." He laughs.

"I'll take all the sage you brought and flush it down the toilet."

His expression turns serious. "Don't you fucking dare."

My phone vibrates in the back pocket of my jeans. I take it out and look at it.

Bennett: I heard we're moving in together

Me: I'm going to kill him

Bennett: I want to

Bennett: Move in with you, not kill your brother

Me: Okay good.

Bennett: Want me to come help you pack?

Me: Right now?

Bennett: Why not?

Me: Because we just got back from an exhausting trip and we have all the time in the world to pack and move?

Bennett: Fine, then I'll just come over because I can't stand the thought of not sharing a bed with you another night

Me: Okay : -)

I put my phone back in my pocket.

"You're smiling," Devon says. "What did he say? He's coming over?"

"Yeah."

"Yes." He lifts a fist in the air. "I brought *Madden*."

I groan. "You're joking."

"Hey, that's what you get for dating my best friend." He shrugs. "Now you have to compete for his affection."

I laugh at his ridiculousness and go to my room to unwind. I fall asleep before Bennett gets there, but wake up to the feel of his arm wrapping around me and his mouth on my shoulder.

"Did you play *Madden* already?" I turn in his arms and face him.

"Not yet. I wanted to kiss my girl before I kick his ass."

"Hm."

He kisses me, a sweet peck on the lips, and then my eyelids and cheeks.

"I love you, baby."
"I love you," I murmur.
I fall asleep smiling.

CHAPTER FIFTY-ONE

BENNETT

I SLIDE into the booth with two drinks in my hand, sliding one to the beautiful woman sitting across from me.

"Thanks," she says, looking around. "This seems like a good place to pick up women."

"If I came in here, you'd be the only woman I'd look at."

"You're just saying that because I'm the one sitting across from you," she says, smiling. She glances out the window. "It's such a pretty day."

"It's a beautiful day to get married."

Her gaze flashes back to mine. "That was random."

"Was it?" I frown. "Because ever since you moved in with me, the only thing I seem to think about is marrying you."

"Wha . . . what? We've only been living together for like four weeks."

I shrug. "I've been struck with Cupid's arrow."

"You're . . . are you serious right now?" She searches my face.

"Dead serious."

"Are you proposing to me?" she asks, frowning.

"I'm proposing we go down to the courthouse and get married."

"Today," she says, as if she's still trying to wrap her head around this.

"We took the day off. We're sitting at a bar with alcoholic beverages in our hands at ten o'clock."

"Mimosas," she says. "You make it sound like we're having whiskey straight."

"What's the difference?"

"Mimosas are acceptable at ten o'clock in the morning."

"Let's ditch this place and go get married, Morgan Elizabeth." I reach for her other hand. "It's going to happen anyway, whether we do it today, tomorrow, in twenty years, so why beat around the bush?"

She's quiet for a long moment, just staring at me, as if she's mulling over every single scenario. If she says no, I'll accept that. Maybe she wants me to propose with a grand gesture or plan a formal wedding like Devon and Nora. Maybe she wants to wait a couple of years. Either way, I'm not going anywhere.

"Hey, Ben," she says after a while.

"Yeah?"

"Let's go get married."

EPILOGUE

ONE YEAR LATER . . .

Morgan

MY MOTHER HAS BEEN in and out of rehab since I dropped her off, not because she's been using, but because she's had weak moments. Weak moments that Devon and I have been with her for. We all started family counseling. At first, I thought it was ridiculous, us going all the way out to California once a month for counseling with someone we didn't even live with. It turned out to be the best thing we could've done for ourselves and our family.

Mom and I aren't best friends by any stretch, but we are definitely closer. We speak on the phone almost daily, and I'm not the least bit threatened whenever she asks about Bennett, which was a big no-no in the beginning. I trust Bennett, but it has been really hard to let go of past grudges, even if they were things that had absolutely nothing to do with him.

Bennett whistles as we stop in front of Rodney's house. "This is the place?"

"Yep."

"He must own a very successful production company."

I laugh. "He does."

He glances over at me. "You sure you're ready to be back here?"

"I'm ready." I reach out and thread my fingers through his. "As long as you're with me."

He grins, bringing my hand up and pressing a kiss to it. "Always."

We walk up to the house and are greeted by my mother, who's wearing a pretty spring dress and a huge smile on her face. She throws her arms around me.

"Thank you for coming. I'm so happy you're here." She pulls back, holding my hands as she looks at my face before turning to Bennett. "She's such a beautiful girl."

"The most beautiful girl," he says, grinning at me before kissing my mom on the cheek. "You look well."

"Oh, I feel so great. Yoga has done wonders for me." She steps back. "Please come in. Make yourselves at home. Rod will be in later on. He had a corporate golf tournament today that he, unfortunately, couldn't back out of. Do you play golf, Bennett?"

"Not well." He chuckles. "Devon should come out here and play with Rodney."

"I've been asking him to. He says he will in a couple of months when Nora is out of the first trimester, you know she's been having a difficult time." Mom smiles over at me and walks over to the stove as we reach the kitchen.

Devon and I were so skeptical of Rodney and this entire arrangement in the beginning, but after a year of seeing the guy, we decided he really is that kind. I guess it's hard to accept kindness for what it is when you grow up in the environment we did.

"The butler isn't with us today. He had a family emergency, so my food will have to do," Mom says.

"Your food is great," I say. "What'd you make?"

"Chicken Cacciatore."

I smile at her. That was always my favorite dish that she used to make when we were growing up.

"It smells great," Bennett says.

"Bennett, please, sit down. Morg, will you grab the lemonade from the fridge?"

I walk over and take it out of the fridge as Mom finishes setting the table. Once we sit down and start eating, I have a moment where I can't quite believe I'm having a meal with the love of my life and my mother, and it's not at the rehab center, but in her beautiful house, and we're not fighting or arguing, but genuinely happy. I bite down on my lip to keep my emotions in check.

"I don't want to be the nagging mother," Mom says, "but now that Nora and Devon are having a baby, I feel like I have to ask . . . "

I laugh. "No baby here."

"Not yet anyway," Bennett adds, raising an eyebrow at me.

We've been going to specialists for months, not because we're in dire need to start a family, but because we want answers as to why his sperm count is so low. We've both decided to foster and hopefully adopt when we're ready, and if later on, we want to have a child the traditional way and can, we'll go that route.

"We just found each other," I say, "Sometimes it feels like a lifetime ago, but in reality, it's been just a few years. We're both so busy with work right now and we're just happy to have each other." I reach over and squeeze Bennett's hand.

"She's right. I have everything I'll ever need right here." He says it with so much conviction and love in his eyes, that I absolutely believe him.

"Well, you're both young. You definitely don't need to be rushing into anything," Mom says. "But I just want you to know that grandkids, whether they're adopted or not, are always welcome in our house."

Later, we're outside on her massive deck, watching the sunset, when Rodney gets home. He walks through the back doors like he only has eyes for Mom. When he reaches her, he throws his arms around her and gives her a huge kiss on the mouth.

"I missed you."

"Missed you." She smiles. "We have company."

He laughs, standing straight and glancing over at Bennett and me. He shakes Ben's hand first, giving him a pat on the back, and then turns to me and gives me a bear hug that doesn't replace all of the ones I missed from my own father, but definitely fills some of the void. Not for the first time, am I completely blown away by the way things have turned out for all of us. I take a seat beside Bennett and he wraps an arm around me. Rodney takes a seat beside my mom on the other side of the deck and wraps his arm around her, and we watch as the desert sky begins to bleed orange and red.

"I love you, Morgan Elizabeth," Bennett says against my head.

"I love you." I look up at him. "You're my favorite match."

"Your only match." He raises an eyebrow.

"Well, I didn't have much of a choice on the matter."

"You didn't, and that's why I know we're the perfect match."

I laugh.

We've discussed this before, and every time he finds a way

to bring it back to the idea that any app would match us together because we're perfect for each other. I always argue that, but I love that he feels the same way I do.

"I don't know," I muse. "There are a lot of people in the universe."

"A lot," he agrees. "But there's only one for me."

"Yeah?"

"Of course, Mrs. Cruz." He winks.

ACKNOWLEDGMENTS

Nana Malone - thank you so much for listening to me go on and on about this story and for helping me "un-fuck it" numerous times.

Sarah Sentz - I am forever in your debt for the feedback you provide me. Seriously.

Tiffany - THANK YOU for reading this and giving me your feedback! Come braid my hair <3

Clarissa LaFirst - I don't know what I would do without you. Probably die. In a very messy state. LOL I love you.

Kimberly Brower - for being in my corner

LBEdits - I love working with you!

Nina Grinstead - for always having my back

My ST girls - your wisdom is invaluable.

DT girls - thank you!

My Crew - THANK YOU for being so supportive these last 7 years. - If you want to join us on Facebook, please do. We love newcomers!

All of my friends, you know who you are because I can't live my life without you - thank you, I love you, I appreciate you, it's a privilege to walk this earth with you. Xoxo

ALSO BY CLAIRE CONTRERAS

More books in Kindle Unlimited:

The Consequence of Falling - Enemies-to-lovers

The Player - Sports romance

Kaleidoscope Hearts - Brother's best friend

Paper Hearts - Second chance romance

Elastic Hearts -Sexy, arrogant lawyer

The Wilde One -Music industry

Then There Was You - Childhood friends turned lovers

Fake Love - Fake fiance

Romantic suspense titles:

Because You're Mine - Mafia romance

There is No Light in Darkness - Mystery, second chance romance

CPSIA information can be obtained
at www.ICGtesting.com
Printed in the USA
LVHW041404150719
624133LV00002B/182/P